BETH OVERMYER

HOLES IN THE VEIL

This is a **FLAME TREE PRESS** book

FLAME TREE PRESS
6 Melbray Mews, London, SW6 3NS, UK
flametreepress.com

US sales, distribution and warehouse:
Simon & Schuster
simonandschuster.biz

UK distribution and warehouse:
Marston Book Services Ltd
marston.co.uk

Thanks to the Flame Tree Press team, including:
Taylor Bentley, Frances Bodiam, Federica Ciaravella, Don D'Auria,
Chris Herbert, Josie Karani, Molly Rosevear, Will Rough, Mike Spender,
Cat Taylor, Maria Tissot, Nick Wells, Gillian Whitaker.

The cover is created by Flame Tree Studio with
thanks to Nik Keevil and Shutterstock.com.
The font families used are Avenir and Bembo.

Flame Tree Press is an imprint of Flame Tree Publishing Ltd
flametreepublishing.com

A copy of the CIP data for this book is available from the British Library
and the Library of Congress.

HB ISBN: 978-1-78758-583-6
US PB ISBN: 978-1-78758-581-2
UK PB ISBN: 978-1-78758-582-9
ebook ISBN: 978-1-78758-584-3

Printed and bound in Great Britain by Clays Ltd, Elcograf S.p.A.

BETH OVERMYER

HOLES IN THE VEIL

FLAME TREE PRESS
London & New York

Know what is to be; everything, you see:
Drink from the Goblet of Seeing.
Lighter than air, float without care:
Drink from the Goblet of Drifting.
Strength and survival, no beast is your rival:
Drink from the Goblet of Enduring.
Strategic and cunning, to war shall be running:
Drink from the Goblet of Warring.
Take what you can, banish at hand:
Drink from the Goblet of Summoning.
Luck is your friend, all others must bend:
Drink from the Goblet of Questing.
Immortality to he who drinks from one and the rest –
And a curse for the soul who was born as a Blest.

PROLOGUE

Meraude

Rage was today's companion.

The Circle had been extinct for nigh thirty years, yet the mage queen found herself looking over her shoulder, wondering when the awful men, the Elders, would come for her. Perhaps it was insanity that drove her to take the measures she had in order to prevent the impossible or the inevitable, or perhaps it was genius. Armed women flanked her night and day, and they were paid well to do so. These sisters-at-arms were rotated six times a day, and spies, *women* spies, brought whispers of schemes and plans, which were immediately and mercilessly dealt with.

All doors bore six locks and six bolts, and the keys were kept by one trusted adviser and the mage queen herself. Every lock, every bolt, every window was checked six times a day by six sets of six trusted women, who were rotated. No one, however, was allowed inside the mage queen's chambers – not to clean, not to bring food or counsel or whatever might be required. The mage queen alone held the keys, three of which she wore around her neck on a silver chain. The keys were heavy and cumbersome inside her blouse and jerkin, perhaps, but she hid the bulk with her mane of black hair, which her adviser had begun to suggest she might wish to cut, for security reasons.

The two children were moving south, out of her sight but not out of her mind. Pawns on a board, that's what they were. They would find the Summoner, free him from the nymphs, and send him on his way. *Or they could betray me*, she thought, her hands shaking inside her sleeves. So much could go wrong. The children could betray her, the Summoner could be smarter than she had anticipated and take the Questing Goblet for himself, and Lord Dewhurst might decide to work for himself as well. She would kill the four of them when they had played their part in her plan. But how long must she wait?

She soaked a slice of bread in her lentil soup, watching as the firm loaf became soggy and red. Her cupbearer had tested the food in her presence moments before, but the girl had been acting strangely as of late. *Perhaps she has been corrupted.* The mage queen would have her questioned and executed later. The thought of one of her sisters-at-arms betraying her caused the mage to lose focus and break the bowl into shards in her lily-white hands. She cursed and sent the remains scattering across the floor. Her lovely linen trousers were ruined.

Calm yourself, she thought, before taking a few deep gulps of air. If she did not maintain control of her emotions, the Circle would win. It seemed as though they had been winning a lot lately. Men had been sighted outside of the breeding grounds, naked yet armed. They had been swiftly dealt with by the sisters and volunteer mothers.

The mage queen moved to the window and recited the only words that could comfort her inner turmoil: "They all will burn." Again she said it, her promise. "*Every last one.*"

CHAPTER ONE

Aidan

Before he and Slaíne even reached the front gate of his former estate, Aidan felt the repulsion of a great amount of iron. That metal always had proven impossible for him to manipulate, though he possessed the ability to control almost any other material due to the power the Summoning Goblet had given him. He looked over to see if the iron's presence was affecting Slaíne as well. The young woman's shoulders were hunched as if against a chill wind, and she gave an almighty shudder. "I'll bury the bodies a ways in," he reassured her. His shoulder prickled with cold, but he said nothing on the score of that weeks-old wound.

Soon enough they were clear of the rusting gates overgrown with ivy and piles of yesteryear's leaves. It would have been sad, seeing the old mansion at the top of the hill falling into disrepair, if it didn't hold the memories it did.

Aidan quickened his pace. The repulsion he felt from the gates eased, and he thought it wise to reach out to see if he could sense any other humans nearby. It only took him a moment's concentration to determine that they were quite alone on the premises, but for some wild game that had wandered onto the estate.

He sensed Slaíne's Pull – the invisible, attracting sense he had of every human and object – move next to him. "How deep, sir?"

"You can stop calling me 'sir'; we're friends now. And we'll dig just a few inches," Aidan said with a grunt. He did not want to say the word 'grave'. So cold. So final. Aidan felt a hand on his shoulder, but ignored it and kept at his work.

"Inches?"

"Yes," he said, not bothering to explain what he meant to do.

Mercifully, the girl did not ask if he kept a shovel in the land between the mortal realm and the land of the magical dead, nor did she complain as she got to her hands and knees and worked by his side in silence. The tools that he did have in Nothingness were useless for this task. "They were kind," he said to no one but himself. Something ought to be said about his parents. "I just wish – I wish they would have told me."

Slaíne made a noise between a grunt and a sigh.

The work was not easy, not after what he had endured for the last two weeks: near-starvation and bleedings. He was weak, but his anger was not, so he poured that into his toiling. "Mother and Father could have told me about my abilities." *Dig. Just dig.* He thrust his hands into the soil and continued to work like a dog. "They could have told me about the Circle." He struck the ground. "Warned me about Meraude, if they knew." The heat went out of his anger. Lord and Lady Clement Ingledark might not have known anything about the woman partially responsible for their own murders. Aidan needed to be fair.

Not for the first time since the night previous, Aidan felt the strong presence of the strange man at the back of his mind. The one he'd begun to think of as his inner friend. The being stirred, perhaps wanting to say something, but Aidan shrugged him aside and returned to his work in silent vigor.

Once he was satisfied with the two inches they had cleared in a six-by-fourteen-feet rectangle, Aidan closed his eyes, concentrated down as deep as he could, held on to the Pulls and Dismissed a few hundred pounds of dirt. Then, quick so he would not have to see or smell the decaying corpses of his parents again, Aidan Summoned the bodies into the open ground before him and Summoned the dirt to cover them. And with that, the deed was done.

Perhaps the strange man's presence had been to blame. Or maybe Slaíne's ridiculously strong Pull was at fault. But it was at that moment, all but too late, that Aidan felt a familiar presence enter the estate's grounds.

"Who goes there?" said the familiar voice, which made Slaíne whip around, her face paling.

Her hand shot out to catch Aidan. "Shouldn't we hide, sir?"

But Aidan shrugged her off. "No." This was the last person he wanted to see, but now that the man who had betrayed him to Dewhurst was here, Aidan was ready for a taste of vengeance. Without further hesitation, he used up his remaining stores of energy to approach Tristram, whose face had just come into view.

"Aidan?"

Aidan did not break stride. Pulse ticking in his forehead, he was only somewhat aware that Slaíne was gaining on him.

Tristram let out a laugh of relief and closed the distance between them. "Thank heavens! I was so worried that—" He got no further, for Aidan threw a punch at his jaw. Dazed, apparently, the fool fell onto his bottom and sat there bleeding from his lip. "Aidan, I can expla—" He was not given a chance to explain; instead, he was lifted to his feet and punched again.

You want me to kill him? asked a faint voice in the back of Aidan's mind.

With a start, Aidan let his fist drop. "You again?"

Don't say it out loud. I can comprehend your thoughts perfectly, friend. The voice belonged to the same stranger who had helped him escape Dewhurst's manor with Slaíne.

"Am I possessed?" he said, shaking his head.

"Is it that thing again?" Slaíne asked, touching his shoulder.

Tristram joined the chorus. "What thing? Who are you? And why is he talking to himself like he's insane?"

"He ain't insane. He's possessed."

"Quiet, both of you." Aidan clenched his jaw and concentrated. To the being inside his mind, he said, *What are you, exactly? Am I possessed?* In his mind's eye, he beheld the same dark-haired man whom he had spied before, standing in the middle of the old Ingledark Estate as if he belonged there.

The man laughed. *I don't think you're ready to hear all of the details yet, Aidan. But no, you're not crazy and you're not quite possessed.*

"Oh, that's comforting." He ignored the stares he was getting from his traveling companion and his former friend.

Cheer up and answer my question: do you want to kill Tristram or let the matter go? Because I've heard some of your thoughts about him just now, and I can't believe he betrayed you like that.

Aidan felt his wrath double, though half of it was not his own, he realized. His fists clenched and it was not he who clenched them, and they began to swing out with such power that he could have knocked Tristram's head clean off. "Stop." Aidan felt the being's disappointment and disapproval, but the man obeyed him and faded out of his mind's eye, and only an echo of his power remained.

Shaking from the sudden loss of strength, Aidan nearly collapsed, but Tristram had risen and was trying to support his weight. "Get off," said Aidan.

"Who is he?" Slaíne took Aidan's other arm and helped Tristram pull him toward the house.

"Who am *I*?" Tristram scoffed. "Who are *you*?"

Aidan tried to stop the two from helping him, but he was too weak to resist. "Tris, I swear – if you don't let go of me, I'm going to strangle you."

"Ha," said Tris. "You can barely stand. What happened?"

Slaíne had stopped and pulled Aidan closer, as if she meant to play tug-of-war. "Is this the same Tris that sold you out to Dewhurst?"

Aidan had told her all about how Tristram had lured him into his home and attempted to turn him over to the now-deceased lord. Said lord was the reason Aidan was still a wanted man, having blamed Aidan for murders he did not commit.

She did not wait for a response, but let Aidan go and attacked Tristram herself.

"Slaíne," he said as she knocked his former best friend off his feet and began pummeling him. He hadn't known Slaíne long, having stolen her from the hideous elves she once called masters a mere month or more ago. And even though they'd been through so much together, her loyalty to him was proving greater than he had first realized. Much to Aidan's satisfaction and embarrassment, Tris began to scream at a pitch more suitable to a woman than a man. Aidan had been on the receiving end of one of Slaíne's attacks; this was far more brutal. "Enough."

She seemed to notice what she had done, her fists ruddy with her victim's blood. As one bemused, Slaíne pushed up off Tris and stood staring at Aidan. "I…."

Of all things, Aidan found himself reassuring her. "It's all right." He held out his hand. "Next time, though, leave the punching to me."

With a nod, she backed away.

Tristram sat up, his mouth working furiously, but no sound came out until, "You're comforting the witch? She nearly killed me."

Aidan gave him a pointed look. "Speaking of one person almost killing another…."

Tristram had the decency to look pained, though it could have been due to the split lip and bleeding nose. "Ah, that."

"Yes, that."

For a moment, Aidan thought Tristram would come up with some excuse and then crawl back to his house. Instead, he staggered to his feet and held out a hand for Aidan. "You look dreadful. Do you have any water?" He studied Aidan more closely. "Or something stronger, perhaps?"

Aidan was about to tell him where he could stuff his water and liquor, but he was too tired and weak. Maybe if he and Slaíne rested for a while, the going might be easier…. What was he thinking? No, Tristram was not to be trusted. They must leave at once.

Perhaps sensing Aidan's inner turmoil, Tris held up his hands in surrender and said, "Easy, my dear fellow. There are reasons for what happened. But first…." He paused. "I need to talk to you. It's about Dewhurst."

Aidan sank down into the grass. "What of him?"

Tris's shoulders heaved and he shook his head. "His manor burned down last night." He lowered himself back down, wincing as he looked over at Slaíne.

Aidan laughed without humor. "That is old news, my friend."

Tris gave him an odd look and said, "I guess he burned to death with his horrible wife. The rest of the household made it out all right, though."

Next to him, Aidan could hear Slaíne's sigh of relief. "I hoped as much."

"But you seem to have heard all of this. How—" He looked more closely at Aidan, his face paling. "I thought you had got away. There's been no news of you since…. Well, since I last saw you."

"Then how did you know I was back in town? You are obviously not surprised to see me," Aidan countered.

Tris had the decency to blush. "I might've paid a few urchins to be watchful, in the event you should turn up again to murder me, which I can't say I wouldn't have deserved. One of those young messengers came running to the estate this morning with the news about Dewhurst. Then he mentioned seeing a man of your description entering the nearby…woods. Blimey, the two pieces of news are connected, aren't they?"

Aidan made no comment.

Of all things, Tristram laughed. "You burned down Dewhurst's manor?" He began to laugh in earnest, and Aidan might have joined him, if he had more energy and less anger bubbling in his veins. "How did you manage it?" Tris swore. "I wish I could have been there."

"No, you don't," said Aidan, and he meant it.

The look on Tris's face spoke a dozen apologies, none of which he voiced. Maybe Aidan would have hated him even more, had Tristram made an excuse and pleaded for forgiveness and mercy. It might have been satisfying to Aidan's pride, but it would have been a hollow victory. Something in his chest prickled, and he swallowed down the emotions that threatened to take over his better senses.

Again Tristram spoke. "What happened? Why were you there in the first place?"

Aidan and Slaíne exchanged a dark look. "He don't need to know," she said. "He's as good as done it to you himself." Perhaps that was the truth…or was close enough to the truth.

"I do know Dewhurst wanted you for some reason."

"Right," said Slaíne. "He wanted him for his blood, if'n you nay knew already."

"Slaíne," Aidan warned, uncertain how much information he could trust Tris with. But his traveling companion kept talking.

"The devil half starved him and bled him for more than a week. We only just escaped with our lives. And you've the nerve to call Mr. Aidan your friend still? I can nay abide to look at ya."

Tristram jabbed his finger at the girl, his expression one of disbelief. "See here, witch. You have no right to tell me off." He looked at Aidan, as if expecting help in the matter, but on receiving none, he opened his mouth again and was interrupted.

"You are not to call her a witch," Aidan said, the deadly calm in his voice surprising even himself.

The silence that followed stretched an uncomfortable two minutes at least. The one to finally break it was Tristram, who asked, "Why are you here exactly?" Absently he dabbed at his bleeding nose with a monogrammed handkerchief that he pulled from his sleeve.

"To bury my parents. And before you ask, your friend Dewhurst is at least partially responsible for their deaths." He made a slight pause to collect himself. "I found their bodies last night in his stables." After a short moment, he Summoned a water bladder from his cache in Nothingness into his waiting hand and took a gulp before handing it over to Slaíne, who also partook. Making the object materialize in the mortal plane, Existence, took a slight toll on Aidan, and he had to stop a moment to clear his thoughts. "I buried them not ten yards from here. I hope you don't mind." His tone was caustic, but his friend only looked confused.

"That doesn't sound possible." He, too, stood. "And why are you asking me if it's all right?"

Aidan snorted. "Don't be stupid. I no longer own this land. I sold it."

"You sold it to Dewhurst, yes." Tristram blinked. "I suppose he's not able to complain now."

Now it was Aidan's turn to be confused. "I meant to *you*. You bought the estate from me as a trap." He Dismissed the bladder and began limping away from the view of the house. No matter that Dewhurst was now deceased, and by his own hand, not in the blaze as Tristram assumed; Aidan still was a wanted man. It had been foolishness telling Tris as much as he had.

It didn't take long for Tristram to catch up and walk beside him. "Dewhurst gave me the money to buy your land." Before Aidan could ask, he continued. "I've been in debt these past three years, Aidan. My estate was about to be foreclosed on. I had nowhere else to go."

Aidan stopped where he stood. "All right, I'm listening."

Tristram drew in a deep breath and raked a hand through his hair. He explained about the blood oath he had made to Dewhurst to save his estate, about the clause he had missed that put him at the wicked man's disposal.

Though unsurprised, Aidan was disgusted. Only Tris would have missed something that important when signing for a loan.

"When he found out about your request to sell your estate, he pounced." Tristram showed Aidan a mark on his hand, a faint old scar, one where blood would have been drawn for an oath. "The Roma fortune-teller was meant to keep you there that day, but she wasn't playing her part right. I was relieved, as it seemed she was trying to lead you away from the trap."

"Larkin," Aidan murmured. He had never trusted the seer, another Blest, a person with special abilities thanks to one of the magical Goblets Immortal. There were six Goblets in total, each of them imbuing those who drank from them with a different magical ability. Larkin had the ability to tell some of the future, thanks to the fact that her mother had drunk from the Seeing Goblet. Aidan and Slaíne had left the seer in Abbington when they'd made their escape from a superstitious mob a week or so prior. If Tris was to be believed, the woman might yet prove an ally in their quest to kill the mage Meraude. Aidan looked at Slaíne, who was worrying her lower lip, then turned back to Tristram. He was about to question him, but felt four new Pulls approaching, not half a mile off. "Quickly, Slaíne."

She did not hesitate or ask what he had sensed, but helped him up the hill to the house. Tristram was fast on their heels.

"What? What's wrong?"

Aidan gave him a withering glare and kicked in the battered front door. "You know well, old friend."

If he was found here, he would have to either lie about his identity or fight his way out. There would be no Dismissing himself into Nothingness like he had done the last time he was trapped. He could only Dismiss himself, and if he left Slaíne, the curse that bound her to him would be triggered. The curse had been put on her when she was a mere child, and it bound her to whomever she called master. She could only travel so far away from that person before the curse caused her excruciating pain. He would gain an hour if he Dismissed himself, but he would most likely return to find her dead and himself captured. Aidan Summoned Slaíne's blade and led her inside.

"Is someone here?" Tris asked, his voice squeaking. He cleared his throat. "You hide, I'll send them on their way."

Before Aidan could stop his old friend, Tristram was already heading out the door. This was not a good plan, but what choice did he have? Aidan knew himself to be in no shape to fight; he hadn't the energy or the stamina just then. They could sneak out the back, but he heard voices and knew it was too late. He hurried into his uncle's old study, wincing as the boards groaned beneath his feet, unable to mask the noise. Once inside the old workspace, he ran to one of the only hiding spots he could find: the rotting wood desk in the corner. Slaíne crawled behind the sheet-covered sofa. If anyone found her, they'd just think she was a vagrant, not an accused murderer like Aidan.

The Pulls were growing closer, and Tris was going out to meet them.

Slaíne's Pull had moved. There was a scraping noise, and then a short silence followed by voices and several bangs that echoed within an out-of-tune pianoforte in the adjoining room.

Aidan all but held his breath as footsteps sounded in the antechamber, and he strained to hear the conversation taking place. His breath had kicked up a fistful of dust, which tickled at his nose and made his eyes burn. He staved off a sneeze by licking the roof of his mouth and praying.

"Can't have gone far," said a rough voice belonging to a man. "There's a reward. A big one, innit?"

Tristram's Pull moved toward the other end of the house. "Yes, a big reward indeed," he was saying. "I'm sorry I can't help you."

A third voice chuckled, an unpleasant nasal sound, followed by an almighty fit of coughing. Once he had recovered, the man spoke. "What is a good fella like you doing in this godforsaken place? It's said to be haunted these days."

"I was looking around."

Something was said too softly for Aidan to hear. "That's right," said the second voice. "I'm in debt as well, as thou well knowest."

"Care to split the reward?" Tristram asked.

Aidan bared his teeth in silence. His hand clutched the sword so tightly it was going numb. He could not fight off several men, even with his ability to make objects disappear and reappear at will, and Slaíne with her ability to fly, not in the tired and mentally exhausted state he was in. If Slaíne weren't bound to him by a curse, she could run away from there right now without raising too much suspicion. There was no helping that at the moment, though. Breaking an old curse was the least of their worries.

There was more laughter. "You know where he is, do you? And you'd be willing to split the reward money, just like that?"

"Of course. I am a gentleman, after all," was Tristram's cool response.

"Well, then, show me to him," said a fourth voice, a woman's.

Someone cleared their throat. "Show *us* to him. And no betrayals. I've got the law on my side."

"After Dewhurst's death, the law is scattered."

The woman said, "Ah, but after Dewhurst's *murder*, the reward went up several hundred."

Better and better. Should he catch them by surprise now and at least kill Tristram and maybe one of the others? He swallowed hard at the thought. Killing Tris would buy him some time, but how to co-ordinate an attack with Slaíne without being able to openly communicate? If he moved from where his side was cramping, Aidan would be sure to make some noise on the unsteady floor, and then he would be caught for certain.

"I don't want my wife to get in trouble," Tristram said, taking his time with his words. The others were silent. Aidan frowned and stilled his breathing so he could better hear. "She doesn't know, but...."

"But what?" asked the woman, only to be hushed by the others.

Tristram let out a sad laugh. "I hid him overnight in our coal cellar. If he's true to his word, Aidan Ingledark is still down there, waiting for me to bring him rations."

Aidan didn't dare trust the words. The slippery rat could be saying one thing aloud for Aidan's benefit and pantomiming what he meant the others to do. But if it wasn't a trap, it was a terrible lie; no one would truly believe it.

"Wherefore are you telling us this?" asked one of the men. "You could have kept the reward money for yourself." A Pull moved nearer the study. "Ingledark's got to be hiding here or somewhere nearby."

The flesh of Aidan's shoulder prickled uncomfortably cold, and the strange presence lingered nearer in the back of his mind, offering help if needed. But Aidan shoved the presence aside for the moment. The possessor interfered with Summoning and Dismissing, and he had the beginnings of an idea forming, an idea that would require full use of Pull manipulation.

"Why would I lie?" Tristram was insisting, obviously trying not to sound desperate. "Besides, this place is falling down around our ears."

"Then what're you doing here?" the woman demanded.

Tristram laughed. "I was an idiot and bought the place off him. I thought I'd stop by and check on my investment."

There were some murmurs, and then a rumble of laughter. "You'll excuse us if we don't take your word for it, Prewitt."

"If you want to look around, be my guest. Just be careful. I think this place might indeed be haunted."

Aidan felt and heard the reward-seekers separating, spreading out as they began their search of the house. The study was likely one of the first places they would look, so Aidan needed to act quickly to keep them away. Most often when he Summoned an object, it would land within a close distance of himself, as that was what took the least amount of mental strength. This would be difficult. Closing his eyes, Aidan Dismissed a tin cup on top of the desk, concentrated, and Summoned it to a spot at the other end of the house. It clanged a few rooms over, on top of what sounded like more metal.

The person who had been approaching the study hurried off in the direction the noise had come from. "Someone's here, all right," one of the men shouted, and the others' Pulls joined him at the far end of the house.

Exhausted and near-hallucinating, Aidan laid his head down on his arm and tried not to drowse. This wasn't over yet. As soon as he was certain they all were inside the far room, he tugged at the door's Pull and was satisfied to hear it slam shut.

"Stop playing games, Prewitt." The door creaked open, and Aidan gave it another firm tug with his mind. Again the door slammed shut, and the small company began to shout. The force with which Aidan had made the door close had caused what sounded like a disturbance in the room's structure. The house groaned and shook, and there was a deafening thud followed by a scream.

"The house is collapsing."

"Let us out!"

"She's hurt."

The front of the centuries-old house was shifting on its foundations, causing boards to loosen and fall from the ceiling. The screaming in the other part of the house grew louder, and the company's Pulls hurried away, though one was moving more slowly than the others.

As the ceiling began to collapse in the study, Aidan used his last reserves of strength to Dismiss it, and then promptly fainted.

CHAPTER TWO

Aidan

Aidan was standing in the middle of the parlor, which was fully intact and immaculate. He was alone for the moment, though he could sense a few human Pulls nearby. "Hello?" he called out. The aroma of baking bread met him as he wandered through the doorway.

"We're in here," a distant voice called.

"Who are 'we'?" Somewhere in the conscious realm, Aidan knew someone was trying to shake him awake, but he ignored their attempts and continued into the back part of the house and down the servants' staircase. He marveled at the coldness of the metal rail beneath his hand; it felt so real.

"It is real," said a familiar voice from behind him.

Heart racing, Aidan turned and prepared to Summon Slaíne's sword. When he saw it was the man who had been taking over his body and thoughts, he swore. "It's you."

"Yes, friend. It's me." The two men stared at each other. "Auntie's making bread. It should be done shortly. Care for a smoke? Something to drink?"

Aidan shook his head. "Where am I?"

The other motioned for Aidan to join him in the parlor. The man sat down on the white satin settee, the one Aidan's father and mother had always scolded him away from as a small child, and put his feet up. "You can sit. No one here will harm you."

"I think I'll stand."

The man shrugged and lit his pipe. "Do what suits you." He puffed in silence for a moment, ignoring Aidan's pointed stare.

"Where am I?" Aidan repeated.

"Oh, I heard you the first time. I just — I don't know how much you really want to know. Sure you don't want some liquor? It's not as good as the stuff in Existence, they say, but it isn't anything to turn one's nose up at." Still he did not rise from his seat to pour himself a glass, but sat there, puffing, and tapping his fingers on the seat.

"So this isn't reality?"

The man laughed. "It is my reality, Aidan. As you might have guessed, I'm dead."

Aidan swore. "Who — why are you so familiar?"

That caused the other to sober. "One question at a time, please. To answer the first, this is the Beyond."

"Beyond what, exactly?"

"Beyond life." He pointed at his chest. "I am one of the magical dead. The Beyond is where all magical beings go after they die."

Aidan shook his head. "How am I here, then?"

"Oh, you're not exactly. Your soul can come here when your defenses are low. I'll have to teach you how to control that. And before you ask, yes, Nitchoo is responsible."

Aidan stared at him without comprehension.

The other man put out his pipe and placed it on the glass table next to where he sat. "The ice blade that the nymph queen stabbed you with. Nitchoo. Very powerful, complicated spells went into its making. The queen used her last bit of strength to…well, to make it possible for your soul to come here and for me to talk to you."

"And you're dead."

"Yes and no."

This was too much. Aidan could feel a powerful headache coming on, and it had little to do with his head hitting against a board in Existence. What were they doing to his body in the land of the living, he wondered? "Yes and no? How is that possible?"

"It depends on your perspective. Now, tell me, if I could convince the elves to return the maps to you, what would you do?"

Aidan shook himself. This had to be some weird dream that he would soon wake from. "Maps? The ones that disappeared from Nothingness?"

The man looked at him like he had lost his mind, which might not have been entirely far from the truth. "Yes. The maps. The ones you took from Dewhurst and then Treevain took from your cache. The maps to the Questing Goblet." When Aidan didn't respond but continued to stand there, dazed, the strange fellow sighed and got to his feet. "Right. Maybe you're not ready for them." He walked past Aidan, bumping into his shoulder, nearly knocking him to the floor. "Ooh, sorry about that, Aidan. I still forget my own strength sometimes."

Aidan ignored the man's offered hand of assistance and backed off a few feet. "I have need of those maps, sir." If even just to burn them. "And I am willing to go to great lengths to get them." He braced himself, but the man just laughed.

"Sir? Aidan, you always were formal, but this is going entirely too far. It's just S-Salem. Just call me Salem for now." He looked guilty about something, but shook himself like a dog and changed the subject back. "Tell me why you want the Goblets Immortal."

This felt more like an interview for a job than anything else, but Aidan knew more was riding on his answer than he wished to consider. "Meraude is dangerous," he began carefully. "She shouldn't be allowed."

"Allowed to...?"

"Exist."

Salem, if that was really his name, clapped his hands together and smiled at Aidan. "Good answer. Very good answer. One that we were hoping to hear."

"We?" Aidan looked around, hoping to be enlightened. They were still alone.

"That mage has too much power, Aidan. And she's using it to kill much of magical kind."

Aidan nodded. "That much I know."

"The Goblets are the best way to defeat Meraude. You must find as many as you can if you are to confront her. Especially the Questing Goblet. That cannot be allowed to fall into her hands. Think of what she might do with it." Salem seemed ready to say something else, but stopped, squinting at Aidan. "It looks like you're about to leave. Say hello to the redhead for me; and tell her to eat something. She's far too light."

*The room grew bleary, and things began to spin and fade to gray. Aidan
tried to hold on to the settee, but it was no use. He was ripped out of the
Beyond, and his soul landed back inside his body with a great wheezing sound.*

"He lives," said Tristram's voice. "Fetch him some water, Slahva."

"Fetch it yerself. And it's *Slaíne*; I ain't no toad. Get the
water yerself."

That caused Aidan to laugh, albeit weakly. He blinked, and
the room came into focus. The ceiling, he noted, was partially
missing, and he could make out a bit of detail of the above floor. So
that hadn't all been a dream...though perhaps parts of it had been.
"How long have I been unconscious?" Aidan blinked and tried to
sit up, but it felt like his brain was going to leak out of his ears, so
great was the headache that flared.

Slaíne helped him lie back down, propping his head on a
musty-smelling pillow. "Easy, sir. Afraid Tristan dropped you at
one point."

"It's Tris*tram*," Tris retorted, but he did nothing to refute her
accusation of his having dropped Aidan.

Aidan noted that he was laid out on the settee in the parlor, the
same one Salem had lounged on in the Beyond – if that vision were
even to be believed. It had felt so real, yet not quite as real as this.

"To answer your question, you've been unconscious for one
and a half days," Tris said, causing Aidan to groan and try to cover
his ears. "Too loud? Sorry." He didn't sound as sorry as Aidan
would have liked. "The reward-seekers ran off and haven't been
back. They think this place is haunted."

Slaíne snorted. "Near soiled themselves, I imagine."

Between the two of them, Tristram and Slaíne gave him a
short summary of what had transpired. The unwanted company
had fled the premises and hadn't returned, though Tris had been
keeping watch on and off again. They had needed to move Aidan
while he was unconscious, because the remainder of the ceiling
looked ready to collapse in the study. Some had collapsed in the
room where they stood now, bits of wood and dust and paint

scattered about. The one and a half days had gone by without much excitement.

"I don't know if you're aware, but you Summoned a few things while you were unconscious," Tris said, raking a hand through his hair before pointing to a small pile on the floor. "A map to goodness knows where. It all seems rather absurd." He studied Aidan a little too intently for Aidan's liking.

"I told him about your plan," Slaíne said. Before he could panic, she told a smooth lie. "But your friend don't like the idea of selling off Dewhurst's private papers. Thinks he's better'n you." She winked at Aidan, who could have kissed her out of relief. The less Tristram knew of the Goblets Immortal and Aidan's quest to kill Meraude, the better.

Blushing, Tris muttered something about lies and an apology. "It's just that it could reflect badly on the Ingledark name when you reestablish your position here. No one's going to respect a thief, Aidan." His voice trailed off and he frowned as he again studied his old friend. "You are reclaiming your birthright, aren't you?"

It was tempting, sorely tempting. Aidan thought a moment. Could he return to the land he had once called home, find a way to clear his name, and stake his claim to lordship? It seemed like a possibility. But who would avenge his family? "I can't, Tris. I can't stay."

"Aren't you tired of running?" Tristram continued. "You can make it work. *We* can make it work. I know a good solicitor in town. He's new, mind, but he has won a few serious cases...."

Hesitation gripped Aidan's stomach. Could he? "I'm afraid not, old friend." Before Tristram could argue, Aidan cut him off with a groan. "Times change. People – change." He gave Tris a pointed look. "I'm moving on, Tristram. This land has nothing for me anymore."

"But your family, the land, it—"

"My family is dead," said Aidan. "The land is yours." He sat up a little and clapped his friend on the shoulder, though he felt far from congenial. He was, after all, a man without a home and without any real hopes of ever having one again.

Tristram's frown deepened. "You're up to something. Aidan, what are you getting yourself into? And don't tell me any lies about selling off Dewhurst's things and settling in your mother's homeland."

One look at Slaíne confirmed that she had told a complete lie, but apparently had not been convincing enough. With her help, Aidan was able to sit up all the way, though the world spun and his head felt light. He accepted a tin cup of water that she had on hand, and drank it in one large gulp.

"Aidan." Tristram's tone was a warning one, as if he were scolding a young child. "What are you doing?"

He did not respond at first, but Summoned some food from his cache in Nothingness, and bit off a mouthful of brown bread from the Romas. Chewing in silence, he reoriented himself with the Pulls in the room. There were three human Pulls: his, Slaíne's, and Tristram's, and no other human ones for at least a mile, as it should be. Aidan finished the small loaf of bread and then Summoned some dried and salted meat, which he tore into. He hadn't eaten in two days, and he was feeling the effects. At last he answered Tristram, who was still glaring at him. "The less you know, the better."

That did not seem to sit well with Tristram, but he made no further comment or objection on that matter, and changed the subject altogether. "Why don't you rest some more? I'll keep watch." He looked at Slaíne with apparent dislike. "I guess she can sit with you. Hasn't left your side, hardly. Like a dog, that one." And with that said, Tris rose and left the room.

Once he had gone and his Pull had moved out of earshot, Aidan tried to get to his feet.

"What're you doing?" Slaíne demanded, pushing him back down without much difficulty.

Aidan bit down on a smile and decided to tease her a bit.

"Now, see here. I managed just fine before you came along to boss me around."

Slaíne snorted. "Right, but before you was half-starved and ready to fall over." When he appeared ready to argue, she threw up her hands. "Fine. Ain't my place to say." She perched atop a sideboard as if she were a bird ready to take flight, making nary a sound.

How does she do that? Aidan shook himself and Called into his hands the maps he had Summoned. The use of his abilities made him even more lightheaded, but he ignored the sensation and went over the papers, looking for anything familiar to orient himself. After a moment, he swore. "North. Cedric's grave is closer to Meraude than I would have liked." He scratched his chin.

"So you do mean to go after the rest of the Goblets, then?" As she spoke, Slaíne produced the sack containing the Goblet from Dewhurst's manor. "Which one do you suppose this is?"

Aidan concentrated on it, as if that might enlighten him. He had held the Warring Goblet before; at least, that was what he assumed from what Meraude had told him in a vision. After a moment, he gave up and put his hand out for it.

But Slaíne made a face and seemed unwilling to part with it. "Are you sure—"

"Hand it over, Slaíne." He paused and amended his statement to, "Please hand it over." He was getting a strange, pulsing feeling from the Goblet, something he hadn't been able to decipher before. It was almost as if...but no, that couldn't be.

"What?" Slaíne asked as she reached to place it in his hands.

In that moment, with her hand on the stem of the Goblet, and his on the rim, the cup grew warm and glowed a rosy hue. Strange words were impressed on the back of Aidan's mind: *At last. Well met, brother.* Salem's presence could no longer be felt at the back of his mind, but had been replaced with images of birds in the sky and clouds scattering through the air.

Startled, Aidan tried to drop the Goblet, but his hand held fast and the glow intensified until he had to look away or risk being blinded. The cup began to vibrate, and pain shot through Aidan's veins, which had begun to glow as well. He did not cry out, could not cry out, and he knew by instinct that Sláine was having a similar experience. The pulsing from the Goblet grew stronger, and the pounding in Aidan's head increased tenfold. Closing his eyes tightly shut, he waited to die.

Thud, thud, thud. His pulse slowed, the pain ebbed, and slowly, ever so slowly, the light dimmed to the point where he could chance another glance. The Goblet fell from both of their hands as if it had a mind of its own, and then rolled across the floor and back again, resting against Sláine's heels.

Breathing hard, Aidan looked up at Sláine. "What...?" he began but did not finish.

"I dunno," Sláine said with a frown.

Aidan looked at his arms to make certain his skin wasn't still glowing, and was pleasantly surprised to find that he didn't feel as weak or as tired as he had but moments before. Curious, Aidan held out his hand in front of himself and flexed his fingers. The tin cup flew into his grasp, along with a glass decanter that had been resting on the sideboard. Well, he hadn't exactly meant to do that. Then, with a breath, he Dismissed the objects, along with Sláine's silver sword lying on the floor. There was no accompanying headache or lightheadedness.

"Do ya think...." Sláine scratched the back of her neck. "Did you hear things?" She picked up the Goblet gingerly, and then replaced it in the sack, which she set back on the sideboard. "It called me 'child'."

That made Aidan laugh. "And that offends you?"

Sláine did not respond to that. "The Drifting Goblet." Her face brightened. "This has to be the Drifting Goblet."

"What makes you say that?" Aidan felt stronger now, so he got to his feet and picked up the maps that he had dropped.

"It did nay call me *a* child, but *child*. I'm a Drifter, child of the Drifting Goblet, if you want to be poetic." She thought for a moment. "That don't explain what happened to you." Slaíne studied him as though the answer would pop out at her from his forehead. "You heard something, yes?"

With a shake of his head, Aidan Dismissed the maps. "I heard a voice, but...." He went to the sideboard and pulled the Goblet out of the sack with the tips of his fingers, fearing that perhaps it would do something to him again. When it did not, he held it firmly in his grasp and looked at it in a beam of light streaming through a broken window. "There are no markings that I can discern."

"I know, sir. I've already had days to look."

Aidan frowned. "There is only one way to find out for certain." He looked around for a pitcher or anything the girl might have obtained water with, found nothing, and then Summoned a water bladder. Hands shaking with anticipation, he unstopped the bladder and poured a meager amount of the water into the Goblet. Would that be enough? The explanations from Larkin the seer had been vague, but it seemed that whosoever drank of one of the Goblets Immortal took on its powers for a limited amount of time – in truth, until they expelled the liquid from their system. The only reason that Aidan, and Slaíne apparently, had the abilities without limits was because their mothers had drunk from a Goblet while the two were in their respective wombs, the magic elixir becoming part of their makeup. At least, that was what Larkin had claimed. Could he trust her?

He raised the Goblet to Slaíne. "To your health." And then he drank. Nothing happened. Was he supposed to flap his arms? Take a running jump off something tall? No, best not to attempt that in front of an audience; not only might he injure himself or Slaíne, but it was a humiliation he did not think he could bear.

"Sir," said Slaíne. "Do you feel any dif'rent?"

Aidan thought on it for a moment. He did feel different. Lighter, less tied to the Pulls around him, except for Slaíne's Pull, which nearly drew him to her as a magnet. Maybe that was why his feet were both still on the ground. "Should I feel lighter?"

She scratched the base of her neck. "Probably."

"What do you mean, 'probably'? This is supposedly your Goblet." But he was not angry with her, rather with himself. What was he doing wrong? "I'm sorry, Slaíne. My temper is—"

Her face darkened. "Ain't 'my' Goblet. Just what my mam drank of. I can feel it. It's got to be the Drifting Goblet. Maybe if I—" She approached him, but he backed away…or, at least, attempted to.

Instead of taking a step backward, Aidan skipped off the floor and nearly hit the ceiling. "Well, that answers that question."

Slaíne clapped her hands and let out a burst of laughter. "I told ya. I knew 'twas the right one."

"Splendid," said Aidan, still aloft. "Now, how do I get down?"

It took them the better part of twenty minutes, trying to figure out how to get Aidan off the ceiling. He tried waving his arms about, imagining himself swimming downward. When that did not work, Aidan explored the Pulls on the floor and attempted to latch on to one to anchor himself. He made little progress with that, as the Pulls felt different with the Drifting Goblet's water in his system.

Slaíne suggested little in the way of helping him and giggled a lot.

He might have laughed too, had he not feared Tristram discovering him floating around like some great bat. That would raise questions, and his old friend might piece together enough information to follow, stop, or report them.

Finally, after much sweating and swearing, Aidan felt himself growing heavier. Slowly he began to sink. "How do you manage it?" he asked, hovering inches above the settee.

Slaíne stopped laughing and seemed to turn the question over in her mind. "I dunno. I just will it to happen, and it happens. How do you make things disappear and reappear?"

"I tried using the same principles I use for Summoning and Dismissing, but they did not work." Aidan frowned as his boot tips scraped the back of the settee.

"And you could always control your abilities?" she asked, giving him a curious look.

Aidan shook his head. It had taken years, and that time he did not wish to think of. "I think the water is almost out of my system." Indeed, he was drenched with sweat. It took another ten minutes, but at last he dropped onto the settee, somewhat dazed. He did not land a minute too soon: Tristram's Pull moved back into the house, followed shortly after by the sound of his boots thumping across the rickety floorboards.

"Uh, Aidan?" he called out. "Aidan, there are two lawmen coming down the lane. What should I do?"

—

CHAPTER THREE

Aidan

Tristram continued to stand there, staring at Aidan for direction. When he spoke again, his voice was shrill. "What do we do? If I'm caught with you, I'll be arrested for conspiring or some other nonsense."

Aidan went to the sideboard and picked up the sack containing the Drifting Goblet. "You're not going to be found with me. Delay them, and we'll sneak out the back way." Not pausing for a proper farewell, he grabbed Sláine by the hand and led her to the back of the house.

"Good luck," Tris called after them.

The mansion had been built into the side of the hill so that the front was at ground level, but the back of the house was three stories from the ground. There used to be a set of stairs leading to the ground, but when Aidan opened the door, he was not surprised to see that they had long since rotted away. "Go ahead," he mouthed after feeling the Pulls of four humans at the front of the house. At least the house wasn't surrounded…yet.

Sláine did as he asked, lowering herself onto the ground by means of her gift. She looked up at him, her expression somewhat visible from the distance at which she stood.

Aidan should have thought to send the Goblet with her, as having it on his person would make lowering himself difficult. There was no chance of that now; the human Pulls had entered the house, and words exchanged might be heard. Hands shaking, Aidan tied the sack onto his belt and lowered himself over the edge, searching for a foothold or handhold. His boots touched a wooden frame below, but it made a horrible creak, so he at once removed his weight from it. Now there were voices approaching the back room, followed closely by two human Pulls.

"I can assure you that I was simply surveying my new property," Tristram was saying at the top of his lungs, as if to warn Aidan that they were coming. "I am well within my rights, sir."

"Miss Emelie Lewis said you threatened her."

"I asked her to leave the grounds, that much is certain. She and her friends were trespassing." The inside door creaked open, and Aidan lowered himself so that he was just dangling by his fingers. "I am well within my rights."

There was a grunt. "So you said."

Aidan could let himself drop to the ground and hope that he didn't break any bones or make enough noise to attract attention. It was a risk, though, one that he might not easily walk away from. His fingers were beginning to slip and they might be seen at any moment. Sweating, he reached again for the wooden frame below with his boots but could not find it.

"Nothing here seems to be amiss," said another male voice.

Tristram sighed. "Of course there isn't."

"But why is that door open?"

Aidan could have kicked himself for having left it open even a crack. Now the man's Pull was moving closer to the door.

"I wanted to get a cross breeze flowing through here, air the place out a bit, you know." Tristram was moving nearer.

Any second now, Aidan would be discovered. He had to do something, and fast. Closing his eyes, he felt for Pulls, latched on to one that felt like glass, Dismissing and then Summoning it. Out in the hall, there was a great crash, just as he put his full weight on the window frame below. He didn't stay to see if the noise from the decoy worked to cover his descent; he needed to move quickly.

The Pulls moved away from the doorway, and Aidan climbed to the windowsill below. It groaned in protest beneath his weight, but he didn't stop moving. Lowering himself to dangle from the bit of wood, he stretched himself out as long as he could, and then dropped to the ground below. He landed on his bottom, though he had tried to roll. "I'm going to be sore tomorrow," he muttered and he got to his feet with Slaíne's help.

Shouts were taken up in the house, though Aidan was certain no one had seen his face. It was up to his old friend now to make up a decent lie about who had been hiding on the estate; Aidan certainly was not going to stay and explain things for him.

Slaíne picked up the Goblet from the ground since it had rolled out of the sack attached to Aidan's belt, and they ran into the woods behind the house. Aidan had not entered this particular part of the woods surrounding Breckstone since he was a young boy, though he guessed he still knew them better than anyone who might pursue them. New trees had shot heavenward since the twenty years had passed. Undergrowth was a problem, but he and Slaíne managed to push through every obstacle without wasting much time.

They were heading farther south than he would have liked, but they could rectify that later; now they had to put as much distance between them and the estate as possible. The ground began to even out. Water gurgled from the brook just around the bend. They followed the water as it bent east, hiding their tracks by wading in up to their ankles. The going became slow as they neared the edge of the rapids and the woods thickened again to the north. "We should refill our waterskins," he said to Slaíne above the roar.

She nodded and they moved out of the water and onto the rocks surrounding. They were both breathing hard. Sweat trickled down Aidan's back, and he swiped at his brow before Summoning two of the six water bladders that he always kept in Nothingness. First they each drank to their hearts' content.

Once they had drunk what they needed, Aidan filled both of the bladders, stopping after each was full and then Dismissing anything harmful that he found so that they would not become sick later on. Two bladders' worth of Dismissing took a minimal toll on his mind, but he dared not exert himself further. It was a wonder he had regained his energy and strength after touching the Drifting Goblet.

He would have to ask Slaíne about that later. Right now, he wanted to sit in peace.

Aidan Summoned two beef-and-potato pasties from Nothingness and handed one to Slaíne, who tore into it like she hadn't eaten in a week. He realized with some guilt that she might not have eaten for the last two days, considering he'd been unconscious and unable to bring forth any of their foodstuffs.

After they had dined on their simple fare, Aidan got to his feet and climbed down from the rocks, holding out a hand to help Slaíne down.

She smirked and flew off the rubble like it was nothing. "Are we safe walkin' on the banks now?"

Aidan nodded. "Just try to walk on rocks when you are able. Or you could always—" He made a gesture that indicated flight. They moved toward the woods. "I'm not overly concerned about being pursued this far. We're outside of Breckstone here. Anyone chasing us has either given up or gone back for reinforcements." He wasn't sure that was true, and there were possibly hunting dogs to contend with. Still, there was nothing he could do about it and, therefore, there was no reason to worry Slaíne.

The look on her face told him she didn't trust all of his words, but she said nothing more on that score.

At this time, the sun had reached its highest point in the sky and begun its descent. And though the air held the promise of summer, Aidan knew from the clear sky that the night would be cold. "There is a small town a few miles east of here. Grensworth. We should reach it before nightfall."

Slaíne was already shaking her head. "But folks is knowin' that you're in the area. Won't they be lookin' in towns nearby?" She was right, but they needed a place to rest their heads and study the maps that he had taken from Dewhurst's manor, and he told her as much.

"I thought you was done with the Goblets."

"So did I," he admitted as they crashed into the woods, steering the path farther east. He had been through with them, having discovered his parents murdered, and apparently by Meraude's hand. That

Meraude would enlist his help in finding the Goblets Immortal made no sense to Aidan, but her involvement could not be denied, not after Dewhurst's alliance to her had come to light. "But if we're going to kill Meraude, having possession of the Goblets Immortal is the best chance of gaining an advantage."

"Do ya think she might have a few?"

Aidan shrugged. "I doubt that she does. Why would she send me after the Questing Goblet if she already had the other Goblets?" He paused for a moment to look for familiar landmarks in the form of large rocks and certain trees. Satisfied that they were on the right course, he started walking again. "She seems to want the Questing Goblet most. That would give her success in finding the others."

Slaíne made a scoffing sound. "If that's how the Goblets' magic works, even."

He let that remark go. Arguing would get them nowhere quickly. "Let's worry about that bridge when it's time to cross to it, yes?"

"If you say so, sir."

Birds chirruped overhead. Mist cloaked the travelers' steps as they walked, making the way more treacherous. Slaíne Drifted a few times, pushing off the ground to avoid anything the mist might be hiding from them. Aidan used his ability to sense Pulls in order to avoid bracken, roots, and rock, though it took more concentration than he would have liked to use, the Pulls not being as substantial as others and thus requiring more skill to detect.

Eventually he became drenched from the mist and sweat. What might have been a sunny day out in the open had turned into a cold and damp one below the tree cover, and its effects were more pronounced every time they took a rest. If only he could Dismiss the water from their clothes. That would solve his problem. They stopped for only short periods of time, just long enough to eat a handful of berries each, and to slake their thirst. The red fruit the Romas had procured for them the other night was bitter and hard. "Must have been picked too early," Aidan murmured. He'd thought it early for starberries, so he guessed they had been grown in a hothouse.

"How much farther?" Slaíne gasped after they'd gone two hours without resting. "Is there anythin' else to eat?" As if to punctuate her point, her stomach roared at them both.

He had felt human Pulls on and off for the last two miles – faint Pulls traveling parallel to them on either side. Now he and Slaíne stumbled onto a well-traveled dirt road, worn with hoof prints and wheel tracks. "Grensworth isn't far," he said, looking around before Summoning a hunk of bread and handing it to the girl. "I can feel hundreds of human Pulls now, so I'm assuming we're within five miles."

Slaíne tore into the bread with vigor and, after a time, handed him the other half. Through a mouthful of crust she said, "We'll use dif'rent names again, yes?"

Aidan did not remind her that it had not worked so well the last time they had tried, but nodded. "Keep your name, if you like. Remember—"

"The less made up, the easier to remember?"

He smirked. "Yes, or something like that."

With the town nearing, their steps quickened, and the more uncomfortable Aidan became. Living life as a nomad on the outskirts of society for nigh twenty years had made him antisocial. If this town was like any other he had experienced, there would be customs to contend with and maybe even small talk. He shuddered at the thought.

After a quarter of an hour, the human Pulls became more pronounced. The pair passed a few travelers on the road who were headed in the opposite direction to them. None made direct eye contact, much to Aidan's relief. Looking – and perhaps smelling – like peasants had its advantages: people might regard them with suspicion, but only if they deigned to regard them at all.

The road broadened as they walked, and soon a gate came into view, though it was rusted and dangled from its hinges. Slaíne walked a little closer to him than was perhaps necessary. "What happened here?" she whispered.

"I don't know," Aidan replied. "Poor towns can hardly afford to keep up their entryways, I suppose."

Slaíne snorted. "Seems stupid and unsafe."

Aidan shrugged and quickened his pace. He hadn't heard anything bad about Grensworth, other than it was small and cheap…as if those were truly bad things. For a moment he paused at the gate, taking in several wanted posters pinned to a community notice board. Thankfully, there were no notices for either him or Slaíne – at least, not yet. He wondered if rumors were flying back in Breckstone. For their sakes, he hoped something new soon would occupy idle thoughts, something more exciting than sightings of a wanted man. "If anyone asks," he said after a moment, "we're from the north. Do not mention my hometown."

"Wasn't plannin' on it," she countered, though not crossly. She grabbed at her side. "Gotta pang."

"We'll find lodging soon. Then you can rest your pang."

The crowds weren't much to speak of as they made their way onto a cobbled inner road. Men and women peddled their wares between worn-down and empty buildings, catcalling Slaíne, who stood out from the others with her flaming red hair. Fortunately, she did not rise to take the bait, but balled her fists at her side and quickened her steps with a tight expression on her face.

It took them ten minutes of walking to find the first inn, and it would have been hard to miss. The purple-painted building stood three stories tall and boasted a wraparound porch and two balconies. Several men sat in rocking chairs out front, smoking and watching passersby. None seemed overly concerned with the two strangers approaching.

"'The Spinning Cup'?" Slaíne muttered. "What sort of name is that?"

Aidan did not care, just as long as they served hot food and had locks on their doors. Two of the men removed their hats when Slaíne walked past, and it seemed to surprise her so much that she stopped watching where she was going and ran right into Aidan.

The two men laughed, and then went back to smoking their pipes as the travelers stepped inside.

"We would like a room with two beds," Aidan said to the innkeeper, a plump woman who looked to be in her seventies.

She stared at him with shrewd blue eyes as if determining whether or not she could trust him, and leaned in to say, "There be a two-night stay fee. Pay up front."

When else he would pay was beyond Aidan, but he pulled his money pouch out of the sack still hanging from his belt, and began counting out what he thought was a decent amount of coins. When she held out her hand and took the money, she then proceeded to hold out her other palm, as if expecting more. "How much?" Aidan asked, unmoved.

The woman licked her papery lips and murmured something about hot meals and baths. Then she gave him a price – another seven of the coins he had already given her – and pocketed what she had already.

Aidan shook his head. "Hot food tomorrow, no baths."

The woman wrinkled up her nose and murmured something about smelling them both from where she stood. Finally, she brought the price down to four more coins, which Aidan handed over. "Welcome to the Spinning Cup. Top floor, first room on the left." She gave them a tile to hang next to their door. "Dinner is served before sunset." After a moment of fumbling in her apron pocket, she produced a small square of soap and slapped it into Aidan's palm. "Here, it's free."

He pocketed the heavily perfumed soap, mustered his manners to thank the woman, and then he and Slaíne tramped up the stairs behind her to the left. They passed two people who were on the way down, and judging by the scarcity of tiles hanging next to doors, those two were the only others who had rooms at the moment.

"I s'pose there's bedbugs," Slaíne said darkly. "Expensive bedbugs."

Aidan made no comment. The rate had been outrageous, but they were in no position to complain; they needed rest and respite from the events of the day. He hesitated outside the first door on the left, slipped the tile into its hanger, and walked inside the room. It was perfectly ordinary. And, thank any powers that might be above, there were two beds.

"Right," Aidan said, throwing the bolt into place after Slaíne had made it in behind him. He walked over to the bed nearest the door and Summoned all the papers and oilskins that he kept in Nothingness, and swore. The maps had become confused in the great pile, which threatened to fall over onto the floor, so he hastened to divide it into four smaller ones.

Slaíne's Pull moved toward the fireplace that sat next to the window. "I'll start a fire."

"Wait a moment," Aidan said, not looking up from his work. He Summoned the flint and magnesium stick and tossed them over to her. "Here. Send no sparks in this direction, mind. The whole stack is just waiting to go up in flames."

She grunted in response and began breaking sticks. Soon the smell of burned leaves filled the air, followed at once by cursing.

"Don't cut your fingers off." Aidan did not turn from the task at hand, never mind how colorful the vocabulary behind him was becoming.

Most of the first stack of documents contained business information from Dewhurst's dishonest dealings in Breckstone. Those were of little interest to Aidan now, so he Dismissed them and moved on to the next stack. The top handful of papers here were varied: some were lists of debts and debtors in the area, others receipts from businesses that had long since ceased to exist, but the last few papers were covered in handwritten children's rhymes. "Why would Dewhurst hold on to these?" Aidan puzzled over one page and realized these so-called rhymes were none that he had ever heard as a child.

Cervain the Cunning
Took off fast running,
For of his blood folk wanted to drink.
Killed him plus four,
The likes seen no more.
Cervain, not so Cunning, you'd think.

Aidan read it once more with a shudder. Were all children's rhymes so unpalatable? He recalled one about a drowning bat, but it did not produce the strong feelings that this one did. "Slaíne," he said after some time, once the fire was crackling in the grate. "Do you know any children's rhymes?"

She laughed. "What? Me?"

Aidan waited.

"'Course not. Never was no child – least, not after Treevain and her lot took me." Treevain had been the eldest – and perhaps meanest – of the four elves that used to be Slaíne's mistresses. Slaíne would have escaped them, had a curse not been placed upon her, preventing her from being more than several yards away from whomever she called master. Now Aidan had taken on that role, though he wished he could set her free, which is perhaps why Slaíne continued to insist on calling him sir.

"So the elves never told you any rhymes?"

The look she gave him could have withered a grape on its vine. "They told me rhymes, all right. Rhymes about what might 'appen to me if I did nay put a hurry in my step. Why ask me?"

"Because," Aidan said with a sigh, "you are – well, you used to always be singing."

Slaíne only shrugged in response and went back to poking the flames with the iron poker, though she seemed to be using the hem of her skirt so her fingers would not touch the metal directly.

"Why would Dewhurst have a collection of children's rhymes in his house?" Aidan flipped to the next paper, which contained another rhyme about Cervain.

> One was let to slip away
> Five others died before their day
> Cervain, the last
> No one's surpassed
> His might to charge unto the fray.

This made no sense. Granted, Dewhurst had had a child once upon a time – a child that he had murdered. Would she have enjoyed these songs? Did little girls like to hear stories about vampires and wars? He opened his mouth to ask Slaíne, but thought the better of it; she already seemed to be in a mood.

Sorting through the rest of the second, taller pile produced a mixture of receipts and more morbid poetry that spoke of Cervain, and others of 'the Slippery Fiend', who was always getting in and out of difficult situations. The latter Aidan only glanced through, as they were partially written in a language that he recognized as belonging to the Northern Isles. He'd never bothered studying those foreign tongues, and had had no dealings with anyone from outside of the country's mainland. Other names and titles came to his attention as he read: Melnine, Edell, and 'the Tight Fist', who was reputed to be at odds with 'the Slippery One'.

Aidan scratched the back of his neck. He was missing something, something vital…unless the words were all ramblings of a madman. "Highly likely," he muttered.

"Huh?" Slaíne's Pull moved nearer. "What're you lookin' at?" She was so close he could feel the warmth of her breath seeping through his collar.

He closed his eyes and thought very cold thoughts. "I can't make any sense of these children's riddles," he ground out after a moment, deciding that raging would be a better course of action than what he had been thinking about a moment before. *Keep your mind on what matters, Aidan.*

The girl reached around him to grab one of the papers, her hand brushing his ribs. She seemed oblivious to his turmoil, as she did not jump back at once in order to put a proper distance between them. "These are in Abrish."

Aidan sighed, and only then did she move back. His insides hurt at the sudden distance, but he shook himself and said, "I thought as much."

"Wait a minute," she said after a moment of study.

He turned to her. "You recognize some words?"

Slaíne hushed him and squinted at the paper. "These aren't no children's songs, Mr. Aidan." The maddening girl was quiet then, studying the rest of the paper and then reaching to pick up more.

"You can read Abrish?" he asked.

"'Course. The elves made me learn." The fire spat out sparks at the hem of her dress, which smoked as she cursed and stomped out the glow. Still she did not take her eyes off the papers. "My reading's poor," she said after some time, her dress charred in places. "But these riddles are clues."

"Clues?"

She snorted. "That's what I said, innit? Not all of them, mind. Some are a history of sorts. Others have got to be make-believe. Fairy stories."

"What makes you say so?" Aidan asked, starting in on the third and tallest stack of papers and oilskins.

"Because some of these things are nay possible."

Aidan raised an eyebrow at her, a challenge. "Come now, Sláine. I can Summon and you can fly. Many things are possible."

Sláine let out a laugh that came off as more of a snort. "I don't remember hearing about no seven wizards ruling the land with an iron hand." She scoffed. "The elves always said wizards left these shores an age and a day ago – did nay want nothin' to do with humans and other magic-kind."

"Wait," Aidan said, putting down the papers he had lifted and approaching her for the ones she had taken from him. "So they're talking about wizards?"

"I dunno," she admitted, holding the papers away from him. "Very well could be. Or could be about dragons."

He glared at her and dove for the documents. "Now who's being fanciful?"

She stuck out her tongue and handed back the papers. "Here. Lemme know if you find anythin' useful." Now she was just provoking him. He saw that familiar fire in her eyes, recognized the hunger that must be mirroring his own.

Aidan shuddered. *Two rooms would have been a better idea....* He refused to take the bait; he needed to keep a clear, focused mind.

"Care to open the window?" he said, keeping his tone casual.

"I just lit a fire," she snapped.

Aidan shrugged and turned his back to her. "Suit yourself." He busied himself. "I might need you to translate some more later. First I'm going to look for the map."

"You lost it again?"

He bristled but ignored the implication of carelessness on his part. As if he could keep everything in order in Nothingness. What was he? A maid? Muttering to himself, Aidan closed his eyes and tried to recall what the map's Pull had felt like to him. Then, satisfied that he had a good impression of it, he located a similar Pull and Called it out of the pile, making certain that the papers left behind on the bed did not scatter. "Got you," he said, grasping the map. Aidan frowned as he spied a riddle where there should have been a legend. "More rhymes?" He read it once aloud, his heart thudding hard in his chest:

"To my dear slippery fellow:
They may search high
They may search low
Ask yourself why
And drop all pretenses
Find me by using all your good senses.
Yours ever,
The Elder."

They looked at each other as Aidan said, "The Elder...could that mean Cedric the Elder? What if—"

"The poems are about the wizards who made the Goblets Immortal?" The words hung in the air between them like a lightning storm.

CHAPTER FOUR

Aidan

Between the two of them, Aidan and Sláine sorted the mounds of papers into eight piles: one for each wizard, equaling six piles; one for anything that looked like it might be about a different wizard but they couldn't tell which; and a rubbish pile that consisted of receipts and other useless things. The 'might-be' pile was the largest by far. In second place was the rubbish stack. Aidan kept the map with Cedric the Elder's pile, to be studied once they'd finished sorting.

Sláine translated whatever Aidan could not make out, scribbling hasty notes in the margins if there was room. By the time they'd made decent progress on finding clues for each wizard, and thus each Goblet – since each Goblet was made from its corresponding wizard's blood – the sun was but a small half circle through the warped glass window. The fire had long since died down, the embers smoking gently.

"We should eat something," Sláine said at long last, setting the quill back into its inkwell. Her stomach growled in agreement as she stretched her arms above her head and yawned. "I feel like me brain's gonna leak out me eyes."

Aidan grunted his response. He would have plenty of time for food later. The feeling that he was on the brink of some discovery burned bright within his breast, and he continued to pore over the same page over and over again, hoping to absorb the true meaning behind the words. "Each wizard seems to have his own title to go with his name...and strange ones, at that. Cedric the Elder is normal enough, but he must have been the head wizard, their better. No, maybe their eldest."

Slaíne yawned pointedly, but he ignored her.

"If we can find Cedric's grave, and drink of the Goblet that is reputed to have been buried there, then we shall be able to find all of the others at the very least. At the very most, we can kill Meraude." He laughed and went back to his studies.

The girl was not done with him yet, it would seem. Her Pull approached, and her footfalls made her presence known in a none-too-quiet way. She cleared her throat. "Sir? You forgettin' somethin'?"

Aidan blinked and all of their food stores appeared on the bed nearest the window. "There. Eat what you think is best."

"You're not going to ration it?" She sounded horrified. Her tone then turned suspicious. "You don't mean to not eat, do you?"

He could scarce absorb her meaning, but it didn't matter. He had a few questions of his own. "Who do you think this 'Slippery One' is? I see many mentions of him in fights with the 'Knowing One', who must be...." He turned the page over. "Ah, the Knowing One must be the originator of the Seeing Goblet."

"Uh-huh," Slaíne muttered through a mouthful of food. "Sir, don't mind me saying so, but you're talkin' an awful lot." She paused. "Are you all right?"

What sort of question was that? Of course he was all right. In fact, he hadn't felt so hopeful since...well, for a very long time. "I'm perfectly well," he assured her, setting the page in his hands aside and picking up another one. "Why do you ask?"

Slaíne muttered a few very choice words. "Are you— I mean, is that thing still in your head?"

That caught his attention. "What the devil are you talking about? What thing in my head?" When she gave him a pointed look, it occurred to him what she meant. "Oh. The person who took over my body? That?"

"Yes, that."

Aidan shook his head. "No. I can't feel him right now." Something hard hit him in the back of the head, and he spun around with a few choice words of his own on his lips as an apple rolled to a stop on the floor. In pain and confused, he looked at her. "What did you do that for?"

"You are obsessed."

Stupidly he stood there, staring at her and then the apple. "Obsessed? Slaíne, this is important work. You want to find the Goblets Immortal, don't you?"

She shrugged. "Not particular like." Before he could start an argument, she forestalled him by tossing a hunk of bread at his face, which he Called into his hand. "All I'm sayin' is you gotta be careful."

"Careful?"

"Mm."

"Careful of what?"

Her eyes flashed. "Wantin' revenge too much."

Aidan couldn't help himself; he began to laugh, a true belly laugh. He went back to his work when she leveled a glare at him. He needed to think, not be distracted by feelings he didn't deserve to have. "Slaíne, you of all people are one to preach about the dangers of vengeance. You want Meraude dead as much as I. She did, after all, kill your family, too."

"Yes, maybe. But I still take care of myself."

Now looking at her, he tore off a hunk of bread with his teeth and chewed it with exaggerated savagery. It was easy to be angry, easier than.... "There," he said, crumbs flying from his livid lips. "Happy?"

It was Slaíne's turn to laugh. "Men." Then she went back to her small meal of dates and dried meat, facing away from him entirely.

After a while, Aidan took another bite of bread and a few gulps of water. He hadn't realized how hungry he was until then, and allowed himself to sidle up next to Slaíne. "Forgive me."

Apparently nonplussed, the girl looked up at him. "What?"

"This is important to me, Sláine." He picked up one of the remaining pasties and bit into it. "I spent most of my life believing that I had killed my family or made them disappear to somewhere in Nothingness. Now that I know Meraude killed them, I can avenge my parents. And my brother, Sam." *And finally have peace.* He chewed in silence for a moment, well aware that she was watching him, but not wanting to see her expression. The pasty was dry crust stuffed with savory onions and potatoes at one end, and raspberry jam at the other. He ate it with gusto, enjoying the tartness at the finish.

Sláine sighed again before saying, "You eat like an elf."

* * *

Aidan studied the map long after Sláine had turned in for the night, neither saying a word to the other. Her soft breathing now filled in the silences between crackling logs and crinkling papers, and it was more distracting than anything he had ever experienced. Perhaps he should give up for the evening and get some sleep himself. Dawn would break before he knew it, and then he would be sorry when they had to make their way on the road again.

The map was unlike any Aidan had ever seen. Instead of many names of towns and roads, there were mostly drawings of landmarks: curves that could be a mountain or a molehill, gnarled trees that could be a forest or an orchard, and scattered throughout in a tiny scrawl was the occasional riddle. Again Aidan read the poem at the top of the map, and again he wondered if he would end up bald from tearing his hair out. "The Elder is Cedric," he said, causing Sláine to snort and turn over in her sleep. He tried to ignore her. "He talks of the Slippery Fellow, who I assume is the Summoner, whose name I'm yet unsure of...."

Sláine groaned and tossed over again. "Ruddy well go to sleep already." She muttered some nonsense about rotting turnips and began to snore.

The lantern ran out of oil then, and the light died. Aidan swore and Dismissed it, and searched for the candles in Nothingness, but thought better of it. He would wait 'til morning's light before having another look. Sleep tugged at the corners of his eyes. He stretched and yawned, and set the papers back on the floor. They would keep.

Aidan rose to check on the fire once more, pulled on the door handle to make certain everything was secure, before crawling beneath the coverlet of the single bed nearest the door. As he began to drift off to sleep, he felt the now-all-too-familiar cold tingling in his shoulder and tried to wake himself. It was no use. Aidan began to dream...if that was what he would call it.

The man who had taken over his body now more than once was standing next to the intact barn back on the Ingledark estate. His dark eyes were crinkled in good humor, but he soon wore a scowl. "Are you sure it was wise to leave Tristram alive?"

Aidan groaned as his eyes adjusted to the light; it was morning here. "I can't go around killing everyone, you know. People will talk."

"Talking people are the problem. I shouldn't have let you stop me."

That made Aidan snarl. "Let me? See here, friend, this is my mind and my body. You just keep inviting yourself in. I won't have you—"

Salem started laughing. "Easy, Aidan. I'm only giving you a hard time. Though I am questioning if you're going soft."

Aidan leveled a glare at him. "Is there a reason you're here?"

Was it his imagination, or was the stranger hurt? It must have been a trick of the light, because the next moment Salem was smiling and laughing again. "I wanted to know how you were getting on with the map."

"I've been puzzling over it and the other papers all night, but I'm not really getting anywhere with them. What?"

Salem was looking at Aidan as if he were missing something. "Aidan, I think Meraude might have wanted you to have the maps. Do you know why?"

Aidan shrugged. "No, not really."

Salem shook his head. "You are the only one who can find the Questing Goblet." He looked at Aidan as if letting the idea sink in.

What did he mean? "Does the Goblet have a certain Pull?"

The man was already shaking his head. "Not the Goblet. The place."
When that did not enlighten Aidan, Salem began pacing. "Let me teach you
some magical history." *He cleared his throat self-consciously before continuing.*
"Forgive me, I've only learned this since I was…well, since coming here. It's
still new to me, in a sense."

"Go on."

Salem nodded his appreciation and started again. "Around five hundred
years ago, there was the Great War. *Not a human war, mind, but one where
magic-kind battled for their freedom from the seven wizards in power at the
time. Many elves, centaurs, goblins, and the like lost their lives in two three-
day battles. One of the wizards sided with and fought alongside the creatures,
which put him in favor when the wizards lost and their blood was drained.
Anyway, where magical blood is spilled, that is where you will find Cedric
the Elder's tomb."* *He stood there looking at Aidan, as if that was enough to
explain how Aidan was going to find the Goblet.*

Aidan cleared his throat. "Salem, is it?"

The man hesitated and then nodded. "Yes. What?"

"I still don't quite see."

*With a knowing look, Salem perched atop a bale of hay, which Aidan
hadn't noticed until that moment.* "Well," *he said,* "why do you think you
found the elves so quickly when you needed to? How did the goblins and
nymphs find you?"

Aidan shrugged. "Someone said that deep calls to deep."

Salem was shaking his head. "Yes, but no. *All magical beings share a
likeness in their makeup, which allows us to identify each other – sometimes,
if the conditions are right and the being is paying attention. But you're
a Summoner. You have Eldred the Slippery's blood flowing through your
veins, a blood that cries out for all things, especially other magical blood.
That's why the Goblets repel and yet draw you at the same time."* *He looked
rather pleased with himself.* "Unless I indwell – which means I take over
your body momentarily – nothing can stop you from sensing magic but iron,
and even that makes itself known to you. You're our best hope of finding the
battleground where magical blood was spilled. You find that, Aidan, and you

can kill Meraude. Claim the Goblet before Meraude can, and all magic-kind is saved."

This seemed easy…almost too easy. "So you're saying if I simply just reach out and feel for this place, I'll find it?"

The man sighed. "Aidan, I really don't know how to Summon. I'm an Endurer. You know, strength."

Aidan nodded. Since he'd felt Salem's strength coursing through him before, it shouldn't have come as a surprise. "Right. So, I'm supposed to figure this out on my own?"

"Well, the maps should be of some help."

"They're full of riddles."

Salem nodded. "Yes, and they all seem to be saying the same thing: a Summoner can find Cedric's tomb. But there are some other hints." He made a face. "But no one will help me with them. I never was very good at puzzles and riddles."

"No one will help you with them?" Aidan asked, brow furrowed. "Who are you asking exactly?"

Now the man seemed uncomfortable. Shaking his head, he hopped off the hay bale and motioned for Aidan to follow him. "The others. The other, you know, magical dead. We live here in the Beyond together."

A thought occurred to Aidan, one that he had not entertained before. "So my parents—"

"Sorry, Aidan. They weren't magical beings." They made their way behind the mansion and into the orchard at the west end of the property. Salem began picking apples. "I assume these aren't in season yet in the land of the living?"

Aidan shook his head. "No. But they seem to be here?"

"Everything's always in season in the Beyond. Here." Salem tossed a few at Aidan, who only just caught them. "Dismiss these. They should stay in your cache in Nothingness, just like anything from your world that you send." Something was troubling the young man, but he wasn't voicing it.

Aidan wondered if he should ask what was wrong, but thought the better of it. He always hated it when people meddled in his own affairs; why would *anyone else be different? Dismissing the apples, he said, "Why don't the other – er, the other magical dead—"*

"Why don't they want me helping you find the Questing Goblet?" Salem shrugged. *"I'm not entirely sure. No one will give me a straight answer. Treevain was all right with my helping you, but she's a bit mad, if you ask anyone. I had to steal the maps when no one was watching. If they find out you have them…."* He gave Aidan a stern look.

The message was clear: Salem would be in trouble with his magical dead brethren if Aidan didn't keep a closed mouth. He nodded. *"Your secret's safe with me."*

Relief lightened the man's features, and he took a bite of a blue apple. *"These ones taste like pumpernickel. Here, try it."* He tossed Aidan a blue one, one without a bite in it.

"Thank you," Aidan said, trying not to make a face. He'd always hated pumpernickel bread, but he was afraid of offending, so he took a tentative bite. The apple, crisp and cold, tasted nothing like pumpernickel. It was sweeter than honey and tasted like a feast of desserts all packed into one mouthful: jam rolls, peach tarts, apple syllabub, cherry jam spread on a bit of holiday bread. All of the flavors of his childhood came rushing back to Aidan in that one overpowering bite. He felt young, innocent, and carefree, just like before…well, before everything went wrong.

"Like it?" Salem asked, his expression mischievous.

Aidan couldn't speak for a moment, so he nodded instead. *"That was – what was that?"*

Salem smiled. *"No one's been able to agree on a name. I call them Memory Apples. Aptly named, yes?"*

"I was thinking of—"

"Your mother's great holiday parties?"

Aidan frowned. *"How did you know?"* Wonderful, the man was reading his mind. Could Aidan strangle someone who was already dead?

As if scenting danger, Salem took a few steps back and tossed him a yellow apple. *"These ones draw out the truth. They're a cross between the Memory Apples and the regular red variety. Don't bother taking a bite; they taste mostly like any ordinary apple. Catch."* He tossed another yellow apple

and one pink and one blue one, along with an apple the size of Aidan's head, calling out names as Aidan Dismissed each. "The big one is Meat and Potatoes. It'll fill your belly and give you the nourishment you need for three days. The others taste like slop, but they help with eyesight and hearing. And these—"
He threw five shiny red ones at Aidan. "Well, those are just regular apples."

"You don't have to give me all of this."

"Sure I do." He grinned at Aidan. "Now, let's visit the vegetable garden. I think the fairy taters are the best, but we'll see if you—" Salem's face paled and he stopped talking.

Aidan looked at the darkening sky with Salem. Up until that moment, everything had been still and peaceful. Now lightning crackled in the distance. Thunder boomed, and hail fell from the heavens. "What's happening?"

Salem turned to Aidan and put his hands on his shoulders. "Wizards walk the earth again, Aidan. Be – be careful. They did not all fight on our side last time."

"Is that what this is all about?" He gestured at the sky as the wind began to whip through the trees.

With a shudder, Salem released Aidan and stepped away. "Yes, and no. But I think you should probably go now. It's hard for the land when you dwell too long." His expression was rueful, but he offered no further explanation.

"How do I leave?" Aidan asked, looking around to see if an exit would appear.

When he turned back, Salem had a shovel in hand and brought it down hard upon Aidan's head.

Yelping, Aidan awoke to sunlight pouring onto his face.

"'Morning," Slaíne greeted him a tad too cheerfully for his liking.

Aidan groaned and rubbed his head. It felt like he was still being bludgeoned with the shovel. "What time is it?"

"Dunno. But you've been talking nonsense in your sleep for the last half hour." By the look on her face, he must have been saying some amusing things, but he did not dare ask what.

Then she left the room so he could be alone for a moment. Why had Salem hit him with that shovel? That couldn't be the only way of knocking someone out of the Beyond.

Aidan freshened up at the washbasin, gave himself a quick shave, aware that Slaíne's Pull was on the move. Surely she wouldn't go far, but he had to wonder what she was up to. Aidan rinsed off his face and the blade and was about to go in search of his traveling companion, but there was no need: Slaíne returned with two plates of steaming food. When he stared at her in wonderment, she frowned.

"What?"

"How did you get food?"

That had been the wrong thing to say. "I did nay steal it."

Aidan raised his hands in placation. "I didn't say that you stole it. But…."

Slaíne blew a strand of hair out of her eyes. "I gave them some coin you gave me afore, of course, and said to send the food to our room. What else would I 'ave done?"

This was no good. "Slaíne," he said with care, taking one of the plates from her outstretched hands before she changed her mind and decided to throw it at him. "When you say you told them to send it to our room…you didn't give a name, did you?"

A mischievous glint showed in her eyes. "Bartholomew Tripe in the first upper room on the left." Apparently she thought her name choices for him amusing.

He glowered. "No one is going to believe for one moment that my last name is Tripe. Now people are going to know I'm hiding my identity."

She should have looked contrite and worried, but instead the maddening girl laughed in his face and took a seat on the windowsill. "Naw, there's lots of Tripes in the area. The maid asked if you was related to the Tripe family in Brontsville."

"That might have been a trap, Slaíne." He tried approaching her. "If you agreed, and the family is made up, we will have been had. There is at least one price on my head." He thought for a moment. "In fact, once Meraude figures out I'm not working for her but against her, there will be two. I'm a wanted man."

But the girl was tearing into her brown bread with butter and red jam. Once she had swallowed the morsel, she replied, "I said no such thing, Mr. Aidan. I just said I did nay know who that was." Well, that was a relief, at least. "And if you're nay going to eat your bread, I'd like it."

To show how very much he was annoyed, Aidan took a giant bite of bread and chewed. They glared at each other in silence as they ate bread, roasted potato, boiled bacon, and seasoned meat patties. With full bellies, though, the animosity between them did not last long.

"They're supposed to bring up a jug of small beer," Slaíne said after finishing off the last of her bacon. She licked her fingers as a Pull approached the door and someone banged on it thrice. "And that would be them now."

Aidan set his plate aside and opened the door. Instead of being met with a jug of small beer, a fist flew up and hit him in the jaw. "Where's my money?" the red-faced man demanded as Aidan regained his footing. He tried pushing his way into the room, but Slaíne was there, helping hold the door partially shut.

"What did you do that for?" she shouted at the stout little man. "Leave us be." She made a face. "You reek of ale, you drunkard."

"Angus owes me money," he belched.

Prodding his jaw, Aidan shooed the man away. "I don't know any Angus. Go away and abuse someone else."

The funny fellow sputtered mightily for a moment, swayed on the spot, and then tried again to enter the room. "This is a free country yet. I have rights." He hiccupped and his whole broad chest heaved. He pointed at Slaíne. "Yer father owes me. That wood table broke not two years after I got it."

"My father," Slaíne said, her voice trembling with rage, "has been dead for well over a decade."

"Slaíne, lower your voice. You're going to draw more unwanted attention." Aidan pushed the man in the chest and tried to close the door the rest of the way.

But the little man was fast and stuck his boot in the way before Aidan could do any such thing. "You're the niece. I remember everything and everyone, mind, so don't look at me that way. Yer no-good uncle sold me a cabinet and a table one-and-twenty years ago. Woodworkers, the brothers were. Yes, I never forgot the little redheaded brat old Fen and Kate brought home."

Aidan looked at Slaíne, hoping she wasn't going to make a bigger scene than had already been made. He was surprised to find her face had drained of all its color. "Slaíne? Are you all right?"

The man looked at her knowingly. "Struck a nerve now, did I?" He licked his thin lips and put his hands on either side of the doorframe. "I am not leaving without my money, girl. And I don't care what damage I might have to cause in order to get it."

That was enough for Aidan. He released the door and grabbed the man by the collar, drawing him close enough to catch his words. "You might want to think more carefully about dealing out threats, sir."

The man's small round eyes darted to and fro, looking frantically for help or something to hit his attacker with; Aidan wasn't sure which. "I won't be talked to like that. I am not friendless here."

"I am not friendless wherever I go," Aidan said, putting extra menace into his words. Once the other had begun to tremble, Aidan set him right again. "I suggest you leave now, quietly."

The drunk hiccupped again, nodded, and toddled away toward a room at the end of the hall. He paused once and looked at Aidan, then scurried back into his room and closed the door softly behind him.

Aidan waited there a minute, making certain the other didn't come back, then returned inside and bolted the door. "We're going to have to leave at once, I'm afraid." He Dismissed all the maps and papers that he had so carefully organized the previous night, and then sat down to tug on his boots. "We can't afford to cause any trouble wherever we go. People might...." He stopped and looked at Slaíne, who was shaking. His chest prickled. "You know him?"

Slaíne shook her head. "No." Her voice was soft, and out of the blue, she ran to her bed and started gasping.

Uncertain as to what exactly had upset her, Aidan sat there for a moment and tried to decide what he should do. Then, after a short deliberation, he tugged his other boot on and went over to where she was hunched over, swearing. He picked up the water jug, which only had a few mouthfuls left in it, poured that into a glass, and handed it to her.

She took a sip and then another. "Jus' bein' stupid."

"Hmm." Aidan took the glass from her and patted her back until, at last, she seemed to have calmed a bit. He sighed. "You're in no shape to be traveling."

She shot him a defiant look, which might have been fierce had she not looked to be in such a pitiable state. "I'm all right. The worst is over."

"I'll be the judge of that." He put his arm around her and helped her to the bed, though she fought him. "Lie down...please." When she did not co-operate, he gave her a slight shove, and she fell onto her back, her mouth forming a perfect O.

Slaíne snarled at him, but he bent down and put his lips to her ear, and she stilled. "You don't always have to be strong." He wanted to say more, to do more, but he needed to think about his next move, so he settled for a lingering kiss on her cheek and turned before he could be tempted to do more.

★   ★   ★

He left Slaíne to rest, making certain to keep within the confines of the curse lest it seize her and cause more pain...or worse. "Excuse me," he said to one of the maids walking past, her sleeves rolled up to the elbows. "I was promised a pitcher?"

The woman stared at him in bewilderment for a moment before enlightenment dawned on her face. "Oh, you're the newlyweds what want some of our fine beer. It's weak, mind, even for small beer."

Newlyweds? Sláine's fabrications were going too far this time. Still, how could he correct it without exposing himself or shaming her? So he smiled and said, "Yes. That would be us."

She favored him with a polite smile, hurried off, and returned a minute later with the promised pitcher. "It's on me. Only, don't tell the master."

"Thank you, ma'am. I'm sorry to trouble you, but there has been a small disturbance between one of the other lodgers and me."

"Oh? Is it anything that warrants calling the law?"

Aidan shook his head and tried to keep his expression calm. "A man has mistaken my wife for someone and has upset her."

Her brow furrowed. "I don't likely know what I'm supposed to do about the matter…no offense meant, sir."

"I was merely wondering what you could tell me about the short, stocky man at the end of the hall above stairs." Perhaps it was beneath him, inquiring into Sláine's affairs, but if she knew the man and wasn't letting on, he needed to know what wasps' nest they had stepped on.

Now the maid seemed more enlightened. "Ah, Titus. A charity case we house from time to time. He's a troublemaker. Has a grudge against everyone he's ever met, and he don't forget nothing nor nobody, mind." She leaned in closer, her breath reeking of rot. When she spoke again, her tone was lowered, and Aidan had to strain to hear her over the noise of the pub crowd just below. "He's a drunkard." She nodded and blushed, as if this would be news to anyone other than herself. "Don't tell him I said."

"I assure you, ma'am, that I won't breathe a word of it to a soul."

That seemed to set the woman at ease, for she smiled broadly and offered him a cake of soap. "Here." She sniffed what she must have thought was discreetly. "For your, er, missus." Then the woman hurried away, leaving the odor of castor oil in her wake.

Well, that had yielded little, other than another cake of soap. He pocketed the offering and hurried back to the upper floor with the beer. Upon entering the room, Aidan took care to make as little noise as possible, as Slaíne had been sleeping when he left. He saw her eyes were open, though she closed them before he could say anything, so he poured himself a glass and Summoned the papers back onto his bed.

This time he was able to sort them back into the correct piles... mostly. Some of the papers had yet to be looked at thoroughly and translated by Slaíne, while others still simply remained a mystery. He picked up the map to Cedric the Elder's tomb and studied it again. Would it really call out to him, the magical blood spilled on the ground there? If the war had been five hundred years ago, then rain and time would have most assuredly washed away and diluted the Pulls. For now at least, he would have to study the map and figure out landmarks.

Something caught his eye that hadn't before, a small scrawl in the corner of the map that he might have first mistaken for oil stains from someone's hands. He ignored the cold prickling in his shoulder and took the map over to the window, holding the paper up to the light filtering in. It was a different hand than had penned the key on the map, a hastily scrawled note: *Starberry grove?*

Aidan blinked his tired eyes and scanned down the face of the map. When he reached the center of the paper, which appeared to be a drawing of a mountain covered in red dots, he squinted. Could that be what the note meant? "But what have starberry groves have to do with anything?" he muttered. "They grow everywhere. They're a weed." The droplets on the mountain or mound, or whatever it might be, very well could represent blood shed in the Great War. Aidan felt he was missing something. He set down the map and began searching for the word 'starberry' in the other papers.

In one poem regarding a wizard named Edell, a *brute who was known to eat in excess and would often find himself drunk on the juice of dayberries.* That was what Slaíne's translation said in the margin. Next to the name Edell, there had been written a question mark, and both had been circled lightly. Aidan scanned farther down the page, and while he found no more references to food, there was a note that said *Enduring Goblet?* Whether that was Dewhurst's or Slaíne's surmise, he could not be certain.

For the next two hours, Aidan pored over the papers, searching for something, anything, that might enlighten him. He was so caught up in his work that he barely noticed that Slaíne had risen until she asked where the beer was, startling him out of his studies.

"Hmm? Oh, over on the sideboard."

She gave him an inquisitive look, but said nothing as she trod over to the beer and noisily poured herself a glass. Then, disturbing Aidan again, the glass thudded down on the table like a judge's gavel. "Sir, we need to talk."

"Of course," he said, setting the papers aside. He had gotten nowhere with his reading, anyway; maybe he would learn some more about the drunkard from Slaíne. "What is it?"

For a moment she worried her lip, squinting as if she were trying to remember something. When she spoke again, her voice was low and serious. "I think that man might know who cursed me."

That brought Aidan up short. He stared at her in wonderment for a moment, but then came to his senses and said, "I thought you said the elves had you cursed?"

Slaíne nodded. "I think they did. Only, I was so little, it's hard to remember exactly. I do remember a strange man coming along after my mam and pap was killed by Meraude. The man worked for the elves or...." She frowned. "Or maybe he ran afoul of them. It's all so muddy in my head."

"But you think that the drunkard down the hall might know something about your past?" He watched as she poured herself another glass of beer. "What makes you think that man knows anything connected to you?"

She downed the glass of small beer in one large gulp, and then hiccupped. "Because he mentioned my parents' names."

CHAPTER FIVE

Aidan

Aidan stared at Slaíne in contemplative silence for a moment before saying, "So you *were* the little girl he remembered?"

Slaíne shrugged. "I dunno. But he spoke their names." Her nose wrinkled up, scrunching all of her freckles together. "Least, it *sounded* like them. It's been so long since anyone's spoken of 'em, I can't be sure."

"And this man believes your parents – your *father* owes him money?"

"What of it?" she said. "Papa made good furniture out of the best wood. I remember him making my cradle, and I never had no complaints."

He scratched his chin. "Right. I'm not saying that your father made poor furniture, what I'm saying is that I need to know if you remember anything or have heard anything in the past about this man, your parents, the Circle, and the Blest. No more secrets."

She frowned. "Why?"

"If this man is going to be trouble, we need to leave before word of our presence here is spread around. Surely you must see that any familiar face is a danger to us now?"

Her mouth opened and closed a few times. Slaíne jumped to her feet, crossed her arms, and moved over to the window. At length, she spoke. "Papa was a woodworker, Mam was a maid. I don't remember no one complainin' never."

"How old were you when they...."

"Died?" She shrugged. "I was four when they was killed, and

shortly after I was wanderin', then I was taken, and— What?"

How could she possibly remember so much of her early childhood? She must be fabricating things, wittingly or not. "You wouldn't have known if there were any complaints. You were but a babe."

She seemed to lose confidence. "Some things are kinda – what do you say? Murky. But I remember my parents very clearly." Her look became distant, wistful, as she said, "She had the finest black hair, shiny as the night sky. And Papa was handsome, though he was balding. They loved each other. Loved me. He always joked about how I was his little doll that he carved out of one of his trees." The memory seemed to have soured, for her face crumpled. "It almost seems right."

"What almost seems right?"

"What? Oh, that they died. Happy people always end up dying tragic deaths." She couldn't have meant that, and Aidan didn't believe for a moment that had been what she was going to say, but he let the matter go. "What I'm sayin' is that maybe this man knows who cursed me, or maybe he done it himself 'cause he was angry about the furniture. And if he can lead us to who cursed me, then surely the curse can be undone."

Aidan thought on it for a moment. What she said made some sense, but what sort of mood might this fellow be in to help them? It did not seem likely that he would come to Slaíne's aid; and even if they did ask, what would the repercussions be? "Slaíne," he said, "if we're going to ask this man what he knows about your curse or whoever cursed you, we need to make certain that he isn't going to hand us over to the authorities."

She gave him a look and said, "I ain't stupid."

"I'm not saying you are. You just…." He gestured vaguely.

"What?" she said, her eyes darkening.

"You have a temper."

Of all things, the girl threw back her head and howled with laughter. "You are one to talk about tempers, sir."

That made him crack a smile himself. "You know, you do have a point there. I'm simply worried that in the heat of the moment, you might say something amiss – if provoked." He turned back to his maps to hide the concern on his face. "I just don't want y— I don't want either of us to get hurt." He sniffed dismissively. "I was stupid, walking straight into Dewhurst's manor. His wife knew who I was all along. What if this man figures things out? I don't want a repeat of what happened before…or worse."

"Sir," she said, not impatiently, "it's a risk I need to take. Please, lemme take it."

If he can help break the curse, what happens then? After a moment, he nodded. "Right. So, how are you going to question him?"

That seemed to throw Slaíne off guard, for she opened and shut her mouth, her brow crumpling. "Hmm. I was rather hoping you would do it with me."

He had thought so. With a grunt, he put the papers aside and turned back to the girl. "Right. We should probably wait until he's sober."

"Yes, that would perhaps be best."

"Maybe we could rent a dining room downstairs, invite him for a meal, on the pretense of figuring out a way to pay him back for the table or whatever it is he claims was flawed." Aidan poured himself some of the beer and took but a sip before setting it aside. "No, we both need a clear head. And we had better be ready to run, should he turn on us." Overcome with some conflicting emotions, he went back to the maps on his bed and Dismissed the ones he didn't think he'd get around to studying. When he trusted himself to speak, he said, "We'll leave early tomorrow morning. Now, I'll try to figure out where our next steps should take us."

"Thank you, sir. Means a lot to me."

Aidan simply nodded and went back to work.

*   *   *

After studying the map and papers for an hour, Aidan realized he would have to try something else. The map was incomprehensible, save for the fact that they would need to head north, and the clues were all vague riddles. It was time to see if Salem's words could have any worth, though he was still cross with and uncertain of the man who had hit him in the face with a shovel.

Seeing that Slaíne was on the other side of the room and otherwise occupied, Aidan sat on the edge of his bed and closed his eyes. Her Pull was going to be a distraction he would have to feel around, and he needed a clear head that evening, but he reached out and started exploring different Pulls. He started with what was closest and strongest: Slaíne's Pull. Having located and centered in on it, he reached beyond it and into the inn. There were dozens of individual human Pulls, nothing familiar or distracting, so he moved beyond those and into the outer village. Here was where it started to become more difficult. The Pulls outside were distant, weaker, and more easily confused with the inanimate Pulls of things like trees and buildings, and the living Pulls of horses and dogs. Aidan did not try sorting out and separating those Pulls, but reached out farther still, into the woods surrounding. Soon he felt his connection to all things beyond and pushed his senses farther. There was something out there, something he had ignored before, to the north of the inn, a dull pulsing....

"Sir?"

Cursing, Aidan lost focus and his senses drew back from the pulsing enigma and latched on to Slaíne's Pull entirely. He was met with a blinding headache, and something heavy hitting him solidly in the side. "What the devil?"

"Sir," said Slaíne from right next to him. "Next time, shout a warning before you Call me."

Temples throbbing, Aidan opened his eyes a crack and saw that he had in fact Called her, and was sitting with her glued to his side. Again he cursed. "Just a moment." Her Pull seemed to have strengthened, and feeling around it was impossible. The world was

Slaíne, and Slaíne was the world. Footsteps echoed outside their door, and Aidan forced himself to search for the Pull they belonged to, and only then was he able to Release Slaíne, who seemed more than eager to get away from him.

Her cursing and spitting followed her to the other side of the room. "What was that all about?"

Aidan groaned and let himself fall backward onto the mattress. "I should have warned you, I'm sorry. I didn't know it would be that difficult." He then explained what he had been trying to do: find the tomb of Cedric the Elder with his abilities. That raised more questions.

"How exactly did you know to look for a magical Pull to lead you there?" She visibly stiffened. "Tell me you ain't talking to Meraude in no visions again."

He was quick to shake his head, and the whole room seemed to spin. "No, Meraude has not visited my dreams since the nymph stabbed me in the shoulder. But...."

"But what?" she pressed.

Aidan made a face. "I have been talking to someone in the Beyond."

That made Slaíne stare at him like he had announced he was there and then going to dance around naked. She blinked furiously and shook her head. "The Beyond? You mean the land of the magical dead?"

He wondered at her. "You've heard of it, then?"

She sniffed. "'Course I have. Was raised by magic folk, weren't I? How is you able to talk to them?" Aidan didn't get a chance to answer before Slaíne gasped and stared at him, visibly awed. "That was no regular blade, was it?" She took to pacing. "So, if you was stabbed with a blade that makes you able to communicate with the magical dead...."

Trying to remember what Salem had told him, Aidan frowned. "The man I've been speaking to in the Beyond—"

"The man that's possessed you?"

He cringed; that was not a word to throw around lightly. "Yes, or whatever it is he has been doing. He says that he wants me to find the Questing Goblet, but that most of the other magical dead are against it. At least, that's the impression he gave me." Aidan rubbed his temples, which throbbed out of time with his pulse and in time with the rising and falling of Slaíne's chest.

"So, did you find it?"

Aidan shook his head, but then stopped. Had he found it? There had been that strange pulsing sensation north of there, but was that really what they were after? "I think I might have a general sense of where it lies. But before you get excited, I don't think that it's close by. It could be in the center of the country or perhaps farther north." With care he sat up in increments, making certain to close his eyes and breathe slowly. After a time, he opened his eyes a fraction, and the room at least had ceased spinning. "What time is it?"

"It's later afternoon, nearing suppertime." She brought him a glass of small beer from the side table. "Looks like you need a drink after all."

He accepted it without comment and took a tentative sip, pulling a face as it did not quite agree with his stomach. "Let's hope a private dining room is still available for our meeting with your friend."

Once he was certain he was not going to collapse and make a fool of himself on the stairs, Aidan Dismissed the papers, and he and Slaíne went down and talked to the owner of the Spinning Cup Inn. It took some haggling and a few extra coins, but they managed to secure a room for the evening. Aidan passed a missive on to the maid he had talked to earlier. "For the man at the end of our hall."

She gave him an odd look, but took the note. "Are you sure you want to be on speaking terms with Titus? I told you, that man is trouble, if'n you ever seen it."

Aidan ignored the confused look Slaíne gave him; she did not know that he had already talked to the maid about the strange man earlier. "Thank you for the warning, but I'm quite certain."

The maid looked at the back of the folded and sealed paper. "Who should I say this is from?"

"Tell him that an old acquaintance wishes to mend things with him."

"I might be needin' a name to go with that."

Wonderful, now I've aroused her suspicions. "Mr. and Mrs. Tripe, at his service." He ignored Slaíne's elbow, which had slammed into his ribs.

Though she had an odd look on her face, the woman nodded and took the note back above stairs. Once she was out of earshot, Slaíne shoved him.

"Mr. and Mrs.? Really?"

Aidan fought his temper. "Would you rather they think we're living in sin? Besides, you told them we were newlyweds."

Her lips trembled a moment, before she burst out laughing, a sincere, spritely sound which Aidan hated to admit to sorely missing. "Right, I told 'er that." She snorted. "And pigs just might yet fly."

Was he truly that offensive to her? He gave her a look. "Right. Pigs, indeed."

The girl let out a great huff of air. "Don't you go getting all offended at me, sir. You know as well as I that it's all rubbish." And with that, she preceded him into the small dining room they had reserved.

Ignoring his hurt feelings – or at least trying to keep them to himself – Aidan followed her inside. He wanted to familiarize himself with the room and the Pulls contained within, as well as the exits. There were two windows, side by side, that stretched from near the floor and almost to the ceiling. Feeling no iron in the frames, he knew that they could crash through them or he could Dismiss the glass, should they need to make a quick exit that way. Next Aidan judged the distance between the tables and the door, took stock of what inanimate Pulls lay outside, and thought about which objects he might use as a weapon. There was a fireplace in the corner of the room, with an iron grate and poker resting before the smoldering embers. The iron he would have to beware of without drawing attention to the fact that he was leery of the metal.

Once satisfied that he had a handle on the layout of the room, Aidan led Sláine outside, where he sat in one of the five unoccupied rocking chairs. He did not want to be too hopeful that things would go his way; they never did, especially when he thought they were going to. It was always best to prepare for the very worst.

Sláine took the chair next to him and started rocking. "Think of it. This time tomorrow, I might know how to get rid of the curse."

He swallowed. "Don't raise your hopes too high. They might just come crashing down around your ears."

She narrowed her eyes at him. "Aye, always the optimist."

That made him look at her. "And *you* are?" Before she could retaliate with another remark, he said, "What will you do, once you're free?"

"Kill Meraude, if she ain't already dead – by your hand or another." She leaned back in her chair and squinted against the setting sun. "Other than that, I guess I've not thought on it much. Ain't got no family to return to...well, not that I know of. That fellow seems to think I have an uncle. Maybe I'll find him and see where I stand." She looked over at Aidan. "What will you do once you've had your revenge?"

Should they find the remaining Goblets Immortal and defeat Meraude with them, his revenge would be complete...if he survived. A glum thought for an otherwise bright evening. Instead of voicing his concerns, Aidan edged his way around the question. "There will be many opportunities for magical folk, I'm sure. We've lived in the shadows long enough, and I assume we might have Meraude to thank for some of that."

They sat in companionable silence for the next half hour, and then went inside to see if the room they had reserved was ready for their meeting with the man named Titus. Aidan doubted Titus would know anything about Slaíne's curse, but he would never hear the end of it if they moved on without confronting the man.

Inside, the smells of dinner wafted over from the kitchen. Aidan had ordered a good-sized meal: roasted leg of lamb, poached pears and sugared strawberries fresh from a local hothouse, asparagus in a cream sauce, brown bread with butter and raspberry jam, and a spice cake for afters. It had cost him a good amount, but he hoped it might loosen the curmudgeonly man's tongue.

Aidan was going to wait inside, but a young woman breezed past, yelling incomprehensibly.

"Wonder what she's going on about?" said Slaíne.

Aidan watched with trepidation as a young man followed her, shouting as well.

"Is there a doctor? A man's collapsed," the young man shouted. "Says he's been stabbed."

Aidan moved away from the door slowly. If someone had been stabbed, the lawmen would be called, and if they recognized Aidan…. He shuddered to think. "It might be time to take our leave," he said below his breath, hoping Slaíne could hear him. Knowing their supplies wouldn't last them long, Aidan concentrated on Pulls in the kitchen. There was one human Pull moving nearer the front of the inn, perhaps responding to the cries that had been taken up. It was now or never. Aidan Dismissed everything of a smaller size that he could sense in the kitchen, hoping that he was mostly taking food. He hated to steal like this, but there was no time to stop and buy all of the supplies that he needed.

People were pushing their way out of the building now, some shouting, some sobbing, most looking solemn. "What's going on?" a little girl asked Slaíne.

"Dunno," she replied as she and Aidan moved out of the way.

Aidan seized her hand and they allowed themselves to be absorbed into the masses, moving toward the outer perimeter of the crowd. There was too much noise to speak quietly, and

Aidan did not want to be overheard. They needed to put this town behind them as quickly as possible, though it would make them look suspicious, if anyone had in fact been stabbed. Hopefully the poor soul was all right, whoever it might be, and Aidan possessed a feeling that he knew who.

They continued to be jostled to and fro until they reached the edge of the crowd. Here and there people were asking questions of each other and had obviously heard some of what had transpired at the Spinning Cup.

"Sir," Slaíne said as they rounded a corner of a building and turned their backs to the masses. "Where are we goin'?"

"If someone was hurt by another's hand, we will be brought under suspicion," he said, trying to keep a casual pace. "I don't fancy anyone figuring out who I am."

To his surprise, she pulled against him, attempting to wrench her hand out of his. When he looked, her expression was furious. "I need my answers."

Aidan sighed. "Slaíne, please don't make a scene."

That had been the wrong thing to say. For the second time since he had met her, she slapped him hard across the face. "Is all you ever worry about yourself? You selfish...."

"Finish it," he said, unblinking. "You think me a coward."

She rolled her eyes. "'Course not. I need the curse reversed, Mr. Aidan. If'n I ever want to be free, that man is what's got the answers."

He gave her a tug and started walking again, meeting a little less resistance. "You don't know that for sure, Slaíne. You're clutching at straws."

"At least I've got straws to clutch. Better than air." She looked at him with such pleading in her eyes that Aidan was tempted to give in and return to the inn, which had no doubt been thrown into complete confusion, what with the alleged stabbing and the food disappearing from the kitchen. No, they could not return.

"Slaíne, I know what this means to you...." He let his words trail off, for he knew they would not be sufficient to mollify her. Instead, he started anew. "Here's what we can do. We'll return to the crowd, see if we can find this Titus fellow out among everyone. We can talk to him there, outside, and then we can make our departure, hopefully before any lawmen make an appearance."

Before he could finish getting all of the words out, Slaíne threw her arms around his neck and bussed him on the cheek, her face glowing. "I knew you was no coward."

He froze, strange thoughts whirling through his mind. There was no time to call the words back: Slaíne grabbed his hand and dragged him in the direction of the inn. They had hardly made it within a street of the Spinning Cup when they ran into a crowd of people, which had tripled in size within minutes. Folks were talking excitedly, but over all there hung an air of dread.

"He'll be all right," said a man on Aidan's right. "I reckon he was imagining things."

His friend seemed to think differently. "Imagining? Someone stabbed him. That's nothing you imagine. 'Sides, there was blood everywhere. Don't think he made that up."

"More like stabbed himself," said another.

Some grunted in agreement.

"Was there blood, though? No one's actually said."

"Well," said a woman, "it would not surprise me one bit if he imagined the whole thing. Always fond of the drink, that one. Floating knives, my hide."

Aidan and Slaíne exchanged puzzled looks.

"What's 'appening?" Slaíne asked the woman, who pursed her lips.

"Ain't really my place to say," she said, before eagerly filling them in on what had transpired. "Apparently, he was in his room all by his lonesome when a knife appeared out of thin air and stabbed him in the shoulder. I think he was drinking, but he claims to not have had a drop since this morning."

"Ah," said Slaíne. "Who was this again?"

A few of the men and the woman exchanged dark looks. "Titus the Mad, but of course." She leaned in and said, "Wants attention, that one."

"I don't like it," said another woman. "Someone said they heard two voices in the room before the stabbing."

Aidan had heard enough. They needed to move on, if there was any chance the wound was not an accident, and it sounded like it wasn't. A knife appearing out of nowhere? He needed to get Slaíne's attention. "Well, we had better find a safer place to stay."

It seemed that Slaíne had not heard him, as she asked the second woman a question. "What were they talkin' about? Mr. Titus and the other voice?"

"That's where it gets interesting," said the second woman. "There was something about not meddling in a curse. Titus screamed and said he knew nothing about a curse and— Why, miss, are you all right? You look like you're going to be sick."

Indeed, Slaíne had grown pale and was shaking. Before Aidan could stop her, she pushed her way through the crowd, and he had no choice but to follow her. A dog brushed past them, nearly knocking Aidan over. Aidan gave the beast a contemptuous look before turning his attention to the crowd.

At the front of the masses by the steps leading up to the inn, there were two men who seemed to be in charge. Aidan wondered if he could latch on to Slaíne's Pull and give her a Tug before she reached them, but he knew he couldn't risk it without giving himself and his abilities away.

"What's happened?" Slaíne demanded of one of the men in official uniform of red tunics and chainmail overdress.

"Miss," he said, beginning to put a hand on Slaíne's shoulder, which he seemed to think the better of. "You need to calm yourself."

That had been the wrong thing to say. "Calm meself?" she said. "Ya don't get to tell me when to calm. That man is a family friend. I've every right to know if Titus is going to recover."

The other man in uniform came up beside his comrade. "Miss, your friend has had quite a shock. He should be fine, though."

"Then I can speak to him?"

Feeling a bit of a coward for remaining in the background, Aidan approached Slaíne and put a hand on her shoulder. "Please," he said to the men, "my wife won't rest until she knows that Titus is being taken care of."

The two lawmen exchanged a quick glance before the second one said, "He's not seeing anyone." He held up a hand as if to waylay their protestations. "But I can tell you that, though his nerves seem to be frayed, there is no actual sign of him being stabbed."

Aidan looked at Slaíne. "See, my dear? It was all a misunderstanding." He leaned in to whisper to one of the lawmen, "Titus has been known to have those from time to time."

"Where is he being kept?"

"Titus is in his room, resting."

Slaíne opened her mouth, probably to come out with some other falsehood to work her way inside, but there was a cry from within. The crowd behind them surged forward as a young urchin ran outside. "Sirs," he said to the men in charge. "I have a message for you. You asked me to keep you abreast of what was happening with the drunk."

"Thank you, Jon. If you'll give us a minute...." He gave a pointed look at Slaíne and then Aidan.

The urchin took no notice. "He's dead."

"What?" Slaíne squeaked. "No."

Aidan squeezed her shoulder and tried drawing her back. He'd forgotten how strong she was. "How...?"

"Stroke or something like," the young boy blurted out before he could be stopped. "Doc says he could nay take the stress."

"Thank you, Jon, that's quite enough." The lawman turned to Slaíne. "Does Mr. Rifron have any family that should be notified?" The man gave her a knowing look. "Why don't you go inform them, miss." And with that, the two lawmen turned and went inside.

CHAPTER SIX

Aidan

It took a bit of persuasion, but Aidan convinced Slaíne to leave the inn, as there were no answers left for them there. He made a few discreet inquiries from some of the crowd, and discovered that Titus had no family in the area but was a homeless wanderer who took the occasional job to provide shelter and drink for himself. But then Aidan and Slaíne had to leave the area, as an uproar arose from the kitchen about the missing food that Aidan had Dismissed earlier.

The weather was fair, and the lightly overcast sky promised the night would be warmer than the previous one had been. Aidan led the way out of the village, stopping at a butcher's shop and a bakery on the outskirts. The feast he'd taken from the kitchen would not last them forever, and he felt it would only be fair to spend more coin in the town before he left it like a bandit. Steak-and-potato hand pies ordered in a large number would certainly draw attention, so he ordered half a dozen, and Slaíne came in after and ordered five. He also bought bread and jam, and some dried meat to sustain them for the next fortnight.

Their water bladders had been replenished the day previous, so they made no stop at the last well they saw, but instead stopped inside a quilter's shop and purchased bedrolls to keep them warm if the nights grew cold. The tentmaker's shop was closed, so Aidan Dismissed a few items he hoped were tents from the other side of the wall. Arms overflowing with purchases, Aidan and Slaíne entered the woods and, once he was certain they had not been followed and were not being watched, Aidan Dismissed everything they had bought.

Up to this point, Slaíne had been brooding. Now, with the town fading behind them, she talked in earnest. "It's nay any coincidence that the man dropped dead. Who falls over and dies from something they've imagined?"

Aidan opened his mouth to answer, but Slaíne was not finished.

"And another thing, it was nay just his imagination. Someone or something was trying ter keep him silent about my curse." She nodded sagely.

Though he wished she was wrong, Aidan knew the odds were against it being a mere coincidence. "I agree with you, Slaíne."

She stared at him for a moment as they crashed their way back onto the main path leading north. "You do? You ain't gonna argue? Say I'm overreactin'? Take offense at something?"

He scowled at her. "I don't do those things regularly enough to warrant that attack."

Slaíne threw her head back and howled with laughter. "Right. And me name's Bob. But that's nay the point anyhow. Whoever's cursed me's hurt that poor fellow." She made a sign that superstitious folk made to ward off foul spirits. Then she looked at Aidan, her brow wrinkled. "But that don't explain you."

"What of me?" He pushed through a particularly thick patch of undergrowth they could not find a way around, and then helped Slaíne untangle herself from some creeping myrtle.

"Well," she said, "you was trying to help me break the curse and nothing happened to you." She squinted at him once they had availed themselves of the groundcover. "Maybe 'cause you're Blest?"

Perhaps that was the case. It sounded right. But all of this talk about curses was wearing on him. Aidan did not want her to raise her hopes too high or become obsessed with the subject, lest she be brutally disappointed if her curse could not be lifted. She had seen enough disappointment in her short life, he knew. So he tried to move the conversation away from the topic entirely. "We'd better pick up our pace if we want to be left in peace tonight."

She clucked her tongue in response. "I don't think no one's following us."

"That's not what I meant." He moved a little ways ahead. "There are wolves in these parts. At least, there were the last time I traveled through. They should leave us alone, but there's always the odd chance our luck will run out." If there was such a thing as good luck and bad luck, surely the good always ran out for them. Not that he believed in such nonsense…mostly.

The going was trying on both their nerves and their bodies. Slaíne was able to glide over quite a bit of the overgrowth and bracken, leaving Aidan on the ground to crash through what he could or go around it entirely. But she could not fly between trees that were too close to squeeze through no matter how high she went. True, Aidan thought, she could fly over the trees themselves, but if her gift was anything like his, it took its toll on the mind if overused. Plus, he knew she did not wish to awaken the curse's wrath by getting too far from the one it had latched her to.

Eventide was nigh upon them when their pace slowed considerably. They had not traveled as far north as he would have liked, but neither of them was in the shape nor frame of mind to continue onward, so he proposed that they stop. "Let's look for a suitable place to make shelter – preferably something with lower branches, should we—" He hesitated and then amended, "Should *I* need to quickly get off the ground."

Slaíne let out a tirade of swear words as the hem of her dress caught on some briars and tore. After pulling herself free, she joined Aidan in searching for good high ground on which to make their camp. Once they had spotted what they were seeking, Aidan felt in his cache in Nothingness and Summoned what he had stolen from the tentmaker's shop. What he found was the hide of some great animal, weatherproofed and foul-smelling, a length of rope, and three other smaller hides. The first he laid out on the ground, and then Summoned a water bladder and four hand pies; a bit much, maybe, but the walk had been hard and the day had been trying. Better to start the night off with a full stomach.

The sun had set, and the night world around them crept to life. Crickets keened and bullfrogs croaked their songs as a light breeze rustled through the budded treetops overhead. Aidan tore into his pasties and did not need to look to know that Slaíne was doing the same. He passed her the water bladder, and she half drained it. Aidan said nothing on that score, for he knew from the sound of the frogs that water was nearby; he could refill that bladder and any others they drained before they set off in the morning.

"Why did ye nay get a tent or the like earlier?" she demanded after they had devoured their respective meals. "Would've saved you some cold nights."

Aidan rolled his eyes but found himself more amused than anything. "Because I couldn't afford it and, despite what it must seem, I haven't always been so keen on stealing." There, let her think on that.

"You're keen on it now, then, are ya?" She gave him a meaningful look, shook her head, and lay back on the hide. After a moment, she sighed.

> *"The fool of a man'd*
> *naught but his looks*
> *The pity's the more*
> *His love's sight was dark.*
> *T'fool open his mouth*
> *The blind lass appear*
> *Hear nothing but rubbish*
> *Baptize 'im with beer."*

It was the first time he had heard her sing in what felt like forever. The song was obviously meant to provoke him, but it had other consequences that Aidan tried to ignore. He allowed himself to crack a smile, but would not look at Slaíne, fearful of what his eyes might tell her. When the silence became unbearable, he let out a burst of derisive laughter and then lay down himself. As on all nights, he did a quick inventory of Pulls near and far, just to make certain he had not been followed. There were no human Pulls for a few miles. Human Pulls were always strongest, anchoring and slowing him down. On normal occasions, Aidan paid little mind to other, less substantial Pulls that might belong to animals or unmoving objects. Perhaps it was because he had not done a thorough search in a few weeks, or maybe it had something to do with the fact that they had come in contact with a murdered man that day, but whatever the case, Aidan closed his eyes and tried to identify the lesser living Pulls.

There were no repulsions caused by iron, save for the one created by the Drifting Goblet, which Slaíne still kept charge of. He felt her Pull and then moved beyond it to what he thought might be deer feeding on the outskirts of their twilit camp. Aidan froze. There was a stronger Pull than a deer's out there, but weaker still than a human's. He had felt this particular Pull before. Recently, in town. "Concentrate," he murmured to himself.

Aidan ignored every Pull from around him, and focused on exploring this familiar one in particular. It was moving slowly, and truly was surrounded by what felt like deer. It was difficult to tell, though, because nonhuman Pulls were harder to identify if he was not used to them. The wind shifted, and the deer Pulls scattered, along with the familiar almost-deer one.

Slaíne yawned loudly. "Where're we bound tomorrow?"

He could not explain it, but Aidan found himself reluctant to give her a direct answer. "We'll stay our course," he offered after a moment's hesitation.

At once she seemed to catch on to his leeriness. "What's wrong? Do you sense something?"

Aidan ground his teeth, trying to dismiss the anxiety rising inside him. "It's nothing. I feel a mite anxious about the scene we left behind at the inn." He tried to convince himself that was it, and after the Pull moved off into the distance, the easier it became to believe that he had imagined any need to feel alarmed.

The moments crawled by in silence, and the strange Pull disappeared entirely. Aidan sighed his relief and handed Sláine one of the smaller hides to cover herself from the cold night air. He would bring out the bedrolls, should the hides prove to be insubstantial.

She accepted the hide and curled up apart from him. "All's well now?"

Covering himself with the other hide, he grunted and then sat up. "I'll keep first watch." Perhaps it was unnecessary, but Aidan was taking no chances. He yawned, and took another swig from one of the water bladders. "You should get some rest. We'll be doing a lot of walking tomorrow."

"Like we don't ever," she mumbled, but Aidan pretended not to hear her.

Bats flittered overhead, and owls hooted their early songs. The air cooled, and Aidan's shoulder prickled uncomfortably, so he rubbed it with vigor, hoping to stop or at least delay any visions for that night.

"The Questing Goblet gives the drinker good luck, yes?" Sláine said after a moment, making Aidan jump. She laughed. "Sorry. Did nay mean ter startle ya. I was just thinking…. Maybe that would break the curse."

Having nothing to add to the statement, Aidan merely sighed and thought some very selfish thoughts. He found himself saying, "Is it so awful?"

She tensed. "Is what so awful? The curse?"

"No," Aidan said, grimacing. "That's not it. Of course the curse is awful. It's a curse. What I mean to say is…." What had he meant to say? He bought himself time by clearing his throat and taking another swig of water. At length he shook his head. "Forgive me. My thoughts are muddled this evening." He could feel her eyes on him.

Slaíne let out a short laugh. "Hardly remember no time before the curse. Just my mam and papa and their lives." She rolled over to face him. "Seems like life did nay really begin until later." Her expression grew distant, and she shook herself. "Seems I've always been, but have nay always been alive, you know?"

Aidan nodded. "I think I know what you mean." He looked at the cloud cover above them. "Sometimes I think I died when my parents and Sam disappeared from my life."

"No," she said gently. "You've got to get past that."

He felt a flash of irritation at the statement, but he let it go with a sigh. Slaíne was perhaps right, after all. If he wanted to avenge his family, he could not let his mind become muddled with emotion. But if rage and sorrow could not and should not drive him, what would? The need to make a better world without Meraude was one reason to pursue this path, a world where magic folk were accepted, valuable members of society where they did not have to hide their gifts. Yes, freedom for all was a noble thing worth fighting for, but anger bubbled around the edges of it, like an overfilled pie pulsing with heat in the oven. Aidan thought he might burst.

Slaíne startled him out of his musings with a sad laugh. "I am nay one to talk. Not gettin' past me own curse. Vengeance drives me too."

Aidan chuckled darkly, his breath clouding the air before him. "We find these Goblets, Slaíne, and then we'll see what we're really made of."

"Woe to Meraude on that day."

"Indeed."

*　　*　　*

As the night deepened and the air cooled considerably more, Slaíne's slow, even breathing told Aidan that she had fallen asleep. He watched her for a while, mindful of the Pulls in the surrounding area. Even though he couldn't see her well in the darkness, he knew she was frowning in her sleep. If things were different, Aidan might reach out a hand and smooth out the lines of worry and whisper that all would be well. Yet it was not his place to do so, and he did not know if those words were a lie or not. So he looked away and peered into the darkness beyond, fighting the siren song of sleep and the cold spreading through his shoulder and across his chest.

Aidan, said a soft voice in his head. *Aidan, come out and play.*

Aidan shook his head and blinked against the pull of rest. "No," he muttered, though he knew he was fighting a losing battle. He even went as far as to sit up and slap his cheeks, but they too were growing cold, and after another minute of resisting, he was conscious of falling backward as his soul separated from his body and found its way into the Beyond.

Again he found himself in the orchard on his estate, only this time the sky was clear of any storms, and Salem was nowhere to be seen. Aidan spun in slow circles and considered calling out, demanding to know why he had been struck with a shovel the last time he had unwittingly visited the land of the magical dead.

Wary, he crept into the thicket of apple trees bearing an array of strange fruit. For a moment he reached out his hand, prepared to pick one, but then he remembered he did not know what the fruit would do or whether or not it was poisonous.

"What am I doing here?" he murmured.

A twig snapped nearby, and he began to call out, but thought the better of it. Some instinct told him to remain silent and unseen.

"Thought I'd felt something," said a ragged voice that Aidan recognized. It belonged to one of the she-elves he had met a month or more ago. In faith, it was one of Slaíne's former, now-dead, mistresses. "Now I doesn't feel nuffink."

"It must be the hags. They like to creep in the grasses and among the trees," said another familiar voice. It belonged to the nymph queen, the creature who had stabbed him in the shoulder weeks ago, thus making these encounters in the Beyond possible. "You wanted to tell me something important, you said."

There was a slight hesitation, and four Pulls moved closer. Aidan tried to slow his frantic breathing so as not to be heard, but he soon realized he needn't have worried. Someone, presumably one of the elves, was wheezing and hissing with every intake and outtake of breath, masking well any sounds he made.

"Where is Treevain?" said the nymph. "Surely you would want your matriarch—"

"With all respect due," said another elf, "that 'un's gone wrong, all wrong."

The nymph let out a short bark of derisive laughter. "And you are all saints?" She sighed. "Would you care to be more specific?"

Though Aidan could not see them from his position, he imagined the three elves looking at each other, their eyes shifting from one warty face to the other. Had he not known what they were capable of, he might have let out a laugh.

One of the elves – Reek, perhaps – picked up the narrative of her sister. "We know nothing for certain, milady." There was a hint of malice added to the word 'milady'. "Only that she won't show us the maps."

"Aye," said the third elf, Gully. "Says we'll betray our kind, that among one of us there be a thief and a traitor."

The first elf chortled and then broke down coughing. Once she had recovered, the creature apologized. "The Beyond do nay agree wiff me lungs."

"And you still don't know who or what killed you four?"

Aidan had wondered the same thing. He'd always thought it impossible for one of those formidable creatures to die. When he found out the means, he would take note, in case he got on the wrong side of one or more of the creatures again.

"We told ye once, milady, that we nay know who dealt the blow, only that it was some right powerful magic, not belonging to no Blest. A flash of red and a ringing sound, and that was it."

The nymph queen laughed, and Aidan cringed. "And you're certain it wasn't Meraude who dealt the fatal blow?" Her words sounded casual enough, but Aidan sensed there was some hidden hope or dread behind them.

There was another cough and some sputtering. "Meraude has numbers and a bit o' power. This was power wiff no numbers, if you catch my meaning." A beat later, the she-elf clarified: "*Him was working alone, this powerful being.*"

"*What makes you say 'him'?*"

It was Gully who answered. "*No woman that mighty, not by long and far.*" The air crackled with dread. "*Is there?*"

"*You and your sisters were fools in life, and you continue to be so in the afterlife.*" Her Pull moved nearer to Aidan than he would have liked, and it took a bit of self-control not to move away, lest he reveal his presence. Mercifully, there was a noise in the distance, up by the house, the sound of wood being chopped. It was enough to draw the she-elves' and the nymph's attention. Someone swore. "*What idiot is destroying trees again? Will these fools never learn to use eternal flame?*" Her Pull moved away. "*Come, we've tarried here long enough. We've much to prepare for the door and the key.*"

Aidan frowned. What door and key? Perhaps he had misheard....

"*We should keep this information between the four of us.*"

The elves grunted.

The strange woman sniffed. "*And take a bath, all three of you. You smell like a farm.*" Her Pull moved away and out of earshot.

"*But we is on a farm,*" Gully muttered. Her sisters grunted their agreement, and tottered away, arguing about whether or not they would tell their fourth sister, Treevain, who was curiously absent.

Aidan waited as one by one their Pulls were a safe distance away before he moved out of his hiding spot, and that was when he became aware of a fifth Pull that he had at first mistaken for an animal. It was familiar, this presence, and though it was not as strong as a human's Pull, it was not an animal. He prepared to Summon the silver sword of Slaíne's, but stayed his hand. He could not kill that which was already dead.

Merry cackling crackled in the overgrowth of weeds, which shivered and bent as a stooped form emerged from their midst. "*Fools in life, fools in death,*" said Treevain, the tall and warty she-elf. She peered at Aidan from the corner of her eye. "*What make you of them's words, Aidan Ingledark?*"

Recoiling from the stench of her breath, Aidan shook his head. "*I thought Salem had brought me hence.*"

The ugly creature frowned. "Who be that, I wonder?" She plucked at a hair springing from the wart on her chin. Her eyes lit up. "Ah, yes, the Blest boy. No, he nay brought you hence. 'Twas me." Her back straightened at this pronouncement – as much as it could straighten; Treevain still stood stooped, her old bones bent and her back humped.

"And you brought me here because…?"

"What for? he asks me." The elf cackled and gestured in the direction in which the others had gone. "What is they plotting? I wonders. Keys and maps and mischief." Now she frowned and spat on the ground. "Tell no one you has the maps, Blest one."

Aidan shook his head. "I wasn't planning on it."

Treevain shook her head, her expression grim. "I hear the accusations in yourn voice, Lord Ingledark. I betray my sisters, you says – nay, my kind."

Aidan had thought no such thing, but he let the elf continue while keeping his distance. "I am ancient, Ingledark, the eldest of me kind. The other three of us greats? Not so great. War is coming to this land again, you mark me words on it, milord. Times afore I took a side, the side of the lesser. Now——" Her great shoulders heaved. "Tired o' death, I is. No more magical blood need be shed."

He nodded in silence, hoping to keep her talking. When she did not continue her ramblings, he offered, "You allude to the war between all magic-kind, I imagine?"

The creature hissed and turned a snarling face in the other direction. "Oh, aye." She nodded in the direction her three sisters had gone. "An' they nay do trust me now, the other three of me kin, and rightly so, I reckon." She swore a rainbow of oaths before calming and turning back to face Aidan. "If I only know'd what this key and door be. Feels important-like."

Aidan weighed his words carefully before committing them to the air. "Do you know where the tomb of Cedric the Elder lies?"

She wagged a bony finger in his direction, though there was a smile on her face. "Now you's asking good questions." The elf cleared her throat and began to speak: "Follow the Pull of magical blood, seek the starberry circle in the shadows of the Ludland. There, 'neath the crown, find the dark place. Speak not the name of the Elder thence, lest his spirit rise and o'er-take you.

Wake now, Aidan Ingledark. Find you the Goblet of Questing and stay the arm of war."

The she-elf snapped her fingers, and Aidan awoke in the world of the living.

CHAPTER SEVEN

Aidan

The next morning, Aidan rose before Slaíne and the sun. He had tried sleeping after his visit to the Beyond, but the weight of Treevain's words hung on him like a millstone. Was there really another war coming? If so, whose side would he find himself on? Aidan had been hiding his abilities ever since they manifested when he was ten years of age. He had hidden them from his uncle, who might have seen him burned on a pyre, but he had shared with Tristram most of what he could do. The former he had feared, the latter had betrayed him. If war were to come, Aidan wondered if it would be between magical beings again – a battle for power – or if it would be the rest of the world versus him and his own kind.

He had fallen asleep again for perhaps an hour, but his dreams were wrought with images of battle, of magical blood spilled, and he had sat up with a start, gasping for breath. Now, tired and anxious, Aidan Summoned another pasty from Nothingness, along with the least-full water bladder, and broke his fast as the morning birds twittered their early songs. Perhaps if he behaved like nothing was wrong, his heart would get the idea and slow its frantic pace.

First light crept overhead as he sat and breakfasted. The ground was wet with dew, and Aidan knew they should dry the hides before he Dismissed them, which meant getting a later start than he would have liked. But he would take advantage of every minute, studying and foraging. First, though, he would search.

Warring with queasiness, Aidan Dismissed the remnants of his meal, closed his eyes, and tried to ignore Slaíne, who was beginning to mumble in her sleep. It did not take him nearly as long as it had the time previous to find the strange Pull in the distance, the one he hoped and assumed belonged to the battleground where magical blood had been shed. It was north of there, though farther east than he had supposed before. The Pull was faint here, but if it were as far away as he thought it might be, the Pull was strong indeed.

Aware that Slaíne was perhaps close to waking, Aidan removed his focus from the distant Pull and slowly brought himself back to the small clearing in which they camped. Opening his eyes, Aidan shook his head and blinked against the light.

Slaíne thrashed in her sleep like a madwoman, muttering curses as she struggled against some invisible foe. "No," she said, her hands clawing at the air.

Aidan sighed and decided that he had better wake her before she hurt herself. "Slaíne," he said once, putting out a hand to shake her.

It all happened so quickly. One moment Aidan was kneeling beside Slaíne, shaking her by the shoulder, and the next he was on his back with her astride him, her mane blowing in a breeze as she put a hand to his throat. At first her eyes were unfocused. Then they locked on to his, and her grasp on his windpipe tightened.

Recovering his wits, Aidan grabbed her hand and pulled it away, though it took most of his strength. "Slaíne!" he said. "It's Aidan."

There was no look of recognition on her face for a moment, but at least she had stopped trying to strangle him. "Where is he?" she demanded.

"Where is who?" Only when he was certain she was done attacking him did he release her hand. "I think you've had a bad dream."

Slaíne shook her head. With a scowl, she looked around her, as if expecting the foe from her dream to appear. "Can't see him. He's invisible." Even as the words tumbled out of her mouth, Slaíne frowned, blinked her eyes furiously, and then at last seemed to realize that she was still straddling him. They looked at each other for a moment, and then she scrambled to her feet, nearly kicking Aidan in the face.

Aidan fought a grin and rose as well. "We need to dry out the hides," he said. "But you need to wake up first." He scooped up the water bladder and handed it to her, then he Summoned another pasty. "Here." Why was he blushing like a schoolboy? He passed over the pasty and turned away.

"'Twas all a dream, yes?" she surprised him by asking. Before Aidan could answer, Slaíne's Pull moved closer and then stopped.

He shrugged. "It depends. What was your nightmare about?" Aidan picked up one of the smaller hides and shook it out as best he could. Then he laid it on a low-hanging branch that was getting some sun.

"Oh, it weren't all bad. That's partially why I'm askin'." She dropped the bladder, which mercifully did not burst.

Aidan looked over his shoulder and saw that she had one hand clutched over her heart, smiling slightly, only to shudder, her grin turning into a confused frown. Seeing that something was troubling her, Aidan thought to ask her about it, but then thought the better of that idea. Things between them were awkward and strange enough as it was, no matter inquiring after each other's thoughts and feelings. Instead, he said, "You were thrashing around in your sleep. I woke you up. Nothing else happened while you were sleeping, save for my breaking fast." He chanced another glance at her.

It looked as though all the wind had been knocked out of Slaíne, but she simply nodded and nibbled at the pasty, shoulders hunched. Then she seemed to recover from whatever was bothering her and tore off a larger portion of her breakfast. Through a full mouth she asked, "I nay think we should let the hides dry."

Aidan's eyebrows shot heavenward. "Why?"

"Dunno." Slaíne shrugged. "Just a thought that bad things might happen if'n we stay here long." She finished her pasty and rubbed her hands over her arms. "Please, Mr. Aidan. Let's not stay here."

Not knowing what to make of this change in his plans – and the one in her demeanor – Aidan did not argue with her but Dismissed the hides and reasoned that they would not be ruined in Nothingness. He went to her and picked up the water bladder that she had dropped and handed it to her again.

After taking several long pulls from the vessel, she sealed it and gave it back. "Don't ya feel it?"

He frowned. "Do I feel any Pulls, you mean?"

Slaíne started to nod but then shook her head. "I dunno. Can ya check?"

"Of course." Aidan concentrated beyond Slaíne's Pull, ignored the Pulls of animals and nature, before landing on a Pull similar to the one he had sensed last night. But it was different. Or was it? Aidan closed his eyes and tried to Call it, but it was alive, and therefore would not heed his mind's commands. Shaking his head, Aidan opened his eyes and squinted against the sun. "There is something out there," he said, and then regretted it at once, for Slaíne's face paled.

"What sort of Pull?"

How could he explain such a thing to her that he himself did not understand? Aidan had never felt any Pull quite like this one before, and yet he had. "I'll be mindful of it," he said carefully. "But I wouldn't worry. It's probably some animal – in faith, I'm fairly certain that it's an elk."

She spun in circles, her eyes searching the skies. "It was like this, in my dream. Something bad was followin' us." Slaíne's hair flew out wildly like flames blooming in a breeze as she nearly made Aidan dizzy out of sympathy. "Let us away, Mr. Aidan." Before he could answer, she started out northeast, the path he had intended to take but had not told her.

Gooseflesh broke out on Aidan's arms, and he Summoned his cloak to cover himself with. Then, after one look behind him for reassurance that no eyes were watching them, he followed her.

★　★　★

Morning stretched on for what felt like an eternity. The sun was stubbornly pegged at what seemed to be the same point in the sky for a good deal of their walking, and the air continued to hold a chill. Secretly, Aidan kept searching for the Pull that he had felt earlier. It was still out there, keeping its distance…at least, Aidan thought it might be the same Pull. The quality of it had altered, which made no sense to him. Pulls did not normally change, unless it went from living to deceased, living being the more substantial of the two. If he had to make a guess, Aidan would say that his weary mind was making the whole thing up. But the notion was not so easily dismissed.

The trees thinned in places, opening up patches above them to allow in more light. Now the sun rose in earnest, beating against their faces. Heat replaced chill, and soon Aidan found himself stripping off his cloak and Dismissing it and draining almost half a water bladder himself before passing it over to Slaíne.

They had been walking in silence for the better part of two hours, Slaíne leading the way at a determined pace, though he had not told her the direction of the Pull. Perhaps she sensed it somehow as well, as she could sense the repulsion of iron.

Now, on the third hour of walking, they both were panting and clutching pangs in their sides. One look at each other silently confirmed their plans, and they ate a quick lunch beneath the shelter of a large maple. "Do you wish to move on?" Aidan asked, since their pace had been punishing.

"Nah," Slaíne replied. She wiped the crumbs of another pasty from her lips and leaned against the bark of the tree. "I think that thing what's following us got lost."

Aidan stared at her in amazement for a moment, and then searched for the Pull. He sensed no human or strange Pulls for at least three miles. Perhaps the creature, whatever it might be, had indeed lost its way.

"You should probably take a look at them maps. Might be an age and a day 'til we get a dry moment to do it again." The words held a weight that Aidan could not argue with, so he Summoned the map to Cedric's grave and the only other map in his cache, the one that led to...well, he was uncertain of where. It had no words on it, just drawings that looked like they might belong to such a document.

After lowering himself down next to Slaíne, Aidan handed her the sheet of drawings and studied the one with the poems and sketches on it. "Strange," he said after ten minutes had passed. He held the map up to some light filtering through the tree cover and squinted at the town labeled *Ashborne*, the only town mentioned on the map.

"What's strange?"

Aidan pointed to the dot that was Ashborne and said, "This town was not here when I looked at it last." He pointed to a spot farther east on the map. "This is where Ashborne ought to lie...at least, that's how I remember it."

"Lemme see." Slaíne took the map from his hands and held it up for study. "Huh. If you say."

He checked his irritation. "Have you ever been that way?"

Slaíne shrugged. "The elves went wherever the whim and wind took 'em. Nay ever told me where we was at the time, now I recall. May've thought me too stupid." She sniffed. "Lotta good keepin' things from me did. They's dead, I'm not."

"I must be imagining things." The breeze picked up around them, threatening to tear the map from Aidan's hands, so he Dismissed it and studied the other nonsensical piece of parchment. It, too, was not quite how he had remembered it to be, but he knew he was entirely capable of having been mistaken. At long last, Aidan quit and Dismissed that document as well.

His traveling companion gave him a puzzled look but asked nothing about what he had seen or deciphered. She was the first to her feet. "What was it like, livin' as a lord's son?" she surprised him by asking. When he did not respond at once, Slaíne tried again, adding, "I've a bad feeling and need to be distracted, yes?" Her look was imploring, and Aidan wondered what might be troubling her.

Instead of asking what the matter might be, Aidan rose as well and the two of them continued their journey. "Well," he said slowly, picking his way around some roots. "My father was a busy man, from what I recall. He had the town and the estate to run, and Mother was often unwell, so Samuel and I were raised by a nanny."

Slaíne walked so close, they kept bumping into each other. Each muttered an apology, and continued forward, around trees, through bramble and briar, their arms brushing. "It don't sound near as luxurious as I'd thought," she admitted. "Mam and Papa was poor, but they overindulged me often."

Aidan shook his head. "Oh, my parents made time for us." He steadied Slaíne, who had stumbled into him, and then quickly released her and tried to put a distance between their steps. "And they were both always kind. It's a wonder my uncle was my mother's brother." He pulled a face. "They were nothing alike." He shuddered. "After they died, and my uncle took the title of steward, I was little more than a servant in my own home."

"I'm sorry."

He nodded. "It isn't your fault."

"I'm sorry all the same," she said, and he could tell she meant it deeply.

Aidan cleared his throat. "Er, thank you." The silence between them as they walked was tight as a fiddle string waiting to be plucked, but not in an unpleasant way. Whatever might have been troubling Slaíne seemed to no longer concern her. Before them lay perhaps leagues upon leagues yet to be traveled, and the miles behind them were fraught with troubles, but Aidan found himself buoyed for no reason apparent to him other than the company he kept. His fingers furled and unfurled, wanting to grasp something, but he was unsure of what. Finally he satisfied himself by clenching his fists and ignoring the ridiculous sensation, whatever it might be exactly.

Slaíne, he noticed, took covert peeks at him from the corner of her eye, and their steps continued to tangle into each other's until they were near knocking the other over. They laughed the first time Aidan was knocked sideways into a tree, and Aidan apologized the first and second times when Slaíne stumbled off the path and into some weeds. He dismissed the missteps as clumsiness on his part, and then on hers, before realizing that he did not mind it at all and stopped trying to figure things out.

The air around them was charged. Aidan wondered if a storm might be approaching, but the skies were clear and sunny. The hairs on his arms were raised, as if there were some great danger looming, but not one that he was aware of. Unwittingly he shuddered, and Slaíne gave him an odd look.

"What's wrong?"

How could he say if he did not know himself? Everything felt right. "Nothing's wrong," he assured her. He paused and swiped at his arms. "Though I think I might have walked through some spider's work." Indeed, he felt covered in the sticky mess, and wondered how Slaíne had managed to avoid it.

"Disgusting," she offered in sympathy. Before he could stop her, Slaíne was brushing him off, trying to help free him from the webs.

After a moment, it was only her working, Aidan standing there like a great idiot who did not know what to do with his arms or mouth, the latter of which hung somewhat open, and the former of which dangled like two useless logs at his side.

Her hands were cold, though it did not bother him in the slightest. He could feel their iciness seeping through the thinness of his shirt, and wondered if he ought to be afraid, an irrational thought. More than anything, though, he wished he could kiss her...which was the last thing either of them needed.

Don't make things so complicated, Salem whispered at the back of his mind.

Again Aidan shivered. *Thanks for hitting me with the shovel*, he thought back with as much sarcasm as he could muster.

Salem laughed. *Just kiss her. Again. It's not like you haven't before.*

Sláine had stopped brushing him off and was now staring at him, her eyes wide. She took a few steps backward. "What?"

Aidan shook his head to rid himself of either the voice or the confusion, or perhaps both. He opened his mouth to answer, but was surprised to find himself propelled forward at an alarming pace.

Again Sláine backed away, but still Aidan pursued. "What're you up to?" she asked, a grin spreading across her face. "You look so serious-like."

It had taken him a moment, but now Aidan realized that it was Salem's power moving him forward, and he wrestled for control over his own mind and movements. Prevailing with a soft oath, Aidan came to an abrupt stop. He muttered a confused apology.

Far from being offended, Sláine's grin widened into something wicked and she started toward him, her intentions clear. "What?"

He needed to stop her, to throw cold water on the whole situation. Why, oh why, did he remain mute? Perhaps he should mention her curse...or maybe Meraude. Either of those would do to put a stop to this madness.

Idiot, Salem said at the back of his mind, before his presence faded away.

Now, with the indweller gone, Aidan had no excuse for his thoughts and movements. The two travelers came at each other as if to battle, expressions set in grim determination as first she grabbed him and then he her, neither's strength to be outrivaled by the other's. Whether he swept her up or she leapt into his arms, it was uncertain, but the result was the same. The kiss was just as violent, two affection-starved people clashing against each other in a rough attempt to feel something. They fell over soon after, her astride him.

"Sláine," he said as she clawed at his chest.

She looked down at him, her brows knit and her eyes distant. There was little recognition in that look, just feral hunger.

His shirt tore in her hands, and finally he thought to stop her. Bewildered, Aidan took her wrists in his hands and rolled her off him and onto her back. Now he was astride her, and only then did she stop her clawing. It occurred to him for a brief moment that something was wrong, but he almost at once ceased caring.

The girl lay still and watched him, her expression inscrutable. "Someday," she whispered, yesteryear's leaves crackling beneath her soft form as Aidan leaned down and kissed her hair.

He kissed the tip of her small nose, her brow, her closed eyelids. Every part of him felt vivid, as if it had not until moments before been awake.

Slaíne took one of his callused hands in one of her own and then kissed it. "Someday your heart will be mine, Aidan."

It's yours now, he wanted to murmur. Only he didn't, because she deserved nothing so wretched. Instead he said, "What do you want?"

She grinned and pushed him off her. "Ter be able to walk without you runnin' me off the way." Then she laughed wickedly and leapt to her feet. She helped Aidan to his feet, and he felt that he had never before beheld any creature so beautiful.

CHAPTER EIGHT

Jinn

The world was dark and wearisome, and Jinn foresaw that she and Quick were heading into a trap. It had been one nightfall since she had last used her gift of Sight. Then the way had been clear. It was odd how one decision could alter the course and its consequences.

"Dark," Quick said. As if to confirm his opinion, her twin shaded his eyes and gazed at the overcast sky. He nodded once then glanced at Jinn, his look of expectation barely readable. When she did not respond, he reiterated his stance: "*Very* dark."

Jinn flashed her teeth in a reassuring grin. "Yes, it is dark. Why don't we stop for the night and make a fire?" She shuddered against the brute north wind. "I need to stop and amend our plan."

Quick nodded. "Fire. Make fire." He grunted but did not move. "You foresaw again?"

"Yes."

He sighed and started toward an oak tree. "You foresaw the trap?"

"You foresaw it too?" Foresight wasn't her brother's strength; he shouldn't be peering more than a few minutes ahead.

Quick chuckled. "Sister worries. Always worries for Quick." He reached up for the lowest branch and snapped it clean off from the trunk. The great crack mimicked a shot of thunder, and Jinn had to cover her ears. Obviously pleased, Quick held the branch up for Jinn to inspect. "This good?"

"Yes, that should make enough logs for the night." She breathed into her hands and rubbed them together with vigor. "I'll gather some tinder." But before Jinn could make it five steps into the surrounding woods, a vision overtook her.

It was the burning season, but the day and month were uncertain.

The Summoner lay amid a growth of creeping wintersnaps, in shock apparently. His redheaded traveling companion stared through Jinn to a road marker pointing toward Egethberem, a little too far north for Jinn's liking.

"Not go far, right?"

Jinn jumped as Quick crashed through the overprint of the vision, which dissipated into a mist before her eyes. "Of course." Absently, she tightened her belt a notch and entered the darkness surrounding.

As she gathered what they needed by touch, praying all she grabbed was benign, Jinn remained on high alert and moved swiftly. Was this a necessary risk, setting up camp and chancing a fire now? Jinn closed her eyes and tried to foresee all possible outcomes of the evening as she did every night before they lay down to sleep in a hollow or tied themselves to high branches out of the reach of hungry goblins.

The first vision, the one that showed her returning to Quick immediately with what she had gathered, would result in her brother startling and crying out like an injured bull. Jinn followed that vision further, careful to continue down that course of thought without wavering from it in her intentions. The cry itself would do nothing, but Quick would drop half of the branch on Jinn's foot. She winced at the phantom pain, and at once changed the course of events in her mind.

The second vision, one where Jinn gathered more tinder, appeared harmless at first. She followed the course of events even as she gathered more brush in real time. Jinn stopped her actions, however, when the vision showed her disturbing a rat in its nest and receiving a smart bite on her wrist. No more collecting, then.

The third vision, and the one she followed to near completion, was of her standing still in the dark, waiting for a loud thump and following it back to where she'd left Quick. There her brother would have begun separating the branch into pieces, and would soon be ready for the magnesium, flint, and machete. All seemed well, so when the foretold thud startled the night, Jinn didn't think twice about returning to her brother.

As foreseen, Quick made fast work of the branch, dividing it into sections and then dividing those sections down further. Each break of the wood caused so much racket that Jinn jumped and swore that the entire kingdom could hear.

Quick chuckled as he finished. "Worry."

She shook her head and told him to be quiet for a moment. If anyone were within two miles, they would be able to follow the noise to its source. It was a still night, a clear and cold night. The fire would draw humans, elves, nymphs, or any other warmth-loving creatures to their encampment, and they could be ambushed in their sleep.

When Jinn closed her eyes again to foresee, Quick rested his large hand on her shoulder, weighting her down. "You can't foresee all."

"No. But I can try."

Quick cleared his throat. "Where is he?"

"The Summoner?" Jinn let out a huff. "There are…holes in my vision."

Making a face, Quick held his hands apart to indicate size. "How big?"

She resisted the urge to laugh. There was nothing amusing about losing the man Mother had sent them after. "No, Quick. It's like – it's like someone or something is interrupting my foresight."

He waited for more.

Jinn shrugged and began building the fire, consequences if not forgotten, then at least ignored. "None of the Goblets grant people the power to cloak themselves like that. Besides," she said after a moment, "there's no possibility that the Summoner knows we're looking for him." Jinn frowned at Quick's laugh.

"Mother thinks all are stupid."

"True. She underestimates us, even. Lights above, I've dropped the flint. Can you find it?"

Quick got on his hands and knees and started rummaging in the dark, and that was when Jinn heard the first cackle. Quick froze as Jinn grabbed his arm.

"What?" he murmured.

Jinn closed her eyes and looked two minutes into the future, and then six. Five hags would reach their camp within that time, no doubt drawn by the noise Quick had made. Jinn found and pocketed the flint, hoisted her sack over her shoulders and made sure that Quick was doing the same.

There was no time to hide the evidence of their presence. The hags would arrive from the southwest just off the hidden footpath they'd taken from the main road, and would sight them far before then. Jinn did not believe in coincidence; they were being followed. As they fled into the night, Jinn wondered if this was connected to the trap she'd foreseen them springing.

Branches reached out to snatch at Jinn like so many hands, snagging and snapping as she and Quick upset a roost of fire snakes. Quick yelped. "Bites you."

Indeed, a fang pierced her left heel through her boot, drawing blood. Jinn felt warmth blossom at the spot, and her legs nearly gave way beneath her. Another cackle filled the night, this time closer. Trembling, Jinn grabbed on to Quick, who lifted her and stood stock-still, awaiting orders.

"Hide," Jinn said. "Quietly."

Quick grunted once, ignoring the glowing orange beasts that snapped at his thick heels, and carried Jinn behind a large bush. "Here good?"

It would have to do. They hadn't made it far, and Jinn could hear the evil creatures gathering at their attempted camp. Lightheaded, she stilled her breaths as Quick lowered her to the ground and then hunched down beside her.

"Nicely done, my sisters," said an ancient voice in the distance.

"Finders keepers." Another cackle turned into a shriek. "Four!"

"I see it," said the oldest-sounding voice. "We're almost upon them."

Jinn's wound had begun to burn, but she bit down the scream building up in the back of her throat. She had to keep a clear head. There was no time for pain; Jinn would have to think around it. But the snake's venom pulsed up her ankle, her calf, shot up her leg and circled in her abdomen, threatening to make her sick to her stomach. Nothing. All that Jinn could foresee ended in a dark, sleepless dream.

Quick shook her with what he might have thought was gentle care, but it dizzied Jinn and made the world spin. "Help. You need help."

This was not the time to need help, with the hags so near. And yet…. "Quick, do you trust me?"

Her twin sighed. "You think Quick doesn't?"

Jinn ignored that. "Pick me up and let's go back."

The hags were suspiciously quiet, but Jinn wouldn't worry about that. Yet.

Quick had hesitated. "Go back? You want to die?" If it weren't Quick, Jinn would have called his statement an attempt at sarcasm. "I don't want to."

"Hags have magic, and I need their help. No one's going to die," Jinn gritted out just as a flash of red light was cast around them like a net.

"I wouldn't depend upon it, Blest one," said a hideous, warty hag tinged in a green glow.

"Please, I seek a truce!" The net of light they had been snared in did not dissipate, but as the hags did not attack further, Jinn grew hopeful that they would honor her request. She tried to focus her eyes on the elf who had spoken. "I beseech thee, O Wise Ones, salve for my snakebite, and safe passage from these woods."

Silence reigned for a moment, before all five burst out laughing. "'Wise Ones' the mortal calls us."

"And she wants a truce," said the short one. "Thinks she's entitled to live."

"And wants a salve."

"Dinnae ye ken, lassie? Everything cometh with a price."

They all spoke so quickly and with such ferocity, Jinn doubted she would have followed easily even without the venom-haze addling her brain. "My brother and I—"

"Which are you?" one of the five cut her off, moving in closer, no doubt to have a better look at their catch. "You smell...familiar. Yet not familiar look."

Jinn would have squirmed away, but knew she would be unconscious in minutes. It was amazing she'd lasted this long. "Quick? Could you answer their questions?"

Quick proved to be of no help. He was trying to pull the snare away, only succeeding in tangling himself up further. "Won't break," he said. "Slippery magic."

"Hmm. She might do."

"Not she," said another. "Too small."

"Too...foreign."

The five mumbled in agreement.

"I can pay you for your help." Jinn gave Quick a weak nudge. "Brother, the pouch."

"We dinnae want your mortal gold, youngling," said the tallest hag. She reached through the net and grabbed Jinn's foot in her warty hand, tsk-tsking as she none-too-gently twisted it this way and that. "Fire vipers. You'll be dead in minutes."

"'Twould be dead already."

"Aye, if'n not for bein' Blest."

Jinn did not like the way the five were stealing covert looks at her brother and nudging each other. "Please, we would like—"

The net vanished, and four of the five hags started cursing at the fattest one. "What'n you done that for?"

The fat one picked Jinn up and flung her over her shoulder like an empty sack. "Come, sisters. She ain't goin' anywhere like this, an' he's dog enough to follow."

Paralyzed from the waist down and her arms quickly following,

Jinn could do nothing but croak in protest as she was carried back to the mound of logs. "S-stop."

"How goodly of the creatures. They've what's gathered wood for us."

One of the others cackled. "Come along, my lad. Your twin hath need of you."

Quick grunted and followed after them, though Jinn wanted to shout at him not to; she had suspicions as to what they planned. "Put down sister."

"All in good time. One, you've the salve?"

"Aye, Two." She sniffed. "There might be a drop or seven missing, though. Those elves dinnae take care of their potions."

The others tutted, and Jinn was let drop to the ground, knocking the wind out of her lungs. She lay there like a drowning fish as the hags lolled about, laughing and taunting Quick to do all their work of setting up camp so they could "Boil your sister in a stew."

"She's a mite on the scrawny side, but with the right seasonings, we'll have a nice little feast." One of them belched. "Hurry up, oaf, or we'll slice and dice her without you."

"No dice," Quick roared, causing the hags to laugh.

"Well, then, build up the fire nice and high. And fetch our bags from the carriage. We'll need some good herbs."

Jinn knew Quick thought he was helping, but he obeyed the hags and left Jinn alone with the five. "Please," she rasped.

"Dinner's a touch noisy." The warty hag poked Jinn with a stick. She loomed over Jinn, her ugly face swimming before Jinn's eyes before the world went dark.

★   ★   ★

When Jinn awoke, a fire was roaring, her ankle felt as though it had been tended to, and Quick was watching her helplessly inside another net of red light and looking rather miserable. Jinn was drenched, and she assumed that she had just broken a fever. But the smell! She sucked in a deep breath...and coughed. The aromas of moldy sage and rancid fat tickled at her nose and overwhelmed her senses. *Oh, mercy, I'm being marinated...in my clothes.*

"It's awake. Should we put it in or wait for the fire to die down?"

Jinn sat up with a start, causing the hags to hiss and descend on her. "Wait!"

They froze. "We're hungry. Ain't that right, Three?"

"You poor things," Jinn growled.

The hags seemed to miss her sarcasm, however, and nodded in agreement. "Och, you're not so unreasonable."

"Maybe we should fry it."

Someone's stomach rumbled.

"Would you prefer to be fried or boiled, mortal?"

Jinn pretended to look thoughtful. "Maybe slowly baked, in a very large oven over very low heat. Preferably a thousand years hence."

The five sat back and looked thoughtful. "It might be right."

Before the five could discuss their dinner plans any further, Jinn cleared her throat and said, "You are a wandering bunch?"

"Why, yes. How observant of you— Forgot the apples, Two. Hold that thought, mortal, while I prepare the stuffing."

"I can do it," Jinn blurted out. She hoped to look innocent, but Mother always said her face was a mirror to what was hidden within.

Sitting there with bewildered looks on their faces, the five exchanged strange words between each other that Jinn could not discern. At last the fat, grumpy one pointed a gnarled finger at her and barked out an order to her companions, who didn't move at first. "Do as I says."

"Do as she says," the warty one grunted. "Och! Might'n as well be her servants, what we go through more oft than not."

"Aye," said the other three, their looks mutinous. "See ye here, now, One...."

The fat one hissed, and the others recoiled and one by one slunk off into the gloom surrounding. Once their footsteps faded, One turned her steely eyes back to Jinn and moved nearer. "We've not got much time, mortal. They're off gettin' the apples." She patted her vast waistline. "Too bad I et them all yesternight." She cackled.

Jinn's breath caught in her throat. "You're having second thoughts about dinner?"

"Dinnae say that, daft girl. I need information."

That took Jinn aback. "What?"

With a grunt, the hag moved in closer. "What is Meraude going to do with the Goblets?"

Jinn's stomach clenched as she got to her feet. "Meraude who?"

"Don't play the fool with me. Her smell's all over you. You're lucky the others did nay scent it, or else you would be dead already. Hurry. Tell me what Meraude plans, an' I'll give you a three-minute head start before the pursuit begins."

Covertly, Jinn peered ahead three minutes: the hag wasn't lying, but Jinn would be too slow in a footrace, and Quick wouldn't or couldn't follow her. In her mind, she saw herself asking for ten minutes and Quick's release, but the answer was negative, and the vision grew dark. Jinn cursed. She would have to either outwit these hags or…. She nodded. "You will give me ten minutes, and I will tell you everything."

The hag named One gave her a thoughtful look, but then nodded. "And you dinnae care to barter for your brother's release?"

"There isn't time for all this," she said below her breath, hoping her brother wouldn't hear and misunderstand. "Meraude hopes to unite the Goblets Immortal and start a war with your kind."

For whatever reason, that caused One to laugh. "Lass, there be only me sisters and I. You'll have to do better than that, I fear."

Jinn tried again. "Not just you five. All magic-kind."

"And how is she going to do that?"

Lights above! This was harder than Mother made it seem. She tried again, noticing that the wood surrounding had grown silent, along with the faint magical humming that had been buzzing in her ears since they'd been captured. "Ever since the collapse of the

Circle, Meraude has been…. How do I say this?" What was she trying to say? Why hadn't Mother better prepared her for moments like this?

"Well, you might as well take one more stab at the truth, as it's the last stab you're like to get at anything."

The silence gathered. Jinn looked down at her feet, hoping her face would not tell the truth on her. How to say what she could only guess at? That was when she saw it, a gleam of metal, inches from her left foot: a knife.

Quick crashed through the silence. "Jinn, what should Quick do?"

The hag had apparently let her magic slip, and Quick was just now getting to his feet, uninhibited by any net.

The hag named One turned with a gasp, and Jinn did not think twice before snatching up the small knife and throwing it haft over blade at the creature's neck. Her aim was true. Blood flowed in copious amounts from the creature's neck and mouth. But the image was overlapped with a foresight of four enraged hags cornering Jinn with whips of fire. Running wasn't an option, it would seem.

Mercifully, the hag's death was a silent one, and the other four hags' approach remained more than a minute away. "Quick, throw the body into the fire," she said, trembling from head to boot as she pulled the knife from her victim's neck. Before he could, however, the body vanished with a sickly glugging sound, reminiscent of sludge bubbling in a cauldron. There was no time to worry about what that meant. The hags were almost there.

"Quick, you need to hide in the woods."

He looked down at Jinn, his brow crinkling. "Leave you? No. No, Jinn."

She didn't have time to explain the plan that was formulating in her brain. She could hear the hags' approach. "Hide and be silent unless I say our secret word, all right?"

Quick scowled. "You die." But he did as she said, moving behind an overgrown bush, all the while muttering, until the hags' voices could be heard.

With the blade in her hand, Jinn forced herself to sit down with her legs crossed and her arms behind her back. It was impossible to look innocent or confused, but terror was a strong emotion, and she knew it was the dominant expression on her face right now.

The four hags were grumbling and cursing the hag named One in colorful terms. "That rascal," said the most warty one.

"Aye. There were no apples. She must've et them all."

"Pig," said the third hag, and they all burst out cackling again. Their laughter soon died out, and the four were left looking around them in bewilderment. "Are we missing something?"

The other three stood there for a moment, considering. "The apples?"

"Fool, there art no apples to miss." They looked at the fire, which had begun to puff gray smoke, and then at the place where Quick had been netted before. "Huh. Could have sworn to me mam that there were five of us."

Jinn's palm grew slick with sweat, her eyes following the hags' every move. If only they would turn their backs again, then she could at least get one of them with the blade. But what would happen after that? She would still have three angry hags to deal with, and they would probably kill her on sight, not bothering to give her a ten-minute start as their sister-hag had offered. All be hanged, but perhaps she should have waited to kill the first one until she could form a better plan.

The fourth hag was counting. "One, two, three, four –" she pointed to Jinn, "– and five. I think we're all here."

"Idiot, she's not one of us."

"Oh, aye."

The tall, less heavy one, hissed and spat. "Curses! You, mortal." Jinn jumped.

Four sets of eyes narrowed, and their owners converged on Jinn. "Where is your brother?"

"Forget the boy-man. Where be One?"

"I can answer all of your questions," Jinn said, trying to keep her voice even, "if you promise to let me go free." She waited as the hags deliberated, her throwing hand cramping slightly, as she'd been clutching her weapon too tightly. She cursed herself for being careless. The knife slipped, and she caught it before it could hit the ground behind her. But it cost her. She was now no longer holding the handle but the sharp blade itself, and it was biting into her bare palm. Jinn choked down a yelp.

One hag sniffed the night air. "I've scented blood."

The four looked at Jinn, suspicious. "Tell us what happened here, mortal, or we'll...."

"Boil you in a stew."

The shortest hag looked at her sister in disgust. "Oi, we were already going to do that, remember?"

Drip, drip, drip. Blood trickled down Jinn's wrist. She needed to adjust her grip, but the creatures would not look away, and she could not afford to take her eyes off them or draw attention to her predicament. "All right," Jinn squeaked. "Give me your word that you won't hurt my brother, and I'll tell you what happened."

"All right," said the one Jinn thought might be called Three. "Start talking."

Jinn drew in a shaky breath. "Your, er, leader let the enchantment surrounding my brother drop, and he took advantage of her situation and—"

Two of the hags swore. "She's getting careless. Three and Four, you go find and help One. Five and me will guard dinner."

Four let out a great huff of displeasure. "How come I have to do all the real work, eh? Durst you think you be One?" With a sniff, she sat down. "I ain't going ter be ordered around by the likes of thee."

"Oh, for the love of everything sacred! We'll all keep ter sitting here and wait 'til One returns with the prisoner. Happy?"

The other three grunted.

"Actually," said Jinn, "I'm not." The knife cut in a little deeper. She was getting dizzy and lightheaded at the mere thought of blood loss. "My brother is going to get lost or hurt or worse. At least three of you need to go find him before something horrible happens."

"Why three?"

Jinn had to think quickly. "Three will cover more ground more quickly?"

The four stood for a maddening moment, muttering in their strange tongue between each other.

Jinn peered into the future, just one minute ahead. But the thread was tenuous, hard to hold on to, and the further she looked – five minutes, ten minutes – the more possible threads there were. It was too much for one person to sort through. A mere look from her could tip fate one way or the other, as could bigger variables such as Quick's ill-timed sneeze in three, two—

"Achoo," Jinn said, covering her brother's racket. He must be neck-deep in ridgewood plants. *It would figure that I'd send him to hide in the one fern he's allergic to.*

The four hags looked at her strangely but didn't say anything about the extra-loud sneeze. "Fine," said Two, "Three and Four and I will look for them, and you—" She pointed her bony finger at the remaining hag. "You wilt stay here and watch over this one. And build up that fire. It's startin' to die."

"*Now* who thinks they be One?"

"Hush." And with a parting rude gesture, Three, Four, and Two tramped off in the direction Jinn made sure to stare in.

The remaining hag sized up Jinn. "Why dinnae you stop yer twin from runnin' off, eh? Something don't seem right 'bout this." She approached Jinn, her eyes narrowing. "My sister thought to tie your hands behind your back before running after the boy-man? Don't sound like One. What have you got hidden back there?"

Sweat trickled down the back of Jinn's neck as she tried to think of a good lie. "A knife," she said, knowing the hag would not believe such a thing.

Sure enough, the creature snorted just as a twig snapped several paces behind Jinn. They both froze. "What were that?"

"Probably some beast," Jinn said, cursing herself for the break in her voice. Lying should be easier, and she should be better at it; she'd done enough of it over the past five months. "Or maybe your sisters doubled around and are returning."

The hag scowled. "There is one way ter find out." She glided past Jinn, her hands fumbling for something at her belt. "Curses! Where is me knife?"

Jinn aimed and threw the blade, just as the hag turned her way. This time, Jinn wasn't as lucky. The knife had taken the hag in the right shoulder, a nonfatal wound that would only slow the creature down a little. Jinn needed to act quickly. With a cry, she rolled out of the way as a blast of blue light was aimed at her chest. Her hand pulsed as she pulled herself to her feet and charged at the creature, attempting to throw her off-balance. It did not work.

Her opponent, who had removed the knife with a yelp, managed to grab Jinn by the throat and held her at arm's length, grinning as Jinn kicked and tried to pry the warty fingers away. "You've got courage, lass."

If Jinn could breathe, she would spit at this monster. The hag must have known this, for she only laughed all the harder, her great brown teeth flashing. "Tell me, where is One, really?"

Stars burst around the corners of Jinn's vision and her lungs burned, her head throbbing and begging her to find a way to free herself before it exploded. *No. I need more time. I need to—*

The hag dropped her to the ground, where Jinn lay coughing and gasping. "Where is my sister?" Her black eyes flashed. "You will tell me of your own free will, or I can make things...interesting. Mortals are so easy to torture. You're all so..." She flapped her arms a bit, stopping to wince in pain. "...flimsy."

"I don't know where your sister is," Jinn croaked, rubbing her throat. She needed a moment, just a minute to get her voice to work right again. "Why don't you go look for her?"

The hag laughed and then stopped, her eyes twinkling. "You killed her, didn't you?"

"I—"

Of all things, the creature threw her head back and let out an even louder laugh, one that could easily be mistaken for a mountain lion's roar. "You little snipe. You done the dirty work for me. How you done it?" Suddenly eager, the hag waved her hand and a rocking chair appeared out of thin air. "Poison?"

"No, I—"

"Strangulation?"

"Er—"

Her eyes narrowed. "Magic?"

Jinn swallowed hard, and put her finger up in the air to ask for a minute. The hag nodded.

It was now or never. Jinn sucked in a deep breath and said at the top of what voice she had left: "Wattlewasp!"

The hag eyed her askance. "A wattlewasp killed her, you say? Huh. I didn't know they were venomous."

As to whether or not wattlewasps were venomous, Jinn had no idea, nor did she care. She waited fifteen beatings of her heart, but there was no response, no noise that indicated Quick had heard and comprehended what she wanted him to do now.

"Wattlewasps," the hag said, laughter in her voice. "It's almost poetry, thou knows? One once mentioned beekeeping."

"Wattlewasp," Jinn said again, louder, and the hag nodded.

"Yes, just as ye says. What she wouldst do with them bees, 'tis lost on me."

Curse all, but where was Quick? He must have heard their secret word. What was he doing? Waiting for her to give him step-by-step instructions on how to sneak up and throttle the hag? At once guilt clutched Jinn's stomach. It wasn't his fault. If it was anyone's, it was hers for not absorbing her part of the curse in Mother's womb. All Blest were cursed in some way. In Quick's case, the curse had done damage to his mind. She pushed that thought aside. Blame-dealing wouldn't get them out of this predicament.

There were thirty-three outcomes to this evening, and twenty-nine of them ended in darkness – and then resumed as if there had been no break whatsoever. Holes. There were the holes again, the ones that had clouded her vision before. It was as vexing as it was dangerous.

Foresight wasn't going to save her; Jinn could simply not account for every little move that she or her brother, or the hag, for that matter, might make. Having all but lost hope, she heard a sneeze.

"Bless thou," said the hag. The person who had sneezed – Quick, for she could not figure out who else was near enough to produce the expulsion – sneezed again. Only, it couldn't be Quick: the noise echoed in the south, while Jinn's brother was hiding a few bushes behind her to the east.

After the third sneeze, the hag looked at Jinn, a gleam of suspicion in her eyes. Jinn wiped her nose with the back of her hand and thanked the elf for the blessing.

Before the creature could voice her suspicions, her sisters ran back into the clearing, their eyes wild as they huffed and puffed. "Wizard!" the three beings cried.

Their sister rose, her chair vanishing into a puff of gray smoke. "What do you mean, 'wizard'? Och, there art no wizards in these lands since Cedric took to his tomb." Whatever the three hags were going to argue, they didn't get the chance. An unearthly growl filled the night air, and the sisters huddled together.

After a moment of frozen terror, Jinn crawled away from the three, trying to still her breaths. She needed to get to Quick. She needed to run.

"Where be One? We are not so powerful without she."

"Dead," said one of the hags.

Jinn rose into a crouch, ready to disappear into the bracken behind her without a sound. She spied the hag's knife lying where the elf had let it drop, and grabbed it. Quick had both of their packs, which the elves mercifully hadn't taken from them when they'd been captured. But speaking of her brother.... "Wattlewasp," she said. She had hoped that Quick would hear and comprehend that she meant for him to start running. Her twin did not respond.

Another growl ripped through the trees as a cold, sharp breeze rushed down upon them. Jinn found her footing as the hags began to scream. "Run, Quick, run." She crashed through the brush, arms flailing, foot still stinging from where the fire viper's fangs had pierced, though the hags had obviously treated it.

Quick was crouching by a great oak, his form hidden beneath a pile of leaves. At first he did not seem to hear as Jinn called him, the unnatural breeze and the roaring beast fast upon them. Magic lit up the night in shades of red and blue, and that was when Quick turned, and looked at Jinn. "We go?"

"Yes, Quick. Now!"

Without waiting for an explanation, Quick scooped Jinn into his arms and sped off into the eastern end of the woods, far from where the hags were shrieking in rage or in pain. Exhausted after all that had come to pass – *I killed her. I killed her!* – Jinn allowed herself to be carried as a sack and shook with silent sobs.

CHAPTER NINE

Jinn

Whatever had come to pass between the hags and their attacker, Jinn did not know. Not that it mattered. She and Quick hadn't been pursued…though she kept checking the near future, and Quick kept looking behind them as they trudged on. They traveled until they ran out of moonlight, and then settled down for the night. No fire this time. They could not risk it.

Without speaking, the siblings lay down beneath the shelter of a great tree after eating the last of the dates they had brought from the north. Their waterskins would have to be replenished in the next town…assuming they could reach it. And she would have to wash her wounded hand lest it become infected. Ankle throbbing from where she'd been bitten and then healed, Jinn closed her eyes and meant to look ahead to the next day, when Quick spoke and upset her concentration.

"Smell bad." He sniffed and said again, as if to clarify, "Smell *really* bad."

Jinn checked her annoyance. The whole thing had been terrifying and humiliating, and the grease she'd been covered in caused her not only to smell bad, but it trapped all of her body heat and made her feel feverish. "I'll take a bath when we reach the next town."

For a moment, Quick was silent, but Jinn knew better than to peer ahead again. She would have to wait until her brother was finished with his ruminations. Sure enough, he let out a long sigh and said, "And new clothes."

"You're right about that." It was a good thing Mother had given them a large sum of money for their travels. Avoiding highwaymen had been a slight concern, but with Quick's strength and thick skin, humans were the least of their worries. "Sleep well, Quick." But he was already snoring. Jinn wondered how he did it, falling asleep wherever and whenever. With a sigh, she closed her eyes and sought the day ahead.

It didn't take her long to map out a good course for their travels, a path that would lead them to a small village where they could replenish their supplies and perhaps stay for a night. It would be their third interaction with humanity since setting out from Egethberem one moon cycle ago. Satisfied, Jinn closed her eyes and an hour later succumbed to sleep.

Though she slept, rest eluded her. For the last fortnight, flickers of a nightmare had danced behind her closed eyelids. It was always the same: she and Quick became separated, and Jinn was…. Well, Jinn didn't know where she was going or what happened to her in that vision; there was a giant hole from the moment she left Quick, and her foresight reached no further. She always avoided paths that led to nothing, because that almost certainly meant her future self was going to die. Surely her future self wouldn't be so foolish as to choose a blind path?

This night held a different dream, and the relief and realization that she would not have to replay her seemingly inevitable demise over again nearly jolted her awake.

In the dream, there was a woman Jinn thought she knew but couldn't tell why. The woman glowed an eerie shade of blue, and her hair and face had taken on that color in a darker hue. She looked straight at Jinn and said, "Take heed: the wizard approaches."

Assuming this was a vision, Jinn waited for her future self to respond, but she did not. The strange woman-creature seemed to be waiting for Jinn's present, sleeping self to answer. "The wizard?" her sleeping self muttered. "There are no wizards in the Saime."

The brilliant being glared at her. "There are four." Before Jinn could ask who and where, the woman said, "I am the third, there are yet three others. Don't ask me to speak their names. Names possess power." The words came out a violent hiss, and Jinn's mind recoiled.

But this she-wizard – was such a thing possible? – shot a cord of glowing blue at her consciousness, and latched on with overwhelming strength.

Jinn's world glowed and burned, and pain threatened to pull her mind to pieces.

"You're strong," the she-wizard said. "But there is always a price, Blest One. I don't think you paid yours." It wasn't a threat; Jinn knew who had paid the price for her abilities. "Never mind that." Her voice was gentler now, though she did not loosen her grip on Jinn's mind. "All Sightfuls lose their minds eventually."

Jinn gritted her teeth until she tasted blood. "What am I supposed to do?"

The she-wizard's eyes flashed. "Seek the Goblets Immortal. The rest will play out as it should."

"How can I know you're not some dirty sprite? What makes you think I can trust you or anything you have told me?"

The woman clucked her tongue and shook her head. "Jinn. For someone with that sort of name, you had better watch whom you call a dirty sprite. You think my present self is speaking to your slumbering mind?" The creature threw her head back and laughed. Jinn wanted to slap that smile off her face. "Oh, I'm certain we'll get in some good kicks and punches at each other, eventually. Well, eventually for *you*."

Jinn's mind was reeling. "*Eventually*? You can see the future?"

The creature laughed. "Jinn, I am *from* your future."

"But—"

"Too many questions and too many answers affect destiny. Suffice it to say that my future spirit is speaking to your present spirit. Understand?"

She did not, but nodded anyway.

The she-wizard smirked knowingly but said nothing more on that score. "Now, listen carefully. Your current plans need amending. Do not go to the village. Head straight for Cedric the Elder's tomb."

"But the Summoner is—" Jinn couldn't breathe.

"Leave. The Summoner. Alone. Understand?" When Jinn did not object – *could not* object – the she-wizard loosened the tendril of blue fire still encircling Jinn's mind. She regarded Jinn searchingly for a moment before yelping in surprise and backing away. The tendril of light guttered and went out, and the strange vision faded with the words, "Destroy them all."

Jinn woke up, coughing and choking, her hands clutching her head. She pulled away from Quick, just in time to vomit all over herself, and then began shaking so hard that she could hear her teeth clashing together.

Of course Quick had slept through it all. Nothing ever disturbed his sleep.

For a moment she regarded her twin with envy, but envy gave way to guilt and shame. Quick would do anything for her – *had* done so much for her. Jinn shook her head, the dream already ebbing away from her consciousness. In the stillness of the early hour, she could almost convince herself that it had all been an invention of her unsettled mind, but for the lingering burning around her forehead. When first light came, she would see if there were any physical marks left from the encounter. She hoped not; Quick would worry and ask questions, and maybe even inadvertently sway her from her devious path.

No, neither Quick nor any she-wizard would alter her course. The Summoner would be found, and then Mother would die.

* * *

Jinn didn't sleep after waking from the dream, but instead welcomed the morning in her own quiet way: with washing her face in a nearby stream and praying a hasty northern-faced prayer. Her body was still grease-smeared from the previous night, and her face was the only part she managed to cleanse. When they reached the town, they would rent a room, and she would take a proper bath with proper soap and would take as long as she liked, other priorities be hanged.

Once the sun had crested the horizon, Jinn shook Quick by the shoulder. "Come on, it's morning. We need to be g—"

Jinn didn't manage to finish before Quick's fist shot out and caught her on the jaw. Yowling in pain, Jinn reeled backward and fell onto her rump. For a moment she sat there in stunned silence. What had gotten into Quick? He had never laid a finger on anyone, and had rarely even so much as spoken a cross word to her. Perhaps he was having a bad dream and lashed out at her in his sleep.

Jinn rubbed the spot, thankful that he obviously hadn't used all of his strength. If he had…she did not want to think about how many places her jaw might be broken in right now and how that would look to an outside observer once they reached the town. "Quick," she croaked.

Her giant of a brother was grunting and struggling in his sleep, and it was then that it occurred to her: something was wrong with him. Foam formed at his gaping mouth, and his open eyes now rolled back in his head as he shuddered and fisted at the air.

Avoiding his meaty hands would be a challenge, as he was reeling about everywhere. She tried screaming his name again and again, but her twin only convulsed and spasmed more violently. With care, Jinn stepped out of his reach and looked around for something, anything long enough that she might prod him with. There was nothing nearby but a branch about as thick as her arm. She might be able to break it off, but she had absorbed only part of the Enduring Goblet's gift, and what there was came and went as it willed. Still, she grabbed on to the branch and attempted to break it away from the trunk. When that did not work, she leapt astride it, trying to summon the power she needed. But that power wouldn't come.

At last, after laboring and toiling, Jinn fell to the ground in exhaustion and could only look on and scream his name as Quick's tremors continued. Over the following ten minutes, they grew fewer and further between, and at last, her brother lay still, his chest rising and falling normally again.

Tears ran down Jinn's face. She let out a soft sob, lower lip trembling as she approached him on her knees, very much aware of the pulse throbbing in her jaw. "Quick?" He lay still. She ventured to place a hand on his shoulder. There was no response. "Quick, are you all right?"

After what felt like an eternity, Quick groaned, and his eyes blinked open. "Where is Jinn?"

"I'm here," said she. "What happened? Are you all right?"

He sat up, wiping the drool and foam from his face with his tattered sleeve. "Quick is hungry."

Jinn sat there in silence for a moment, stunned. "Quick? You just had an attack. I don't think you should...." She let the thought trail off and eyed her brother askance. She had warned him so many times not to. It couldn't be. Trying to keep the ire out of her voice, Jinn said softly, "You didn't, did you? Please tell me you weren't looking ahead."

Quick gave her a gentle shove, that sent her sprawling over backward, and immediately looked upset with himself. "Sorry. Quick is sorry. Didn't mean to shove Jinn."

The wind had been knocked out of her lungs, but other than that, Jinn was all right. Well, not all right. She was furious. "How far ahead did you try to look?"

He shrugged and started reaching for his pack, but Jinn pulled it out of his way before his fingertips could brush against the straps. "Sister, don't be angry." It was hard staying furious with Quick long, what with his innocent puppy eyes staring at her. But Quick was no puppy. He knew better than to exert himself.

"What did you foresee?" Jinn asked, rubbing her weary brow.

"Bad man."

She stared at him, waiting for him to finish. "Oh?"

Quick shrugged. "Bad man who didn't think Quick could see. But Quick saw him."

Jinn groaned. "How would anyone know you'd be looking for them? Wait, never mind. This is all beside the point. You're not supposed to be using your part of that gift. It's too dangerous." She stared at Quick, who looked more like a sulky child than anything. With a sigh, Jinn reached out and patted him on the shoulder. "When you're feeling yourself again, I'll come back. I'm going to scout."

"Bad man's looking for you."

That made Jinn pause mid-step. Looking for her? No one knew that she or Quick existed; Mother had seen to that. She was going to ask him if the 'bad man' was a Sightful – highly unlikely, as men didn't usually have the fortitude – but it wouldn't do to encourage him. Later she'd draw the information from him without his knowing. "It'll be fine. You'll see."

The look Quick gave her made it clear that he did not think so but was in no mood or shape to argue.

★   ★   ★

After scouting out a good path for them to take, Jinn returned and they broke their fast with the remnants of their foodstuffs: dried caribou meat, withered cherries Quick had picked off a wild tree, and an onion. There was no choice left them but to finish the supplies. Although it was only a six-mile hike from there to Gullsford, Quick burned through food like a forge in frigid weather on good days. Jinn foresaw that the way would be difficult.

She was about to finish her portion of meat, but noticed her brother eyeing it longingly. "I don't think I can abide another mouthful of this horrid stuff. Quick, would you finish it? Waste not want not, you know."

Quick nodded sagely, and with a fast chew and a big gulp, their supplies were gone.

Their journey started out in silence, besides their stomachs making their complaints known. Jinn saw the path clearly in her mind, and Quick followed her at a restrained pace, bumping into her when she walked more slowly than he would like.

The morning saw hazy gray skies. Humidity prickled the cool air, but in no time, Jinn was sweating and swatting at yellow flies that plagued the byways around the marshes. Quick tugged on her sleeve, and Jinn stopped, her eyebrows raised in question.

"Be quicker through there." He pointed at the swamp, whence came the noxious odor of rotten eggs. "The village is on the other side."

Jinn nodded. "It won't be quicker. I—"

"You foresaw," Quick cut in briskly and moved on ahead.

She raised an eyebrow and resumed walking. Her brother wasn't usually so tetchy about her proficiency in that magical art.

"You're not asking?"

"I'm not asking what?"

Quick took a deep breath and started walking backward. "Bad man is coming. Maybe the village is bad idea."

Jinn frowned. She hadn't seen anything amiss in the village. Perhaps she should check again…. "We're almost there," she said instead. "Do you need to rest?"

He grunted once, his only response, and they walked the remaining four miles mostly in silence. They had to watch their footing, as the way was pockmarked with rabbit and gopher holes. Quick sank into one once and could have easily twisted his ankle, if he weren't nigh impervious to physical harm. Jinn could foresee holes before she fell into them, but there were enough possible and probable steps that they both would take, that she had been unable to warn her brother about any of them.

By the time they reached the wall that surrounded the town, the sun was high in the sky and they both were sweaty and cross.

Quick wouldn't come within five feet of her, lest he smell her 'pig stink'. She really did need that bath.

At the village gate, which sat wide open, there was a tiny watchhouse that held an open-roomed tower at the top. No one was above, but there was a rough-looking little man sitting on a stool in the room below. "State your business," said the gatekeeper, not bothering to look up from his lunch, a pasty stuffed with what smelled like onions and liver.

Jinn looked at Quick before answering, "Lodging and a meal."

The whiskery fellow nodded and jerked his thumb in the direction they should head. "Thanks for visiting Gullsford. Enjoy your stay, and stay out of trouble."

They thanked him and entered.

For a town named for seabirds, there was no body of water beyond a stagnant pond on the outskirts. There were not many people about at this noon hour. The few individuals she did see were sleeping in rocking chairs or even in the grasses with hats over their eyes.

As if in response to what he saw, Quick let out an enormous yawn. "Hungry."

"There should be an inn not too far from here," Jinn said below her breath, not wanting to disturb anyone during this strange napping hour. "We'll hopefully fill our bellies there." She had already looked ahead at seven possible outcomes for the trip from the front gate to the green-doored inn. That was all she had the energy and the stomach for. Experiencing the strange vision and getting punched by her brother earlier had left her tired, sore, and cantankerous. If she had to play out one more possible outcome for the morning, she might go mad.

They walked on for the better part of a half hour, circled the same streets twice, and finally ended up outside a surprisingly new and well-kept inn with a white picket fence and full beds of flowers. Jinn made her way toward the building, but Quick stopped her by putting a heavy hand on her shoulder. "What?" she asked, perhaps not as kindly as she could have.

Quick frowned. "Look first." His own vision must have left him more frightened than Jinn had first realized.

Nodding, Jinn took a fast glance at their surroundings, found no one overtly staring, and then closed her eyes and looked at one path and one alone. *The vision showed them walking up to the inn, opening the green door, paying a weasely looking yet otherwise harmless-seeming innkeeper with a pointy red hat, and making their way to a room. There were many rooms empty, but she and Quick would take just one and save their coins.* Exhausted, Jinn opened her eyes and said, "It's all fine. We're safe to go in." It was half the truth, as she had only peered minutes ahead.

Just as her vision predicted, the innkeeper was an oddity but didn't ask too many questions. "You're not from around these parts," he drawled. His left eye was shifty and wouldn't focus on anything.

"No, we're not," Jinn replied, hoping not to sound guarded. "We're just passing through."

"Visiting family," Quick said at the same time.

Jinn smiled in what she hoped was a calm, benign manner.

The innkeeper narrowed his one eye. "You married?" He gestured between the both of them. "I don't house unwed couples. Ain't right."

"Twins," Quick said and patted Jinn on the shoulder hard enough to make her knees buckle.

The man's good eye grew wide. "How is that even possible? You two don't look anything alike."

"Different fathers," Quick said before Jinn could answer. It was the truth: Mother had been with at least two men and thus conceived her unwanted twins, but judging from the innkeeper's face, he had never heard of such a thing.

"It's a long, complicated story," Jinn said. "Can I ask for a hot bath?"

The innkeeper nodded. "You can ask. Not sure how hot the water will be by the time we haul it up there."

"Any temperature's fine," she assured him, reaching into her money pouch for the exact amount she knew he would ask for. "Here. It's all right that there's no lock, we'll just bolt the door from the inside."

Quick shifted his weight as the man's eyes narrowed.

"You been here before?"

Lights, but she shouldn't have let her foreknowledge slip like that. "No," she answered. "Word gets around, though."

Thank the stars that he inquired no further into the matter but handed them a worn tile that they were to hang on their door to state that the room was occupied. "The water'll be up in a while. Gotta round up my hands to fetch it." He gave her an accusing look, like she was ordering him around, but Jinn ignored it. A bath was worth the trouble, especially considering that her main source of bodily protection was now standing as far from her as possible, nose pinched.

"Hungry," Quick reminded her.

Jinn put on her prettiest smile and said to the innkeeper, "Oh, and it would be lovely if we could be pointed in the direction of something to…eat." The withering look the man gave her put a knot in Jinn's stomach.

"We ain't your servants nor staff to order about here, you understand?"

Struggling to retain the smile, Jinn reached into her money pouch again and pulled out a more-than-generous banknote. "Point us in the direction of the kitchen; we can fend for ourselves." It was beneath her, but she batted her eyes.

The man was not looking at her but rather at the money. "This real?"

"Real," Quick assured him, stomach rumbling.

The innkeeper pointed to his left, which Jinn assumed led to the kitchen or larder. "Well, I guess it's all right. Just don't get in Cook's way." His eyes were still studying the banknote, pupils large.

"Many thanks," Quick offered as Jinn took him by the elbow and steered him away into the adjoining room. Better to get all the food they could before the man changed his mind or decided that he wanted more money. "Still stink."

Jinn sighed. "There's nothing I can do about that at the moment."

Quick walked a little ways ahead of her, breathing loudly through his mouth. "Soon, though?"

She did not dignify that question with a response. The kitchen smells were growing stronger: roasting garlic was most pungent, but Jinn could also make out the yeasty scent of baking bread, the sharp tang of wild herbs, and perhaps a goose roasting on a spit. Woodsmoke bit at her eyes, which began to water. "Let's look in the larder," she whispered, not wanting to alert the cook to their presence and then have to deal with introductions and explanations of why they were in his or her kitchen.

"Hot food. Please." Quick's voice was full of such longing that Jinn hated to deny him that wish.

"We'll take up what we want to our room and I'll cook it there. How's that?"

Quick made a face. "Bad smell."

"Right. We'll sit on opposite sides of the room." As she spoke, Jinn found a big empty basket and filled it with a small chicken, two cold turkey legs, brown bread, butter, a large wedge of cheese, small black berries that she assumed must be currants, and a rasher of bacon. She lifted it, thought it would look strange for a small woman such as herself to show such strength, and handed the lot over to Quick. "There." After grabbing a frying pan and a pitcher of what smelled like small beer, she led Quick out of the kitchen, up the stairs, and into their room, where they hung their tile and set their wares by the cold fireplace.

"Eat now?"

"Soon." Jinn looked around the room. It wasn't overly large, but would do for the both of them. Quick was much too big for the canopy bed; he would probably snap the frame into splinters just by sitting on it carefully. There was a thick rug by the fireplace, where he could sleep with the beige down blanket from the bed. That decided, Jinn removed her pack from her back and rifled through it for the flint, magnesium, and her knife.

"Cold."

She looked up from her work at the small fireplace and noticed that the two warped glass windows were framed by heavy gray curtains. "Close those. That will keep the heat in better."

As her brother shivered and complained, Jinn worked on starting the fire, all the while trying to keep herself from thinking about the fire she had meant to start the night before. If only she had peered ahead a little further, then they wouldn't have ended up ensnared by those treacherous hags. Jinn shuddered and her knife jumped, nearly nicking the skin of her index finger. And what had scared the creatures off, exactly? "What does it matter?" she muttered. "We got away. We're safe."

After building the fire and nurturing it into a brilliant blaze, Jinn set about putting their meal together. First she fried up the bacon, which she cut into strips and placed in the iron pan. She hated touching the metal vessel, as it interfered with her foresight, but there was no way around it if they wanted to eat a hot meal.

While the bacon was crackling in front of the blaze, Jinn cleaned the knife, cut up the hunk of cheese and handed all but a small portion to Quick, who began to devour it like a man breaking an extended fast. Jinn made him eat a handful of currants as well, and they both sipped from the pitcher of small beer until the bacon was almost crispy. The smoky, salty meat proved too tempting to wait much longer for, and they ate it hot out of the pan.

"More cheese?"

"No. But you can have the rest of the bacon." The remainder of the rasher had been frying while they ate the first panful, and Quick ate it half-cooked in a matter of seconds. "So," Jinn said, casting about for a careful way to broach the subject. "Last night was an adventure."

Quick raised his eyebrows and gave her an odd look before reaching for the brown bread and tearing off a chunk with his teeth. "I suppose."

Jinn took the remainder of the bread and slathered on the soft butter with her knife before taking a bite herself. Through a mouthful she said, "It was good fortune that the beast showed up when it did."

Of all things, he growled. "Weren't no beast." Quick did not elaborate on what was meant by that.

Carefully, Jinn placed the cold chicken into the pan of bacon grease and pushed it with a thick stick toward the fire to warm up. "Do you think that perhaps our foresight is being—"

"Jinn," Quick interrupted. "Bad man is coming."

"Right, that. Are you sure—"

There was a knocking at the door, and Quick's face went as white as chalk. "Who there?" he roared.

Jinn dropped the bread and did not retrieve it immediately. Instead, she closed her eyes and peered into the near future. It did not take her long to realize that there were two men outside their door, an enormous cauldron supported between them on a pole. She sighed in relief. "It's the workers with the water. Brother, it's all right. Truly." She rose and hurried to answer the door.

★   ★   ★

After the bathwater had been deposited – not enough to fill the metal tub by the window, but enough to get clean with – Jinn dismissed the two workers and explained to Quick how to tell when the chicken was done. She wasn't going to wait any longer to bathe, so tough luck; Quick would just have to be in the same room with his naked sister. He didn't complain – much – and when he did, she reminded him that they had been together in the womb like that.

Quick shuddered. "Don't remind Quick."

With a sigh, Jinn climbed out of her grimy and grease-covered clothes, which she would later launder or burn, and stepped into the bath, yelping as it stung her skin. "Don't forget to rotate the bird every once in a while." She leaned back in the tub and closed her eyes.

"Yes, Jinn."

She cracked an eye open. "And be sure to spoon some of the pan juices over it every now and again."

Quick made a noncommittal sound in his throat but otherwise did not respond. He was busy stuffing his face full of the remainder of the cooked food with one hand, as he added the turkey legs to the overcrowded chicken pan with the other.

The vision from that morning all but forgotten, Jinn let herself drowse. She dreamed small dreams of no consequence: rabbits and trails and birds in iron cages. Then there was a palace by the sea, salty water spraying up its sheer black cliffs whence the bird from the iron cage dared not fly again. Refreshed, Jinn woke up to the smell of the chicken cooking in the fireplace. The water was cool. Quickly she scrubbed the sleep from her eyes and picked up the cake of soap that had been supplied, lathered up as well as she could, and then rinsed herself in a hurry. The inn workers hadn't supplied her with a towel, which was a bother.

"We can't stay here," Quick surprised Jinn by muttering as she rummaged, naked, through her pack for her one change of clothing. "Town people are strange."

Jinn quirked a smile as she slipped into gray trousers and tightened a red belt around her waist. "Are all town people strange or just these ones in particular?" The food and the bath had restored good humor in her, and she thought it might have with her brother as well.

Wiping grease from his chin, Quick let out an ill-tempered belch, if ever a belch could be ill-tempered. When he caught that she was still half-naked, he turned away. "Have bad feeling."

"You didn't look ahead again, did you?"

Quick made no immediate reply, and Jinn felt her good humor fading.

Jinn groaned. "Oh, Quick!"

"No, no. Didn't look ahead. Honest."

The charcoal-blue tunic she was pulling over her head got stuck for a brief moment, and Jinn could scarce hear what he was mumbling about. Something about a poor bird and weird customs in parts of the world, all said in clipped syllables with the occasional growl added for emphasis.

"Besides, *trap*."

They stared at each other, a veil of Jinn's dripping-wet jet-black hair hanging between them. "The holes in my vision are—"

"Trap."

"The holes in my vision," she gritted out, "make it impossible to see when it will happen, how it will happen exactly, or even if it *will* happen. Maybe there is no trap." She let her shoulders rise and fall.

Now Quick's breathing came harder. "You saw bad things."

She gave him a pointed look. "*We* saw bad things."

He pulled the chicken pan out of the fire with his bare hands, and Jinn shuddered. "We eat, we sleep, we leave." He gave her the same look she had been giving him. "No argue. Just do."

Jinn pointed at the window. "All right. But we have to restock our supplies."

His eyebrows shot up and his mouth opened to argue, but he closed it again and shrugged. "Sister get hurt?" He looked at her with expectation, most likely hoping she would look ahead, since she was so adamant about him not looking himself.

Ignoring the beginnings of a headache and her throbbing hand, Jinn closed her eyes and peered ahead through the next hour. If they continued on their current course of actions, both of them would be lying down to rest. She looked ahead through the next hour, and the hour following that. There was shopping in the marketplace – with a few rabbit trails from seven different decisions they might make, so she followed through with those, which all led to the same conclusion: their packs being refilled and them sitting down for supper. Sifting through various sights and sounds, Jinn came to eight hours later when eventide prevailed. To this point, nothing had been amiss. But now Jinn realized with a start that the holes in her vision had returned and were many and close together. Something or someone was blocking her abilities.

With a gasp, Jinn felt the phantom touch of someone grabbing her by the shoulder. Her future self turned to see who was assailing her, but all she saw was a pair of dark eyes before the vision left her altogether.

"Jinn?" Quick's voice was warped and insubstantial-sounding, as if it were coming from under water. He was now shaking her by the shoulders, but Jinn found herself frozen in terror. She had seen those eyes before, in other visions. And they always led to an impenetrable darkness.

"Quick," she said, licking her dry lips.

"Quick here."

Her whole body convulsed with an almighty shudder as she tried to rid her mind of the terror that had seized it. "We need to pack our things now."

Silence. "Bad man?"

Jinn nodded and then shook her head. "Yes. I mean, no. I don't know." She had to get a hold of herself so that Quick wouldn't be frightened. They needed to leave, but they needed to rest and to restock their supplies. Perhaps her brother had been right; it was a mistake to stop in this town.

While she sat frozen, trying to decide what to do, Quick began repacking both of their bags. "Look again," he said, encouraging her to look down a new path.

Her nerves were frayed. Foresight – oh, what a gift and what a curse – was difficult to summon when she was afraid and distraught, but she had to try. Trembling, Jinn closed her eyes again and pursued a new line of action in her thoughts and intentions. More sights and sounds flashed in front of her mind's eye, and she followed various small routes, three of which led them to leaving within two hours' time. That would put them six hours ahead of darkness. She shuddered. Would six hours be enough to escape her demise? *No, best not think like that.* Even then she could feel her foresight blurring and fighting against her control over it. *Focus.*

The sounds of Quick bustling around, counting out money that they would need to purchase supplies, and eating the rest of their food, were jarring but proved to be more irritating than startling. Jinn focused on his heavy tread and willed herself to relax and concentrate to the sound as if it were to the beat of a drum back home in their cave. *Rat-a-tat. Thump-thud-rat-a-thud-tap.* Her foresight cleared.

They stood by a vendor's tent, asking for directions. Well, that was foolish. If someone was pursuing them, the pursuer only needed to ask this vendor a few questions and Jinn and Quick's game was up. Jinn added a twist to her intentions and saw herself asking the vendor for directions to a city in the complete opposite direction of where they intended to go.

Within minutes, she had scouted out a safe route through the next ten hours, no dark eyes and eternal silence at its conclusion. That would have to do; looking forward was exhausting and confusing. Once they followed the course she had set and her mind had time to rest, Jinn would peer ahead again.

*   *   *

They were packed and ready to leave the inn in twenty minutes' time. Part of Jinn's plan was to maintain the illusion that they were remaining in Gullsford, so they left the pots and pans and Jinn's dirty clothing there in the room, made the bed look slept in, and then went to restock their foodstuffs. On the way out, they made sure to give the impression they would be returning that evening by asking what time they might have supper, even going so far as to pay for the next night's stay.

Now that they were on the move, Quick seemed more like his usual self. He pointed to various items in the small marketplace in the middle of the town, like the bright purple ribbons streaming from a sweets stand whence the crisp, sweet aroma of hot sugar and butter tickled at Jinn's nose. They could afford a treat, but it had not been part of Jinn's plan, so she took Quick by the hand and led him to the butcher's shop. They bought as much smoked meat as she thought they could carry, paid the man, and tucked the stiff strips into the leftover grease paper in Quick's pack.

Next they bought six beef-and-potato hand pies apiece from the baker's, wrapped up and ready to stow next to the jerky. They moved on from shop to shop and stand to stand, but Jinn kept a watchful eye out for trouble and tried her utmost to keep their steps and transactions on the same path that she had chosen to foresee. After new boots had been purchased – Quick's were wearing thin – they refilled their waterskins at the well in the middle of the town, paying the well-keeper for the water and giving him a few coins beside.

"Looks to be a fine day," said the well-keeper after first biting the coins that had been handed to him.

"Mm," was all Jinn could think to say in response. It would be a finer day once they had put this town safely behind them. She swore as some water splashed onto her front. It was a warm enough day, she reassured herself; her shirt should dry before nightfall.

The well-keeper seemed to sense her agitation as he said, "Things can't be that bad."

Quick laughed in disbelief, and Jinn shot him a warning look. "Dark," he said. "Night is very dark."

Smile faltering, the pudgy old man nodded. "Oh, yes. Night can be, erm, very dark indeed." Perhaps a salesman in a former life, he then asked them if they had been to the candlemaker's. "They use the finest beeswax, none of that rendered-fat garbage."

The thought of tallow made Jinn's stomach turn sour. The cave that she and Quick had lived in most of their lives had been lit only with tallow candles, which they would sometimes eat when Mother forgot to send food. "Beeswax is lovely," she replied.

"I used to keep bees," said the man fondly.

Jinn smiled and nodded. "That's lovely."

"They're good creatures. Very gentle...except when they interbreed with wattlewasps."

Quick's ears perked up and he nudged Jinn. "Wattlewasps."

She hushed him. "Yes, wattlewasps. Where is the candlestick maker?" Jinn asked out of politeness.

That brought a large grin to the well-keeper's face. "Oh, it's just across from the sweets stand. Birk's sells the finest candles in all shapes and colors. And the wicks are high quality; they'll burn for hours."

Having finished filling their water bladders, Jinn thanked the man, took Quick by the hand, and started to leave. But Quick was having none of that.

"Candles not a bad idea, Jinn."

Jinn gave him a shrewd look. "You just want sweets from the shop across, don't you?"

Quick nodded. "Yes."

For a moment, they stood there, Jinn worrying her lower lip as Quick swung their clasped hands. She had looked down this thread, but hadn't seen Quick's request coming, which made her at once uneasy. It wasn't quite a hole, though, was it?

"We'll buy you a small package of sweets —" Before her brother could rejoice at his triumph, Jinn squeezed his hand and said, "— but no candles. There just isn't time or need for them."

That took the wind out of Quick's sails. He didn't exactly pout, but there was a slowness in his step that made Jinn aware of his displeasure.

"You were the one who was worried about the bad man chasing me."

Quick tightened his grip on her hand. "You see bad man?"

"No," she admitted and then was quiet about the matter. There was no point in getting him all worked up again. Besides, after the last few weeks they had endured, Quick deserved a treat.

The sweets stand was just closing as they stepped up to it, and it took some convincing to keep it open just five more minutes so they could make their purchase. A little extra money thrown in did the trick, and the confectioner was all smiles and even offered Quick a sample of a new product. Quick liked the treat so much that Jinn gave in and bought a large packet of it. "That will ruin your teeth," she warned him as they left the stand.

Quick said nothing but gave her cloak a tug. They were standing just feet away from the entrance to the candle shop. "Go inside?"

She groaned. "I told you, we don't have time."

"Quick has good feeling about it," Quick said, his face lighting up like a child's on its birthday. "Please, sister?"

Jinn couldn't say why, but the candle shop suddenly sounded like a marvelous idea. Why hadn't she thought so before? It would seem they weren't the only ones with the notion: left and right, people were dropping what they were doing and heading for the candlemaker's. No one pushed, no one shoved. In fact, everyone smiled and was polite, even letting Quick elbow a path through their ranks without reprimanding him.

A cold sweat had formed on the back of Jinn's neck but she forced away any trepidation she felt as she followed Quick through the iron doorway with four words painted above it: *ALL SALES ARE FINAL*. The door itself was wood painted black and it shut behind them as if by a gust of wind. Outside the crowd stood, backs pressed against the exit, forming a solid wall.

"Odd," Jinn muttered. Hating crowds, she moved away from the door and toward a display of soothing oils that made all sorts of ridiculous claims. *Bald no more! Regrow a full mane – two sniffs will do!* read one bottle. "Sell a lot of these?" Jinn called out. There was no immediate answer, just a calm silence. *Fatten up! Slim down! Wake up! Sleep some more! Warts-be-gone!* All the bottles were stoppered with cork, but were attached to an iron charm and a prayer printed on parchment to ward off fey. Jinn stiffened. So, magic-haters did dwell this far south. "Quick, maybe we should think about leaving."

Quick laughed, an unnatural sound. "You worry too much."

Jinn turned and was about to accuse him of drinking too much small beer, but the edge went out of her anger and she found herself blinking sleepily. She fought against the sensation, only for it to hit her again. *I'm worried for naught.* The soothing words entered her mind, but their tenor was not her own. Jinn shuddered. She lived in her thoughts more often than in the real world, and she knew what her own voice sounded like. The intrusive thought tried again. *All is well. Peace. I am at peace.*

Yes, she was at peace...until she realized she was not. They were fleeing this town, desperate to escape the darkness to come. So why did Jinn feel the sudden urge to lie down and sleep?

Something or someone was trying to charm her. It had worked on Quick, that was certain.

Even now her brother was smiling stupidly at the mediocre-looking wax candles that lined the wall. "Pretty," he said, waving his hand a little too wide and clumsily. A freestanding candle fell from its display and thudded onto the ground.

Jinn looked around for the proprietor. "Quick, we need to leave."

Behind the counter there sat a wisp of a man with an oiled salt-and-pepper moustache, and wire-rim spectacles perched on the bridge of his nose. He smiled languidly at Jinn as if he thought it perfectly fine and normal for a giant to crash around his store and knock things over. "Isn't it a fine day?"

She didn't bother answering, but grabbed Quick's hand and gave him a tug. "There's an enchantment, Quick. I don't know how or why, but we need to leave."

Quick smiled down at her. "Sister, all is well."

The words settled on her shoulders and tried to work their way into her veins, but Jinn was on to the spell now and fought against it in earnest. "Quick, be a dear and look at me. Look into my eyes."

"Pretty Jinn has blue eyes."

"Yes, Quick. Look into Jinn's pretty blue eyes."

Staggering as one drunk, Quick turned to better face her. "Why so worried? You're worried for naught."

"Quick," she said firmly. "We need to leave. There is danger. Someone is trying to keep us trapped here."

But her brother wasn't listening. With a big grin, he ambled away from Jinn and plopped down in front of the door as if he meant to take a long nap.

Panic roiled in Jinn's veins, and her breaths came with increasing difficulty. She closed her eyes. One minute ahead – *they remained in the shop and Quick had started to snore.* Two minutes ahead – *the candlestick maker laid his head down on the counter and began to drool all over his brown wrapping papers.* Three minutes, four minutes, five minutes – they all showed the same things: everyone in Jinn's vicinity was falling unconscious. There was no time to look ahead to ten minutes even; by then goodness knows what else the enchantment would do to Quick and all these poor people.

So Jinn did the first thing that sprang to mind: she screamed. She screamed obscenity after obscenity at Quick, trying to get him to wake up and tell her to stop swearing. But Quick just gurgled and sniggered where he sat, until Jinn's voice cracked and she lost him again to his dreams. Quick was hard enough to rouse when he was in a normal sleep, but an *enchanted* sleep? Jinn had no idea what to do. She tried slapping him, once, twice, soft, and hard. Nothing. She shouted in his left ear. Her brother stirred for a moment, before leaning that ear onto his great left shoulder and then falling back asleep. Knowing she couldn't truly hurt her brother, Jinn ignored the snoring shopkeeper and began throwing candles at Quick. They cracked and crumbled against his chest and thudded onto the floor, but drew no reaction.

Minutes had passed. Jinn could feel the nigh-irresistible call of sleep intensifying. She knew nothing of enchanters. Did they even still exist? But there was no good reason for one to be after her of all people; she was near kin. Lights, but this was difficult. Desperate for an idea, she closed her eyes and was about to peer ahead, when she backed up into a display and heard a few bottles clink together. Again she swore, trying to right herself. The sight of the glass bottles gave her pause. Perhaps if she really tried to hurt her brother, drawing blood even, that might wake him. She shuddered and was about to turn away from the vials in revulsion, but froze and looked at them more carefully.

Love potion! See like an elf! Shrink your feet! Odor-be-gone! Jinn tossed those bottles aside. *Catch more fish! Smaller thighs!* For people who had special prayers to keep away the fairies, these strange folk had some pretty magical-sounding oils. "Ridiculous," Jinn snapped at a bottle of *Blondes are best!* She knew from her reading there was something to be said for the ancient art of oils, and she could have sworn she had seen— "Yes!" She snatched the bottle of *Wake up!* off its precarious position on the edge of the display and ran to Quick's side. But when she went to unstopper it, Jinn was hit hard with a vision, which overlaid the images in front of her. *Quick stood lost and alone, calling her name. The rest of the vision was darkness.* Jinn jumped. The vial shattered unused on the floor.

It took her a moment to realize that Quick was stirring and that she scented the strong odor of greens-baro and tanderine blossoms, plants with potent healing and anti-hex powers. She could have cried in relief, but the vision of imminent doom was not fading, even though it had changed by a degree. "Quick!" she shouted, tugging on his hands with all her might. Her giant of a brother grunted and pulled his hands away, scrubbing his eyes in apparent confusion.

"Why is Quick on floor?"

"I'll explain later." She looked out the shop window, where dozens of townsfolk were dozing in their way. Jinn swore. "We need to find a way out. Here, let's wake the shopkeeper and ask him."

By now Quick had stumbled to his feet, causing the floor to shake and the boards to creak in an ominous manner. "Should we bring stinking oil?" Even now the aroma was fading, and Quick swayed on his feet. There was no time to rouse the shopkeeper.

Jinn took her brother by the hand and led him behind the counter. The workspace opened into a small backroom where sat vats of oil and wax for dipping. No doors or windows there. She pushed Quick out of the room and led him through the rest of the tiny shop, and in each tiny room, they ran into the same problem: no windows and no doors.

"What wrong?" he asked as Jinn began pacing.

"How are we going to get out of here?" She pointed at the front of the shop. "There is only one door and one window, and half the village must be in the way."

Quick chuckled. "That easy."

She frowned, and he grinned.

"We make door."

★   ★   ★

Once Quick had pounded a hole in the back wall, the twins ran through the shop abutting it: a sewing supply store. From the woman behind the counter to the ladies next to the calico, everyone was fast asleep. "Why they so tired?" he asked as Jinn and he pushed their way out of the shop and ran through the back streets.

Even as they fled, Jinn felt a strong need to return to the candle shop and sleep. "There's some sort of curse. Or spell...or something." Panting, she handed her sack to Quick; strength was not with her at this moment.

"Bad man," Quick said after a moment.

They ran to the edge of town in silence, and everywhere they were met with sleeping bodies, still and defenseless. Anyone could storm into town and attack the villagers. Jinn shuddered. Should they stop? Find more oils to wake at least a few people?

"What Jinn doing?" Quick asked as they finally reached the border wall. He cupped his hands together, meaning to give her a step up, but she stood undecided.

"What if he hurts all these people?" she asked. "It would be my fault."

Quick groaned. "Jinn, bad man not after them." He jabbed a finger at her chest in emphasis. "He after *you*." And with that said, he grabbed Jinn by the back of her trousers and hoisted her up onto the wall, though he could only just reach it with his fingertips.

"All right, all right," said Jinn, bracing herself so she could help Quick up after her.

But Quick stepped back, got a running start, and threw himself at the wall. The momentum carried him up high enough to get his hands on the ledge, and Jinn helped him the rest of the way over. Panting and cursing, both of them tumbled over onto the other side and into the woods.

CHAPTER TEN

Jinn

The wind shifted, and the sky darkened. Lightning flashed as Jinn and Quick ran into the bracken, not daring to hesitate lest the enchanter catch up with them. Scratched and sore, they had run three miles when the rain began to fall in earnest.

"We can't go much farther in this," Jinn shouted above the roar of thunder. "We need to make a shelter."

But Quick wouldn't stop running. Rather, he scooped his sister up by the waist and ran with her another three miles, nearly dropping her five times and knocking her twice against solid oak trees.

Jinn didn't complain though, she was happy to put more distance between them and the sleeping town, especially since she didn't have to move under her own power. The previous night's vision had interrupted her sleep, and her nap in the bathing tub only left her wanting more.

When Quick set her down, they began to scout for a place to settle. Sheltering beneath a tree in a thunderstorm was far from ideal, but the rumblings and flashes of lightning had grown farther off and farther apart, leading Jinn to believe that the worst of it was over. Still, they looked around for the shortest tree they could find, and began to make camp.

It was past midday now and well into the late afternoon, though the sky seemed to say otherwise. Quick ripped a section of bark from a tree twice the thickness of his own girth and leaned it against where they would build the shelter. Jinn directed him several times, while looking for twine in her pack to secure the materials together.

In forty minutes' time, they had the beginnings of a mediocre shelter but not the energy to finish it. Shivering, the twins crawled beneath the lean-to and huddled together for warmth.

"Remind Quick of the cave," Quick said, sticking his head out from the shelter.

A tremor went down Jinn's spine. "Let's – let's not talk about home."

Quick grunted, and she took that to mean he agreed. After a moment he said, "Any food?"

Jinn suppressed a groan. "Do you think you could hold on a little longer?" The rain had died down to a drizzle, and a fog crept in over the forest floor. She pulled her hood over her head and stared into the haze.

"S'pose." He fidgeted, jostling the shelter and thus letting in a few extra chilling drops of rain.

The droplets pattered against the crown of Jinn's head. Not that it mattered; she was already soaked through. "You should get some rest," she said through a yawn. "We didn't get proper sleep last night."

"You slept none."

"True." Again she yawned. "Still, I don't mind taking first watch."

Of all things, Quick let out a rumbling laugh. "Sister thinks Quick will eat while she sleeps?" Again he laughed.

"I guess I will take a rest." She blinked against the sleep tugging at her eyelids. "Oh, don't forget your sweets."

"Mm," he said, smacking his lips together. "You want some?" He sounded hesitant, if not entirely unwilling to share.

The laugh slipped out before she could catch it, so she disguised it as a small cry of pain. "Must've sat on a bur."

He let out a deep sigh. "So you don't want?"

"It's all yours, Quick."

⋆   ⋆   ⋆

After finding the sweets for Quick and telling him to drink rainwater
if he got thirsty – they needed to save their waterskins – Jinn leaned
her head against her shoulder and closed her eyes. The constant
drip, drip, drip atop her hood was mesmerizing and could have lulled
her to sleep had it been a warmer day. As it was, she was shaking
in her boots. Jinn tried pulling her cloak closer, but as that was
waterlogged, it didn't do much good. Now the cave that they used
to call home didn't sound so bad.

A loud crunching noise shattered any illusion of peace. Perhaps
it had been a mistake, buying the sweets, as Quick was chomping
on them with vigor. But they had only bought half a pound, and
Quick was a fast eater. Soon the crunching ceased, and Quick
began to hum.

With a quiet grumble, Jinn opened her eyes a crack and looked
at her brother. "Quick, would you be a love and hum more softly?"

There was silence for a moment, and then snores cut through the
silence like a great wood saw. So much for his keeping first watch.

Jinn tucked her chin into her chest. They had been traveling for
around a month now, searching for the Summoner, following her
foresight and hoping for the best. The best sure hadn't turned out.
She was cold, she was sleepy, and she was cranky. Some strange man
or beast was after her, and she was no closer to stopping Mother
than when they had started out. In fact, by the way things were
going, Mother's so-called 'secret' plan was more likely to happen.
That plan, as Jinn had figured out, without Mother's knowledge,
was for Jinn and Quick to succeed in finding the Summoner...and
yet hopefully die in the process.

Mother had belonged to the Circle, a cult that bred men and
women to produce magical heirs, the Blest. Though the cult had
long since been destroyed – by Mother's hand – they were still
feared. It was no wonder, then, that Mother hated Jinn and Quick,
the two reminders of her captivity. Though Jinn could not blame

Mother entirely for her hatred, it did nothing to cool her own.

Another yawn escaped her. The sun wouldn't be getting any higher in the sky, not that she could actually see it. They couldn't stay where they were for the remainder of the day; the shelter would not hold, and whoever or whatever was pursuing them could very well overtake them in the dark. With a grimace, she closed her eyes and did what she had been dreading: she looked ahead.

The next hour was clear of anything dramatic. Quick would sleep like a dead man, snoring as loudly as ever. Jinn foresaw herself lying on her back, her chest rising and falling slowly. The rain would stop, and the sun would even make an appearance. There were no holes in this vision. But an hour's time was not long. She needed to look further.

Jinn followed the vision down its course for five hours into the future, sorting through divergent paths that seemed likely when they appeared. The most alternate paths she chose to look at were three. Again, nothing much seemed to be happening. She concentrated and tried to look ahead to ten hours from now, something that was always difficult and required more concentration. The further ahead things went, the more paths there were to look at, and any conclusions became less stable and vaguer.

Once she was satisfied with what she had seen, and having chosen the path that would allow Quick to sleep another two hours, Jinn rubbed her temples and attempted to look for the Summoner. It was one thing looking at one's own fate, but a more delicate feat to try to look at another's. Gauging when a vision's events were going to take place was impossible and had led her in the past to make less calculated decisions.

She waited until Quick's snoring grew softer, and then sought out the Summoner. It took several minutes to find him, and when she did, she wasn't entirely sure what she was foreseeing. *There was a dimly lit cave. Water trickled in an unsteady stream, ploinking on the ground while the air hummed with energy, as it does when a storm is building. There was no sign of the Summoner, and yet she knew he was there…somewhere. Perhaps if she focused harder—*

"Where hast you gone?" a strange voice asked in the darkness. A lantern's blue light bobbed into view. The Summoner did not appear. Perhaps he was hiding. But why could Jinn not see him?

"Eldred!" the man with the lantern called out, his voice bouncing off the stone walls. He approached where Jinn knew the Summoner should be, and stood there with his cloak's hood covering his face. For a moment the man held the lantern aloft in silence, watching the spot where Jinn was also staring.

His cloak was perhaps once fine, but the royal red – if that truly was its original color – was dirt-caked and torn. His feet were bare, and his brown toenails were long and curled back up over his feet. He shifted his weight and called out again. "Eldred. I know your power." When he pulled his hood back, Jinn thought she might faint. Not only was his gray hair long and matted with mud, the man's face was emaciated, his skin thin as paper, so Jinn could see his veins and the blood pumping through them. He drooled excessively.

Jinn gagged and coughed, and the man looked her straight in the eye, frowning. "No," he said, shaking his head as his eyes widened. "Go away, Fistight. No. I don't want to be found. I don't – stop following me. You're dead." He laughed, rearing his head back to show the blackness of his teeth. "Yes, you're dead." The thought seemed to make the man shiver, and he stopped laughing.

Coming to her senses, Jinn decided to try talking to this strange man, though she had only ever been able to interact with one vision, and that had been the night previous. "Who are you? And why did you call me Fistight?"

The man continued to stare at her but said nothing in reply.

She tried again. "Are you from the future?" Immediately she felt stupid. How would this man know if he was from the future or not? Just because the she-wizard from last night's vision had known, it didn't mean this crazy old bat would have a clue.

A great roar of a man or beast was taken up in the distance.

The insane man seemed to forget about Jinn and began wringing his hands. "Oh, dear. More guests. Must prepare the games again." And with that, he hoisted his lantern higher and scuttled back to the tunnel whence he had come.

Jinn swore. Where was the Summoner?

"Jinn?" Quick's voice intruded. "Jinn, you all right?"

She opened her eyes and blinked several times as the world came into focus. No longer sitting up, Jinn found herself lying in a puddle at the base of the tree. She groaned. "How long was I asleep?" The sun sat lower in the sky, and the rain had stopped entirely. She must have been asleep for two hours at least.

Quick yawned, and his stomach rumbled. "Hungry," he said as if in apology.

"Thanks for waking me. I didn't mean to sleep that long."

His head bobbed once in acknowledgment. Standing, he knocked the shelter to the forest floor with a thud. Birds squawked their complaints and flew high into the sky. Quick groaned, his joints cracking as he stretched. "Rainwater tastes bad."

Jinn laughed. "You drank from the puddles, didn't you?"

Quick shrugged and mumbled something unintelligible. What was she going to do with him? "You slept. Quick ate."

That stopped her laughter. She quirked an eyebrow and fixed Quick with a frown. "How much did you eat?" Before he could answer, she broke out the packs and sorted through the papers and crumbs. Jinn swore. "Oh, Quick. Why?" More than half of their food supplies were gone. What should have lasted them three days had lasted maybe three hours.

"Was hungry," he said, thumping his chest, defiance in his voice. Before she could reprimand him further, Quick continued. "There are berries in woods."

She looked around. "What kind of berries? Where?"

Quick licked his lips. "Red berries. Big, red starberries!"

"B-but wild starberries aren't in season, Quick," she wailed. "Quick, the next town is far from here, more than two and a half days' worth of walking." Tears prickled her eyes, and exhaustion washed over her.

Like a child, Quick stomped his foot, kicking up a spray of mud that streaked across Jinn's face. "Quick saw starberries."

Stunned, Jinn sat there in the mud and stared at her pack through a film of dirt and tears. Why had she let herself fall asleep like that? She knew that Quick couldn't be trusted at all times with precious items, such as food and water. Just for good measure, she felt and shook the water bladders. Those, at least, were plenty full. She took an angry swipe at the mess on her face and stumbled to her feet. Of course her right leg was all pins and needles, and her boots squelched in the mud and might have gotten stuck had she weighed more. "What is done cannot be undone," she said, though her voice quavered. "Come, we need to make haste. The sun isn't getting any higher in the sky today."

"Make shelter?"

"You're right." Jinn started walking, pushing aside branches and bracken that tore at her cloak. "We'll walk for an hour." She pointed to what she assumed was the south. "Then we'll make a proper shelter. Perhaps I can forage for root veg." That was optimistic. Any carrots or other root vegetables would have probably long since rotted. They would simply have to ration. And she would have to sleep with the food pack beneath her head.

*　*　*

They walked on for another five miles, stopping several times to readjust their plans as well as their packs. Jinn scouted paths in her mind and, finding the ones that led to the best conclusions, she tugged at her brother to make him follow. One way led downhill to a fast-moving river. Jinn did not like the look of that, since so much could go wrong with rapids. She scouted out a way that led them a little farther west than she would have liked. From what she had foreseen, the Summoner was – or at least would be – headed northeast.

Quick remained impenitent and Jinn tried her best to keep a level temper as she stopped him from eating more of their wares away. In the end, she carried his pack as well as her own. Several times she thought she might collapse beneath the weight in exhaustion, but she only dropped one pack twice, and then figured out a better way to manage them both. When they settled, she would transfer all of the food to her pack. In the morning, she would place some back in Quick's pack, just in case they were, stars forbid, somehow separated from each other.

"How much more?" he said, stopping to watch some birds flying overhead. "Water birds." He grumbled. "Can't eat water birds."

Had her hands been free, Jinn would have rubbed her temples. "The sun is about an hour from setting. So…. Oh, let's just make camp here." She set down the packs with a little more force than necessary and looked for a good spot to build a shelter that would better protect them from the elements that night, for it seemed to be a cold one, judging by the now-cloudless skies.

"Fire?" Quick asked.

Jinn nodded. "I'm afraid we're going to have to light one. We don't want to catch our death of cold." She set about gathering shrubs and branches, hoping to make another lean-to shelter between three trees. While she gathered, Jinn ordered Quick to start collecting anything dry he could find to burn. When he looked at her in confusion, she said, "We don't want a lot of smoke." But he continued to stare at her, confused. "Inhaling lots of smoke could make us faint." That still drew no reaction from her twin. "And it could draw the bad man you keep talking about. Quick? Are you all right?"

Quick shivered and seemed to return to the present moment. "Not feeling so good. Lie down?"

"Once you've found some firewood and kindling. The two of us need to work together if we want to be ready for nightfall." Jinn began to construct a wall between two of the trees by stacking branches and sticks in an interlacing pattern. When she'd finished, she would fill in the empty places with leaves, moss, sticks, anything she could find to block out the wind.

Quick sighed. "All right. Quick find your dry wood."

Jinn ignored him and continued her work. Half an hour later, she had most of one wall constructed and decided that she wouldn't make it any higher. Then she began filling in the gaps. All this time, Quick had been quietly gathering wood and stacking it. None of it looked very dry, but that could hardly be helped. Jinn stopped working on the second wall to build a fire while Quick gathered stones to form a pit.

After another hour of hard work, all was mostly prepared for their night ahead, and Jinn was ready to settle down for the evening. The shelter was decent, if not perfect, and they'd managed to bring a fire to life, stars alone knew how.

Jinn stretched, and put a hand to the small of her sore back. She hadn't eaten or drunk anything since that afternoon, so she unstoppered a water bladder and downed more than she knew she ought. Then, when she was certain Quick was out of sight and hearing, she reached into her pack and searched for a pasty. *He may be bigger, but I am going to waste away if I don't take some nourishment.* She rummaged some more, hoping Quick hadn't eaten the rest of their provisions while she had been busy making camp. With a sigh of relief, she produced one of the hand pies and took a bite, crust and all. The pastry was too salty, and she spat it out at once. "Water," she gasped, reaching back into her pack for the canteen. When she did, something slipped out and thudded onto her boot tip. Jinn ignored it and took a sip of water.

Quick's boots were squelching their way back to her.

She'd have to share the pasty with him or risk dealing with a full-blown tantrum. Or she could hide it. The thought was tempting. Jinn reached for the grease paper in which the pasty had been wrapped, and then she noticed a strange object lying on the ground, presumably the same item that had fallen out of her pack. "Huh." She held the iron dagger aloft, shuddering as she felt her abilities recede deep inside herself and far away from the blade. Ignoring her discomfort, Jinn studied the dagger. "Where did you come from?"

"What that?" Quick asked, startling Jinn so she dropped the blade into the mud at her feet. He shuddered. "Iron?"

Jinn nodded. "You didn't take it from someone back in Gullsford?"

Quick shook himself like a wet dog and backed away from where the blade in question lay. "Bad metal. You know Quick don't like the bad metal." He gave her an accusing look.

"I didn't pack it. It was underneath the pasties and fell out when I...."

His eyebrows knit together as he looked at the unwrapped pasty sitting on top of the pack. "You eat without Quick?"

"I haven't eaten since I broke my fast at noon," Jinn said, hoping to reason with him. "You've already had enough meals for today. Remember, there are two of us and a three-day journey ahead." It was hard to ignore his muttering and foot-stomping, but Jinn tried her best as she studied the dagger. There were strange markings on the sheath, curving and twisting symbols she thought looked a bit familiar, but she couldn't be sure. Mother had taught Jinn to read at a young age, but had soon tired of the chore and had given Jinn old musty books to finish her studies with. Perhaps that was where she recognized the symbols from.

Curious to examine the blade further, she unsheathed it, nicking her already-bandaged hand and drawing a few droplets of blood. At once the blade began to glow green. Jinn yelped and dropped the knife into the blaze, and the whole fire began to glow a deep red.

Somewhere nearby, Jinn was vaguely aware of Quick calling for her to be careful. Perhaps he had been frightened by the strange red blaze as well. Trembling, she tried to find a stick to pull the knife out with. If the fire kept glowing red like this, it would attract anything with a pair of eyes for miles. She had found a suitable pointed stick – "Gotcha!" – when Quick began to cry out in earnest. Jinn turned. "What? What's wrong?"

He pointed to the blaze.

Jinn looked just in time to see a giant pair of glowing black eyes staring out of the flames. After a moment of frozen terror and confusion, she had the presence of mind to grab a stick and wave it in the fire, trying to break up the image. If the eyes were able to see where they were, they might be able to track her and Quick, she reasoned. The stick did nothing to disrupt the apparition.

"What is this?" Quick asked, his voice cracking.

"I don't know," she answered. "We have to put the fire out." It would be a cold night without it, but what choice did they have? Jinn took the stick and started scattering the logs. "Quick, see if you can gather some dirt to throw on the fire. We need to put it out."

"But it gets cold," he said. "Try something else."

Jinn continued beating and stirring up the embers. Something hot and solid rolled over her boot, and the unnatural red hue went out of the flames, and the eyes disappeared entirely. Trembling, she looked down at the object that had been dislodged from the fire: it was the strange dagger she had found in her pack. Cursing, she shouted at Quick to mend the fire, and she dug a hole with her poking stick and buried the blade there in the ground.

Soon the fire had roared back to life, and as no eyes reappeared in the flames, Jinn decided that they should get some rest. "We'll have to move on first thing in the morning," she informed Quick, who groaned. "I think someone is still tracking us."

He pointed to the blaze. "Will it come back?"

"No, Quick," she said wearily, "I don't think it will. At least, not tonight." She had no idea why the eyes had magically appeared in the fire or why the fire had turned red. It might have had something to do with the blade she had found. Or it might have been both of them imagining things. The latter idea sounded slightly more comforting, so she chose to believe that.

Quick was still shaking, the color drained from his face, but he went back to work, gathering more tinder to feed the fire with. The sun was nearly set now, and the temperature had dropped considerably. They would both be thankful Jinn hadn't managed to put out the flames.

"Jinn?"

"Hmm?" She was busy working on their makeshift shelter and didn't look up.

"You never leave Quick, yes?"

That startled Jinn, but she tried not to show her emotions. "Why would I leave you? We're twins. We're supposed to do everything together."

Quick snapped a log in two. "It – nothing. No mind. Just being silly." He let out a laugh, which fell flat, but Jinn pretended not to notice.

What did he know? Maybe Quick was on to her scheme involving Mother. Perhaps he had foreseen something going horribly wrong. She would ask him at first light. Now she needed to get a good night's sleep, as she hadn't had one in a while.

By the time the woods plunged into dusk, Jinn and Quick had gathered enough wood and tinder to last them through the night. Bats skittered against the charcoal sky. Owls hooted and crickets keened. The fire crackled pleasantly as the twins lay down next to each other in the tiny shelter, and for the first time in a while, they both weren't shivering enough to hear their own teeth chatter.

Quick's stomach growled a few times, but he must have been feeling sorry about eating half of their supplies earlier, for he did not say another word about more food. Soon his gentle snores filled the night.

Jinn knew she ought to keep watch, to make certain the strange eyes did not return or the fire go out. But she had been so long without enough sleep that soon her eyelids became too heavy to keep open, and she found herself drifting off.

The dreams she dreamt were nonsense at first, mostly about a lonely castle by the sea and gulls swooping down into the water to feast on tiny fish. But then she dreamed of Quick, all by himself, calling for her. She could hear him, but no matter which way she turned, she was met by a wall of darkness. The darkness surrounded her and was fast moving in, until it was all she could see. Darkness poured out of her mouth and nose as she breathed, and downward she fell, Quick's voice growing louder and louder as the void stamped her out.

Jinn awoke, gasping for breath. She looked around, expecting to see only darkness, and was relieved to find a glimmer of light at her feet. The fire was down to embers, and the moon shone overhead. As Quick was fast asleep, Jinn shook herself and mended the fire on her own. A few logs and some more tinder later, it had repaired nicely, and Jinn lay back down, hoping to get more sleep before sunrise. But her mind was troubled, and sleep proved elusive. After about an hour of trying to rest, Jinn thought she felt a slight tremor in the ground. When she had lived in the cave with Quick, there had been what felt like small earthquakes. Mother always explained that there were feral dwarves mining below them, which had not comforted Jinn in the least. Surely no one was tunneling under them now?

She shook her head and sat up, meaning to drink some water. Again the ground shook. "What the devil?"

"Hmm?" Quick cried out in his sleep as one of the logs fell over in the fire, but soon he was snoring again, unaware of whatever was happening.

Creeping out of their shelter, Jinn removed the hag's dagger, which she had wrapped in leather and attached to the side of her pack. Moonlight glinted off the blade's sharp edge as Jinn wandered a few steps into the night. The earth's quaking had stopped. Jinn listened.

Faintly she could make out the sounds of someone speaking. At first the words were indiscernible, but then she could make out: "Why so dark? Are we below ground?"

"Quick, someone's out there," she whispered at her brother, who didn't stir. "Quick. Give me a little help, please." There was a great scraping noise, and the earth quaked again. Jinn raised the hag's blade and crept toward where it sounded like the voices were coming from, making certain to remain out of view. The sound of scraping became more pronounced, and the voice grew louder.

"Up, a little higher. We must be close. I can sense warmth."

Jinn's gaze darted about, but she could discern nothing in the woods beyond the reach of the fire's light. Since Quick wasn't waking, she stepped out farther from the enclosure, but now the sounds were right behind her. She spun around, ready to bring the blade down on whoever might be standing there, but there was no one.

"There, Master. We're here." Something red glowed on the ground a few short paces from the fire. The earth ceased to tremble, and the light died out.

Shaking, Jinn lowered the hag's dagger and approached the spot where she had seen the red light. There, just discernible by the fire's glow, lay the strange dagger she had buried earlier. Jinn swore softly, and flipped the blade over with the one in her hand. "I must be losing my mind," she muttered. Daggers didn't make eyes appear in fires and then dig themselves out of holes. They just didn't...or at least, *shouldn't*. But then, people should not be able to see the future or lift impossibly heavy objects. A lot of things were that should not be, and this blade was one of them.

Meaning to fling the dagger out into the woods as far as she could, Jinn reached down and picked it up by the handle. Nothing happened at first, so she took aim and was prepared to let it fly, but her hand wouldn't let go. She tried prying her skin free, but it wouldn't move. Trying not to panic, she attempted to release the blade and was prepared to use the hag's knife if it came to that, but a deep voice in the back of her mind said, *Wait!*

Jinn screamed, and the blade grew uncomfortably warm before falling out of her hand. Gingerly she took it by the tips of her fingers, and this time managed to toss it far into the woods, where it landed with a thud.

"What happened?" Quick yelled, crashing his head through the roof of their shelter. "Jinn get hurt?"

"No, Quick. I'm fine," she lied. "I just – thought I saw a snake."

There was a pause as Quick lowered his head back through the roof – or rather, *tried* to. The rest of the twigs and leaves came down with him, and he looked rather wild. "Snake? Not more fire vipers?"

"No, it was just a stick." She picked up her fire-poking stick and came over to him with it. "See? Not a snake."

He took it from her and made a face. "What is on Jinn's hand?"

Jinn shrugged. "Probably some dirt or ash. Let's try to get some more sleep, shall we?" She tried to sound calm, but her heart continued to race. If she didn't know any better, she would say that the dagger she had tossed had spoken to her mind.

"You telling truth?"

"Always," Jinn lied, peering at her hand. At first it looked like a rash, but upon squinting, Jinn could see that they were words written in red on her skin: *Don't run. Peace, friend.*

Quick began to sit up. "Something's wrong."

"No, no. Nothing's wrong. I just have a bit of a rash." She hated to lie to her twin, but they had been through enough already that week, what with the strange eyes in the fire and almost being eaten by hags. "Come, let's sleep."

CHAPTER ELEVEN

Jinn

For the remainder of the night, Jinn slept as one dead. There were no dreams, no visions, no worries whatsoever to disturb her slumber. Not even Quick's snores bothered her. She awoke feeling made new, and with peace in her mind and praise on her lips, Jinn bowed toward the north and said as long a prayer as she could, before her brother interrupted her.

"Hungry," was his first word to greet her that morning.

Jinn could not bring herself to snap at him or even feel irked. Instead, she rose from her incumbent position, wiped the soil from her knees, and went straight for her pack, which she had used as a pillow during the night. "Good morning, Quick."

The look he gave her was puzzled. "Morning?"

Of all things, Jinn found herself wanting to sing. She had not slept so deeply since…well, since she could remember. Not that it was saying much: with visions coming and going ever since she had been Jolted at the tender age of five, Jinn had never rested well. "It is a good morning. Thank you." She reached into her pack and produced enough rations to get them through the first portion of their journey that morning.

"You in good mood. Why?"

Jinn laughed. "I have been a bit irascible lately, haven't I? I'm sorry."

Quick started counting on his fingers, before holding up five. "This many weeks. Since before we left the caves. You are scared."

Yes, that was a fair assessment. They were new travelers to the world, untested and naïve. That had not improved much since they had set out. "Here you are. Don't eat too fast. You'll feel fuller if you savor it." She had handed him some dried meat, cheese, and an apple, and produced half that amount for herself.

It did not take long for Quick to finish and ask for seconds, which he was cheerfully denied. He grumbled and satisfied himself with half draining one of the water bladders. "Quick thinks he likes you grumpy better." He made a face. "Why in a good mood?"

"I don't know," she said, taking back the water bladder. The mark from the night previous was still clear and pink on her right hand: *Don't run. Peace, friend.* A chill went down her spine, and some of the glee went out of her.

Quick did not seem to notice her sudden change in mood. He was too busy licking the last of breakfast from his hands. "You look ahead?"

Jinn's stomach clenched. If the mere *thought* of using foresight made her queasy, what would actually taking a careful look into the future do? It was necessary...or was it? She perked up at once when she remembered the rapids from yesterday. "There's a stream nearby, I'm sure of it."

"Rapids dangerous."

She waved a dismissive hand. "Yes, of course they are. But what if we found a spot downstream of it all? You know, calmer waters?" Bending over, Jinn began scattering the firewood and kindling that had made up their blaze during the night and was still smoldering. When that would not entirely put out their fire, Jinn took a large stick and buried the remainder until it smoked no longer.

"Bladders need filling?" Quick scratched his great head.

"Yes, and...." Jinn cringed. She knew Quick was not going to like this part. "Quick, you know how difficult it is, trying to look ahead?"

He responded with a shrug and shouldered his pack.

Jinn took that as encouragement to continue, so she hoisted

her own pack onto her shoulders and led the way away from their shelter. "What if there was a way to know everything? Not the future, I mean, but everything as it is right now." She pulled ahead of him. "Wouldn't that be nice?"

"Jinn," Quick whined. "You want to make a seeing pool? Bad idea. Very, *very* bad idea."

"No," she assured him. "That would be very dangerous, indeed. This would be much less dangerous." Jinn chanced a look back over her shoulder and was amused to find her brother looking up at a water bird flying overhead.

"Large birds are a bad omen."

She allowed him that, acknowledging the point with a sigh. "Quick, you do trust me, don't you? I would never do anything to put you in danger."

He looked down at her with his innocent eyes, and nodded, albeit reluctantly. "What is Jinn thinking?"

If she told him everything, he would never be for the idea, so she decided to skate around the edges of it. "We're going to seek someone who knows what we need to know." Jinn picked her way around some large roots.

"What we need to know?"

What *didn't* they need to know? "Well, this person will be able to tell us where we can replenish our supplies. Then they'll know where we can find the Summoner. No more guesswork, Quick. Real, solid, unchangeable information."

They trudged southeast mostly in silence for the next half hour, muttering encouragement to each other every now and again when the way became difficult. The sun sat behind clouds, and what light had managed to filter through that and the tree cover was dingy. Thick roots rose up before them in knots, and Jinn found herself wondering how the trees had not managed to choke each other out. The tree trunks themselves were four times as thick as Quick, and Jinn could not begin to wonder at the height. Briars made the path between trees difficult going. More than twice, Quick had to pluck Jinn out of a mess and carry her until they were clear of it.

At the end of the first hour, they paused to catch their breath and drink some water. Jinn took a few gulps and then passed the bladder back to Quick, who might have emptied it had she not snatched it back in time.

"How much farther?" Quick asked, wiping sweat from his brow. "Quick is hungry."

"We'll catch fish there," Jinn promised. "It shouldn't be more than two hours before we reach a good spot."

Quick eyed her with suspicion. "You look ahead or Quick does. No more guessing."

How could she argue with that, after having forbidden him from looking ahead himself? It was unfair. "All right," she said, feeling substantially less cheerful than she had upon waking. Jinn closed her eyes and focused on the next ten minutes, adjusted their path a little and looked ahead a bit more, and was surprised to find themselves arriving at a lagoon not half an hour hence. "If you can endure just twenty-five minutes more, we should reach the spot by then."

Far from looking relieved, Quick frowned. But he nodded and shouldered his pack once more. "You certain this isn't dangerous?"

Jinn nodded. "Of course."

Quick did not look reassured. "Quick knows you read books. Quick does not. Mother thinks Quick stupid." He sighed and helped Jinn overcome a sticky web of spiders. "We look for some great creature, yes?"

She did not answer at first, but she knew her silence would spook him, so she tried to think of something to say to soothe his worries. "It's not some great creature. If my books are correct, and I am certain that they are, these wise people will be no bigger than me." Jinn stole a sideways look at Quick. "Definitely not as big as you."

This caused Quick to sigh. "No big feat." He caught Jinn grinning, and grinned as well. "But what might they be?" The question hung in the air between them for a moment, before Quick was again distracted by the birds flying overhead. One relieved itself on his head, and he swore up a storm before looking down at Jinn, who laughed even more heartily. "Not funny."

"You never swear, Quick. Of course it's funny. Besides, you can wash it off once we reach the water." Her stomach clenched at the thought of what she must do to ensure the creatures would come. Perhaps she should have peered further ahead than she had....

The remainder of their walk was uneventful. Quick asked no questions, and Jinn did not offer any answers. Soon the land grew marshy, only to be converted into solid stone, which gave way to sand just as it met the banks of crystal-clear water.

Heart racing, Jinn set down her pack, and Quick did likewise. "Could you help me find the rope? I can't remember where I packed it."

Quick gave her an odd look but began rummaging as well. "Jinn," he said after a moment.

She looked over and nearly threw up when she saw the iron dagger in his hands. "Oh, I must've packed that again by accident. Put it down, Quick."

"All right, all right. Sister gets drawers in a twist." He set the strange knife down on the bank and kicked it for good measure. It didn't move.

How had it found its way back to her pack? She had thrown it as hard as she could into the woods the night previous. Jinn shuddered, but now she had an idea what she might do with it. She went back to searching her pack for the rope.

"Here it is," said Quick, pulling a coil from his own pack and then handing it to Jinn. "What is it for?"

Jinn forced herself to remain calm. "Help me tie one end around my waist, will you? You've always been good at tying strong knots." She slipped the rope around her waist, tied it once around, and then held the ends out for Quick, who reluctantly tied an expert knot.

"Jinn, what is this for?" His face darkened. "You go in, right? We cannot swim."

"It's just a precaution," she assured him. "I don't plan on going in over my head, but should I accidentally go too far, you'll have something to pull me up by, yes?"

He nodded, though Jinn knew he was far from reassured. "If you say so."

"Good. Now, be a dear and look away when I tell you." After a moment's hesitation, Jinn pulled her tunic sleeve over her right hand and scooped up the iron blade, hoping it would be enough to protect her from any magic. Then she handed the far end of the rope to Quick and began to wade into the water.

"Why does Quick need to look away?"

She wished he wouldn't talk so loudly; from what she remembered, merrows startled easily and were repelled by too much noise. Then again, that might not be true. *Creatures of the Shallows, Volume II* had contradicted some of the information written in the first volume.

Quick repeated himself. "Jinn?"

Jinn gave the knot an experimental tug. It did not budge – *good.* "You'll see. Or, rather, you won't." She grimaced.

"Look ahead, Jinn."

Her good mood evaporating entirely, Jinn threw up her arms. "All right, I'll look ahead." It should be no problem, she reasoned with herself. She used her foresight many times every day, so what was she afraid of now? *Maybe that this plan will end badly.* Jaw set in concentration, Jinn closed her eyes and then jumped. Never before had she come across so many separate strands of potential realities at the beginning of a look. The threads were all tangled in one great ball, the lines of what-might-be blurred. She tried latching on to one, a path that led to the water stirring beneath her hands, but that path at once diverged into ten other paths, which in turn diverged into twenty more. Jinn knew she could not continue looking, as she might drive herself to madness. As it was, her thoughts had already become a tangled mess, and she felt her knees buckle as she released each strand and brought her consciousness back to the moment, grounding herself to the sound of Quick's voice.

When she opened her eyes, Quick had a hand on her shoulder, his expression dark. "Bad things?" he asked.

She suppressed a shudder. "Just a bit confusing."

"Holes? Darkness?"

Jinn started to nod, but then shook her head decidedly. "No, I didn't see any holes, and there definitely wasn't any darkness." Then why was she shaking? Quick asked as much, and she replied with, "I shouldn't have used the gift on an empty stomach."

That answer seemed to satisfy her brother, and he asked her no more questions. "Quick hold rope. You wade in now – before it gets dark again."

She nodded and waded into the clear blue waters, her hand still curled around the magical dagger. The water was as cold as mountain runoff, and Jinn shivered as it came up to her thighs. Surely this would be far enough? "Look away, Quick," she warned. Once Jinn was certain he had turned away, she raised the knife and pricked her finger on its fine point. Warmth blossomed at the tip of her finger, which began to throb in time to her heartbeat. Then, shivering still, she dipped the wound into the water, hoping her sacrifice would be enough.

The frigid water slapped against her hand, which continued to throb. Her feet were growing numb. Had she waded in far enough?

"Nothing is happening," Quick pointed out.

Jinn grimaced. "I know."

He let out a grunt and gave the rope a slight tug. "How long we wait?"

That was a good question, one to which Jinn did not possess the answer. Perhaps she ought to make the wound deeper. "A bit longer." While the two volumes of *Creatures of the Shallows* had contradicted each other on several points, they were both agreed when it came how to draw a merrow. Jinn eyed the knife, light gleaming off the severe edge. "The knife is afraid," she murmured and then shook her head. "Knives don't have feelings." She paused. "Well, knives don't magically reappear in bags, either."

"Can Quick open eyes now?"

She jumped at the sound of his voice. "You still have your eyes shut?"

Quick opened his eyes. "Was getting dizzy." He gave the rope another tug, and Jinn nearly lost her balance. "Sorry." He gave the rope some slack.

Ten minutes passed, each colder than the last. Perhaps the wound had closed itself and was no longer bleeding. With her back to Quick, Jinn lifted her hand and examined it. White and wrinkled, her finger was no longer bleeding, so she took the knife and cut into the wound again. It should have smarted, but her hand was almost too cold to feel anything but the pressure of the blade slicing in. Now she was certain the dagger was terrified, as it began to shake of its own accord and nearly wrenched itself from her grip. Jinn's fingers slipped out of the fabric she held it with, and the haft came in contact with her bare flesh again. In the back of her mind, Jinn was impressed with the need to get out of the water at once, and could even feel her legs trying to move without her permission. She resisted. Her blood dripped into the water, which darkened.

"Jinn," said Quick. "You hurt?"

She was ready to cast the knife into the water as far as she possibly could, but stopped when the darkness in the water spread far beyond where her finger continued to drip.

If she had thought that the water could get no colder without freezing, she was sorely mistaken. She gasped a painful breath and heard Quick do the same behind her. The water churned before her, and the rope around her waist received a firm tug.

"Come back," Quick cried.

Jinn ignored him and tried to wade out farther, though her legs did not obey, seemingly frozen to the spot. A thrill went up her spine as a great ripple formed a mere three feet from where she stood. The blood-red water parted, and a man emerged.

He was tan of skin with eyes darker than night. His hair was a brown so deep that it might be as black as her own, and it blew out behind him in a breeze that Jinn could not feel. "You have called me, Jinn," he said in a rumbling voice, folding his arms over his naked chest, a tail flickering to the surface briefly before sinking again. It was not a question.

Somewhere behind Jinn, Quick whimpered. "Bad man."

The water spirit bared his white teeth in a grin. "No, Quick. I am not the one who pursues. His form is mine – for now." He began to move closer, but looked down at Jinn's blade and stopped. "I will answer three questions."

Her mouth and lips were as dry as paper, and when she spoke to the merrow, her voice was a strained croak. "My questions are—"

The creature held up his hand to stay her words. "I know all that was and all that is. But you, Jinn, know what is to come." His dark eyes pierced hers. "Answer me one question, and I will grant you a fourth answer."

Jinn swallowed, hard. Would it be wise to give this creature any information? What if it was a trap? Trembling, Jinn replied, "We'll see."

That did not seem to please the merrow, but he nodded grimly and spoke in his rumbling voice, "The one you seek is safely in the clutches of peril."

She frowned. "What does that even mean?"

The merrow ignored her. "The one who seeks you is blinded by the very curse that blinds your way. And the object you seek would be your salvation and the grief of many. I am the One Who Knows." He uncrossed his arms and looked at Jinn, expectation written across his face.

"Might I have a moment to think on the matter?"

He hesitated and then nodded once before looking past Jinn at Quick. "A simple, pure soul. You may have three words of advice at no cost."

Quick made a bleating sound and tugged in vain on Jinn's rope. "No need. No need."

The water spirit paid him no mind. "You would do well to separate yourself from the one you ought to love most but love least. You would do better to unite with the one you will hate. You would do best to run as far and as fast as you can from both. I am the One Who Knows." He looked at Jinn again, perhaps reading her thoughts.

What a bunch of rubbish. I wounded myself for this?

Again the being spoke. "If I were to speak plain, would not I alter your course? You know the future, Jinn, daughter of another man. It is not my job to interfere with what is to be."

Now Jinn found herself clenching her fists, even the one around the knife. "Yes, I know the future. Some of it. But there are holes in it. If you had let me choose my own questions, I would have asked why this was and how to see around whatever is causing it. Come on, Quick. Help me to shore." She started to turn her back on the merrow, but at once thought the better of it, and began backing away.

The creature scowled. "If you had been listening, you would realize that I have already answered your questions. And even if you did not like what you heard, that is no excuse to deny me payment." He glared at her, his eyes darkening.

Jinn shuddered. "All right. Your payment." Jinn held out the knife for the creature, but he shook his head. "What? It's a perfectly good knife."

"But it is not yours."

"Nothing I have is mine," said Jinn. Mother had told her this many times. "I have nothing to offer besides this." The creature was unmoved. "You who know everything surely must have known this when you were giving so-called answers to my unspoken questions." Now her whole body was trembling, not with cold or terror but with rage, rage at the difficulty of the last few weeks, at Mother's ridiculous demands, and her own failings. The knife in her hand grew warm, almost hot, and it was impressed on Jinn's mind that she ought to tread carefully with the wild creature.

At length she unclenched her left fist and gave herself a shake, as a dog ridding itself of fleas. "All right. How about I tell you one thing about the future for payment?"

Already the merrow was shaking his head. "That would cost you three." He held up that many fingers, as if he were talking to a slow, small child.

Jinn grimaced but nodded. "All right. But like you chose, I will choose what I tell you."

The creature opened his mouth as if to object, but closed it again, and nodded. He did not seem pleased, but perhaps she had bought herself some respect.

"Quick," Jinn told her brother, "watch him."

Quick whimpered. "B-bad man, Jinn. Bad merrow."

"Do as I said, please." Without waiting to see if Quick was complying, Jinn closed her eyes and peered into the merrow's future. So many paths, all of them tangled. This would take ages to sort through. But what else did she have to barter with? Surely this had been the merrow's plan all along? Jinn chose one thread, one that was as blue as the lagoon had been before her blood had polluted it. She latched all of her concentration on to that, and strained as the future fought her. Finally, head pounding, Jinn could make out two merrows splashing in the water, both quite unlike the man who stood before her, but she knew one was he, and after some focusing, she was able to discern which one. At first it seemed that the two merrows were playing, but the one that was before her drew a knife and drove it expertly into the other's chest. Gray blood gushed out of the wound, and the wounded merrow collapsed into the water and moved no more. "You will defeat another of your kind with a knife," Jinn said. "He will die. You will prevail."

She did not open her eyes to see the merrow's reaction to this, but clenched them more tightly shut still and peered ahead again. The next thread she chose was leaf-green. Again she latched all of her concentration on to it and fought against whatever force was trying to prevent her from gripping the future. The merrow sat alone on a log beneath some greens, its tail spilling over into the water. There was no one else in sight. Jinn perceived that he was triumphant yet sad. The future image called out to his kin in a strange high-pitched wail and then dove beneath the water. No one ever answered. "I'm not sure what this means," she told the merrow, her eyes still closed, her head pounding.

"Perhaps I will. Tell me."

Jinn grimaced. "You seem to be all alone. You are sad, very sad about something. You call out for someone, but they do not answer." She chanced a peek at the merrow, but his expression was unreadable.

"One more," he reminded her.

Quick whined. "We go now?"

"Soon, brother." Jinn closed her eyes and sought another random thread. There was a brilliant red thread spinning and whirling throughout all the others. It felt...familiar somehow. She tried to catch it, but it was tangled up with a black thread in one big knot. With a groan she focused on the black thread with all of her might and was surprised to find a hole. One moment, the merrow had an expansive choice of futures, but this part was empty. Death. Jinn swallowed and wondered if she could lie to the creature, but instead she shook her head and searched after another less complicated thread – a silver-and-green thread, the shortest and least tangled of the ones that the black thread kept brushing against. In the thread she saw herself, much to her surprise. The merrow was angry, his tail splashing the surface of the water. She saw his future self lunge and—

Her concentration was broken by the merrow's voice, "Well?"

Blood pounding hard through her veins, Jinn lost the thread and opened her eyes. "The future is a difficult thing," she said, her voice stronger than she felt. "You have so many threads, and they're all so entangled and confusing, I don't—"

"Tell me what you saw." The merrow's tail swished, reminding

Jinn of the time she had upset a stray wildcat that had wandered into the caves.

Again she tried to compose herself, pausing far too long to obscure the fact that she was hiding something. "One of your possible futures ends in darkness," she said, hoping that would be enough.

"Is that all you have to say for yourself?"

Jinn nodded. "It's all I've got."

The merrow's tail did not splash the surface of the water before he lunged at Jinn, too quick almost to be seen. His fist closed around her throat and he squeezed it slightly. "You. You've brought this darkness upon my kind. The curse that seeks you now seeks me."

Quick pulled on the rope in vain. "Jinn, help. You need help."

Jinn could only just draw in enough air to say, "I don't know what the darkness means. Maybe I could help you."

The merrow scoffed. "You were unwise to seek me, Jinn, daughter of Meraude." He tightened his grip. "Wizards walk the world again. But perhaps I can foil this one's plans yet."

Pinpricks of light formed at the edge of Jinn's vision. Her lungs burned. She needed air. She tried to pry away the creature's fingers, but he was too strong. Her grip on the dagger slipped and the blade fell.

Then a strange thing happened. The burgundy water began to hiss and fizz as bubbles formed on the surface. Screaming, the merrow released Jinn, who collapsed into the water, choking as she tried to pull down air. The rope around her tightened, and Quick made fast work of dragging her to shore.

Coughing and spluttering, Jinn blinked her eyes furiously as the creature continued to shriek. It no longer kept the form of a man, but had taken on the appearance of a hideous beast with slimy green scales, overgrown yellow teeth, and bulging red eyes.

"Curse you," he wailed – at least, that was what Jinn assumed he was saying. It was hard to make out the exact words as he struggled against some unseen force. The water churned, the beast writhed, and then all was still. The lagoon had gone from the crimson of Jinn's blood to a greasy silver, and now a mangled body bobbed to the surface along with a smaller object that might be the dagger.

Quick patted Jinn's back and then pulled her up under the arms. "That was close."

As her throat burned and clenched, Jinn could only nod. Not for the first time was she thankful for Quick's brute strength as he hauled her up over his shoulder and carried her to the edge of the rock landing. "Thank you," she mouthed.

He shook his head. "That was very stupid, Jinn."

She could not disagree with that. "Water," she croaked, pointing to their supplies. While her brother retrieved one of the waterskins, Jinn flopped over onto her back and rested. The merrow had said so many strange things that it would take more wit than she had right now to sort through them. One thing was clear, though: whoever had sent her the dagger must want her alive...at least, for a while longer. Jinn shuddered.

"Sister cold?" Quick handed her the waterskin, and she drank greedily from it.

At first Jinn shook her head, but then relented and nodded. She had lied enough to her brother – not that he knew, but this was a pointless lie. It's not like he couldn't see her shivering. She stoppered the waterskin and set it next to her. Without her voice, she could not order him around, telling him what needed to be done and how to do it.

It was a surprise, then, when Quick walked into the woods behind her and emerged moments later with a dry log. "Quick make a fire." He grinned at her. "Didn't think Quick could?"

★   ★   ★

While Quick made the fire, Jinn sorted through their packs, finally moving most of what was left of the food to her own pack. From time to time, she rubbed her throat, which she was certain sported an impressive bruise. Once the food had been moved around and she had reorganized their supplies, Jinn assessed their waterskins. They had four in total, and two were almost entirely drained. The water here was not safe to go near now, let alone drink from. In one of her books, Jinn had read about the process of draining vines. Unfortunately, there did not seem to be any in the vicinity. They would have to refill their waterskins upstream of the lagoon. Jinn cringed as she tried to summon the mental strength to use her foresight.

"Where is the flint?" Quick asked, interrupting her concentration.

Jinn opened her eyes and tossed the flint and magnesium stick at her brother, closed her eyes, and tried again. She had meant to look ahead for the next hour, but an unasked-for vision overtook her.

The Summoner was standing in a field of starberry plants, ruby-red fruit glistening in the sunlight. He seemed uncertain about something. With him, as usual, was his redheaded traveling companion, her face paler than Jinn had seen before.

"Are you certain it's here?" she asked.

He nodded once, a quick jerk of his head. "The Pull is stronger than almost anything I've felt before." The Summoner shot a sideways glance at the young woman, a look that held some hidden meaning.

She grimaced. "Lots of folks died here, yes?" The girl rubbed her arms, as if trying to get rid of goose bumps. She shuddered.

The Summoner made no reply. He was busy studying the great rock formation standing in the foreground. The structure stood at what appeared to be thirty feet, its length beyond what Jinn could discern. Shrubs grew in front of it, and at them the Summoner now was staring. "I wonder...."

The vision changed, blurring into a new one.

The burning season had yet to begin, and late were the days of summer. Jinn could tell by the slight changing of the leaves, the way they drooped on their branches, the life of spring wrung out of them. The location was familiar. It was the wood beyond the Mountain, near the tower of Inohaim, the Pool of Seeing. Mother was pacing to and fro before Inohaim Wood. She must be truly unsettled indeed, for she had never shown any emotion but rage and disdain to Jinn.

"What are you doing without your Endurers?" Jinn wondered aloud, knowing she would not be heard by her mother's future self.

A twig snapped. The Lady Meraude turned, pulling her pale blue hood over her dark tresses. Her posture stiffened and then relaxed. *"Oh. It's you."* She sniffed and made a face in the waning light. *"I thought I told you to bring me the Summoner."*

Mai Larkin's scratchy laugh grated on Jinn's ears. She had never met the Sightful in person, but had seen her in enough visions to recognize her by sight and sound.

"Just as you sent your twins to find him?" The woman gave Meraude a knowing look and then smirked. *"Wonder what might be taking them so long. Jinn has the Sight as well."*

Again Meraude seemed nervous. *"Speak not of the two to me. You're not even supposed to know of their existence."* Was that why she was nervous, or was she thinking about Jinn's ability to see into anyone's future?

You think you're so clever, Jinn thought with a sigh. I know you want us both dead. If Mother got her hands on the Questing Goblet.... Well, Jinn would make sure that did not happen.

Meraude said in the vision, *"Any rumors to report, seer?"*

Mai Larkin grinned her gap-toothed grin and removed the hood from over her head. Her hair, which had once hung in dirty blond locks down to her waist, was now gone. *"Milady is surprised."*

Much to her credit, Meraude did not seem to be so in the least. *"You've made a vow,"* she said, her voice lacking any emotion, as if she were simply commenting on the state of the weather.

The Sightful simply nodded, her expression unchanging. *"Dewhurst is dead."*

"So I have gathered from reports."

Mai Larkin's expression darkened. *"He found a way around his vow."* Her eyes flashed. *"I assume you did not know that?"*

At first Jinn's mother made no reply but stared on coldly at her servant. *"And I assume that you found a way around yours?"*

The Sightful tossed her head, her looks giving away nothing. *"The one you forced on me? Might have done. Might not have done. But one thing is for certain: Dewhurst betrayed you. He has withheld information from your people."*

Finally, Jinn noted, there was a break in Meraude's mask. *"I compel you to tell me all."* When her servant made no immediate answer, the would-be mage queen pulled a dagger from her sleeve.

The Sightful backed away. *"He has the maps now,"* she spoke, though she was obviously trying to stop herself. *"He is coming for you."* She cringed.

"Dewhurst's corpse is coming for me?" Meraude said in all seriousness.

Mai Larkin was struggling. Her eyes bulged, her face turned blue, and she shook as the words pushed their way out of her mouth, *"The S—"* Again she struggled against her own tongue.

"You know, Larkin, I will find out anyway. But let me hear it from your own lips."

"Su — mmoner." Larkin gasped and collapsed to her knees, panting. Then, before her master could ask another question, the Sightful reached out her hand and the most unexpected thing happened: the dagger flew out of Meraude's hand and into Mai Larkin's, and she drove the blade through her own throat.

The vision ended, and Jinn woke up, panting. "The Sightful is also a Summoner?" she croaked, forgetting about her own throat. Jinn gagged and rose up onto her knees. Again and again she choked on her own spit, until she could slow her breaths and remind herself that she was no longer being strangled.

In the present, Quick had a nice blaze going. She had not seen him at first upon waking, but now realized his clothes were hanging up on a makeshift clothesline made of sticks and twine. He sat nearby, chewing on something.

"Quick," Jinn whispered. "What are you eating?"

Proudly her brother held up a fish bone, picked clean of its flesh. "Cooked trout. Slippery fish did not want to be caught, so…." He now looked guilty. "Might have looked ahead a bit."

Jinn shook her head. She was too tired to express her displeasure in any other way. "I had another vision."

"Quick noticed." He skewered another gutted fish that lay near him and put it on a rock before the blaze. Quick rose and brought

Jinn one of the waterskins. When she tried to refuse it, he said, "Refilled them all."

She frowned. "But the water here—"

Quick laughed. "Not here. Water bad. Went upstream for it, so drink." He pushed the vessel into her hands, and she drank deeply.

The water was cold and refreshing, and Jinn thanked him in a hoarse whisper and handed the skin back. When her brother sat down next to her, his expression inquisitive, Jinn told him all she had seen.

As she spoke, he listened intently, interrupting once or twice for clarification on something she had said. When she told him about the Sightful killing herself, Quick's eyes widened and he shook his head. "Sightful is not a bad person, then. Maybe on our side, even."

Jinn nodded. "It would seem that way. But what of the Summoner? The Sightful killed – I mean, *will kill* herself at some point to stop herself from sharing information about the Summoner. What does she know?" She turned the matter over in her mind, but no easy conclusions were coming to her. The Sightful obviously held no love for Mother and would rather die than help her. But what else might she be compelled to say?

The smell of baking fish reached Jinn's nose, and her stomach snarled. "How long was I unconscious?" she asked Quick, who was rushing to the fire to turn the fish over on the stone.

"Don't know. Maybe an hour. Jinn, we need to stop Sightful."

"From killing herself? Quick, I don't even know when this will happen. Maybe some time this year, maybe in *five* years."

Quick was already shaking his head. "No, we must find Mai Larkin and stop her from going back to Mother at all. She knows things she should not, methinks."

There was no arguing with that. "We'll look for the Sightful after we find the Summoner. We know where he's headed...well, I mean, we don't know where the place *is*, but we know he wants to find Cedric's grave. And, judging from my vision, he will find it. We'll just have to make certain our paths cross."

Her brother did not look convinced. "Why we need to find Summoner, anyway?" He sat back down next to her and wiped his nose on the back of his sleeve. The look he gave her was piercing.

Jinn cleared her throat. "I think he'll be able to stop Mother's plans, whatever they might be." She left out information about a potential situation she had foreseen. The future was so tenuous, one shift of the wind and it might break into a thousand different threads.

"Fish is done," he said, sniffing the air. He went over again to attend to what looked like a rainbow trout.

She tried to disguise her relief. Whether or not Quick would want Mother dead remained yet to be seen.

*　　*　　*

They slept in the open that night beneath a clear sky. Jinn made a half-hearted attempt to keep watch, but she was still sore and tired from her encounter with the merrow, so sleep caught her midway through the night, and she did not awake until the dawning.

When she sat up, covered in dew, her stomach rumbling, she was surprised to find that Quick was already awake and tending to the fire. More fish had been gutted and were baking next to the fire on sizzling-hot rocks. The waterskins were all full, and large handfuls of starberries were mounded atop a clean handkerchief. Jinn marveled at these most. "Quick, how did you find these? They're not in season."

Quick set down his fire-poking stick and came over to her, a big grin on his face. "The strange place let Quick pass."

"'The strange place'? What is that?"

Her brother flapped his arms about in excitement. "Lots of starberries everywhere. Big hills." He held a hand high over his head in measurement. His smile soon wavered. "Felt odd there. Felt...scary."

Still waking up, Jinn took in the information as she picked up a starberry and then hesitated. "Have you had any?"

"Oh, yes. Ate lots, but lots more to be picked. Quick shows you." He ran to the fire and turned over several fish, and then brought one to Jinn on a leaf. "Here. You eat, then we go. Maybe they'll let you in too."

Jinn, who had been taking a large bite into the cold, sweet berry, paused. "They? Someone is out there?" It was as if the berry had turned to ash in her mouth, and her stomach soured.

Quick chuckled. "No, sister. Feelings. Feelings told Quick he could enter."

Now she found herself even more confused and full of dread. "Feelings told you you could enter? What are you talking about, Quick?"

But her brother had lost interest in the conversation and returned to tending the fire and the fish. What was he on about?

Shaking, Jinn set the fish on the ground before her, closed her eyes, and scouted ahead. Five minutes ahead: they would begin to pack up camp. Ten minutes ahead: she would follow Quick. She looked to twenty minutes ahead where Quick would lead her down a path that had not been there the day previous. That was the least of strange things. There were no various future paths to be followed, which struck Jinn as ominous. There were always variations, different paths to be chosen in the future. Why was there only one possible path now? Jinn peered ahead again, thirty minutes. That was when the first hole appeared, a ten-minute gap. When her vision resumed, she was watching Quick's back as he trudged off into the distance. Her sight stopped entirely then, which could only mean one thing. She searched in vain for an alternate route, but none appeared.

"Jinn? Time to pack up camp and put out fire."

Swallowing hard, Jinn opened her eyes and looked at Quick. "Quick, I think you've found something important."

CHAPTER TWELVE

Aidan

Aidan walked the remainder of the day at a distance from Slaíne. *She* seemed to know the way, even though *he* was growing more and more uncertain. Whatever magical Pull the place held, the direction and strength seemed to be changing. For that day, at least, the Pull was mostly north, so Slaíne followed whatever guide she was going by, and as it was in tune with the Pulls that Aidan sensed, he did not question her judgment.

The day was, mercifully, not a hot one. Cooler weather meant less water drained from their water bladders. They would need to refill the following day, however hot or cold the weather might be.

The paths were fairly easy for a while, but the trees soon thinned, and the underbrush gave way to a new problem: marshy soil. *We'll have to be on the alert for quicksand,* Aidan thought with a grimace. And there was another problem: the strange Pull from the previous day was now following them again. He made mention of it to Slaíne at one point, but she shook her head.

"Today looks to be fine," she puzzled him by saying in response.

Something was different about Slaíne. She had been a little less herself since the declarations – or near-declarations – of the morning. It was almost as if she had acquired an air of eccentricity. Or perhaps it had always been present and he had failed to notice before. Or maybe it had been a dormant characteristic that only now had awoken. Aidan did not quite know what to make of her muttering to herself and her sudden sense of direction. Maybe this whole journey was driving her mad. Or maybe it was he who was losing his sanity.

As nightfall approached and they had traveled a good fifteen miles with the occasional break in between, Aidan broke the easy silence between them. "We should find water wherever we make our camp tonight. I don't want to be long in the sun with the amount of water we have left."

Slaíne bobbed her head and veered off to the left without warning. "This way, sir."

Aidan frowned but followed. Sure enough, he began to hear the keening of insects, and felt the Pull of smaller life that might belong to frogs and fish. He crashed through the thicket of marsh plants and nearly stumbled into Slaíne and into a small inlet of water that apparently ran from a stream. "That was fast." He Summoned all six bladders and began to fill them one at a time, cleansing the water by Dismissing the Pulls of dangerous things.

"Sir," Slaíne said as he filled the fourth.

"Are you hungry? Here." He Summoned some brown bread and a cold slice of roasted beef onto a nearby rock that seemed to be clean. Then he went back to what he had been doing. But when he realized Slaíne was not eating, Aidan paused and looked up at her. "Is something wrong?"

Her pupils were huge in the growing dimness, and her small frame trembled. "I don't know if we should find the Questing Goblet," she said in a small voice. "I have an odd feeling. Here." She put her hand over her heart and then over her stomach, before shaking her head and walking away.

Had he said something amiss? "What did I do now?" Aidan murmured before going back to filling the bladders. There was no time to worry over what one should or should not say, nor was there time for going back over things in one's mind. It was enough to drive any man to insanity. He wondered how his father had done it with his mother. The thought brought him little comfort, as he recalled the rotting corpses he had buried back on the estate. Dark thoughts to dwell on, he knew, so he put all of his concentration into filling the bladders and Dismissing anything harmful. The process took him nearly twice as long as usual, but he did not care.

Slaíne's Pull gave him a slight tug, and he at once Dismissed the waterskins and went to look for her. When he found her, she was sitting cross-legged under a tree, finishing up the last of the food he had Summoned. Her looks were of one who was guilty. "Guess I was hungry."

"What?"

She gave him a sheepish grin. "I et all the food. Sorry."

Aidan waved the remark away. "It wasn't much." In truth, he had been meaning to partake of half, and had planned to reward the both of them with a greater meal in the morning. But as his mother had always told him and Sam, "Butchered pork is not for mourning."

"Are we ter make camp here?" Rising, the girl wiped filthy hands on the fabric of her torn yellow dress, the one he had bought her in Abbington a fortnight or more ago. "What?" Her eyes went to where Aidan was looking, and she worried her lip. "Don't mind that I ruined it, d'you?"

"What? Oh, not at all. I have the one still in Nothingness, if the need arises."

Apparently satisfied, Slaíne nodded and looked to the sky. The sun was a little more than an hour from setting. Clouds moving in from the west were tinged red from the brilliance of the waning light, signaling a still evening. Good. No wind to blow them about.

"Are we making camp?" she asked.

Aidan was about to agree, but he stopped himself. There was that obnoxious Pull out there. It was closer now than it had been earlier; closer still than days previous, and fast approaching. He held up a finger for Slaíne to be still and quiet so he could concentrate around her Pull and her sound.

It was as if the man or beast knew Aidan had sensed it, for the Pull stopped where it was, two clearings behind, and came no closer. In fact, it retreated what felt like three paces and then changed. Its essence remained the same, though.

Mindful of exactly where the Pull was coming from, Aidan motioned for Slaíne to come near, and then whispered, "That creature that's been following us...."

Slaíne grimaced. "I knew it was still out there. What is it? Can ya tell?"

Not knowing what hearing this creature possessed, Aidan lowered his voice further still and leaned in even closer. "Its Pull keeps changing."

"Shape-shifter."

The word made Aidan queasy. If there were such things, it would be a difficult type of being to fight against...at least, he imagined. Without further thought, he Summoned the silver sword that he had taken from Slaíne the night he ran off with her.

But Slaíne shook her head and motioned for him to hand it over to her. When he hesitated, she smirked and said, "I think *I* should be the one who kills it."

Again Aidan was impressed with the thought that something was not quite right with Slaíne. Not only was her Pull increasing in strength as the day wore on, something was wrong in her eyes. They were...darker.

The girl's smile fell, and she looked as she always did, her Pull lessening before curling back in around her like a hug. Or had it? Perhaps Aidan had imagined it all. "What was I saying?" she asked in a soft voice.

"You said something about a shape-shifter," Aidan reminded Slaíne, frowning. "What makes you think it might be one?"

"What makes you think it might *not* be?"

Aidan felt his ire rising to meet hers, but he let it cool before continuing. "You just said it with so much assurance. Why is that?" When he saw a glint of malice in her eyes, he continued, attempting to smooth things over. "Don't get me wrong, Slaíne. It seems very likely that this creature, whatever it might be, can change appearances. I've noticed its Pull since leaving Grensworth, but it keeps changing in quality."

She gave him a look as if to say, *I told you so*, but her temper seemed to cool at his words. The grin was back again, only this time it was nowhere near as maniacal. It almost seemed resigned. "Should we both go after it, yes?"

What could he say to that? He dearly wished the blasted thing would simply go away, but he knew they were being followed with a purpose. Here was the opportunity to deal with the menace or nuisance once and for all. Now was the time. Aidan raised the sword and was prepared to charge after the creature, but again Slaíne stayed him.

"What're you going to do? Just charge at it an' hope for the best?" she snipped.

Aidan rolled his eyes. "Fine. Let's—"

"Give me the sword." When he stood there staring at her, unmoving, Slaíne groaned. "Mr. Aidan, the sword is mine. Also, I doubt you've had as much practice with a blade as I have."

That would be a blow to his pride to admit, but it was true. He hadn't taken a blade with him when he had fled Lord Dewhurst's manor as a youth, and he hadn't acquired any on his travels. Aidan knew he was better suited to a dirk or magic, so he lowered the sword and tipped the pommel toward her.

Without hesitation, Slaíne took it by the grip and slunk off into the distance, her feet scarcely touching the ground. Or perhaps they did not touch it at all.

Aidan had lost sight of Slaíne, so he followed her Pull, which was confusing the shifting one who was following them. The strange second Pull changed again, to something far less substantial, and moved high up into the air in the distance. Slaíne's Pull followed suit. Swearing, Aidan was forced to watch from the ground as the girl soared overhead, chasing the creature, who now looked like a bird.

To his amusement and horror, she was flying around after some great bird of prey, her dress catching in a current and billowing up around her. Aidan shook his head and averted his eyes. "Slaíne, you're not going to catch it. You're going to get yourself killed. Come down from there."

Slaíne, however, had different ideas. She paid him no heed, but swooped around in one large circle, chasing the raptor higher and higher into the sky. Surely the curse would take her, what with the distance she was putting between herself and him.

Aidan cringed in anticipation and called out again, "Leave it be. We'll catch the beast another day." He thought she would not listen, so he was surprised when she dove back to earth, barely slowing as she hit the ground.

Her face was livid. "You made me lose it." The dress she wore was torn in places where the bird must have snatched at her, and her hair was a tangled mess. "You blasted fool. We could have ended it."

"You could have died," he pointed out.

She snorted. "Rubbish."

He felt such relief that she was all right that he could not find his temper within himself. Instead, he let out a laugh, which had been the wrong noise to make. She came at him, sword in hand. "Are you going to stab me for that?" he asked, amused.

It was Slaíne's turn to roll her eyes and let out an exasperated sigh. "'Course not." She dropped the sword at his feet, and Aidan Dismissed it before she could change her mind. "I had it." The girl gestured wildly, flapping her arms and stomping her feet. "Its wings were inches from my face, and I reached out, but you—" Her face darkened. "You distracted me, blast you." Exhausted apparently, the girl sank to the ground and put out her hand. "I need water."

Aidan Summoned a bladder and handed it to her, watching as she downed several gulps in one great pull. "If you had flown beyond the limits the curse puts between us, you might have had a fit and fallen out of the air." He gave her a pointed look. "Better the creature got away than me finding your corpse on the ground."

"Better not having no curse on me head." Slaíne thrust the bladder back at him. "That creature followed us from Grensworth. He's what scared that man to his death. There are no coincidences." Her shoulders heaved. "This is all connected."

There was no arguing with that. Aidan held the same feelings about the matter, but what was to be done other than wait for another chance to kill or capture the creature? "We should make camp soon. But might I suggest we travel a little while more today?"

Slaíne hesitated but then nodded, her eyes on the heavens. "You feel it out there?"

Indeed, he felt the strange Pull not that far off. Since it had taken the form of a bird, the creature could watch their progress without worrying about being easily caught or seen. But if they kept their voices lowered, they could discuss their plans without it hearing them. "Let's see if we can lose it." He Dismissed the water bladder, and then he and Slaíne headed northwest.

They traveled in silence until nearing sunset, looking to the heavens from time to time, but no bird seemed to be following them from above. The Pull disappeared entirely by the time they stopped to make camp, and did not reappear while they laid out the animal skins and partook of their evening meal.

When the light failed them and they had lain down for the night, Aidan rolled onto his back and looked at the stars. It was a clear, cold night, and several constellations popped out at him. He thought of the maps and what Treevain had said in the Beyond.

"Follow the Pull of magical blood, seek the starberry circle 'neath the shadow of the Ludland. There, 'neath the crown, find the dark place." He was following the Pull, but why was the word 'Ludland' so familiar?

Slaíne was lying several feet away. His query could wait 'til morning, perhaps, but he wanted to know now.

He called out to her. "Slaíne, I have a question."

At once the girl sat up, her eyes wide in the night. "Mr. Aidan, you about near made my heart stop." Indeed, she was clutching her chest, which rose and fell quickly. Once the shock seemed to have worn off, she asked, "Is the creature back again?"

Aidan shook his head. "The creature is a ways off and hasn't come any nearer since we've settled."

"Then why'd you bother me?" She lay back down, but rolled over on her side to face him. "What do you want?"

"Have you heard of the Ludland?"

Slaíne was silent at first. Aidan was afraid she was falling back asleep or had no intention of answering when she said, "It's a manmade mountain. Well, I should say wizard-made. The elves mentioned it several times throughout the years, usually when they wanted ter scare me into obeying them."

Aidan frowned. This was not promising. "What about it frightened you?"

She laughed darkly. "'Twas said to be haunted by the ghost of a madman. Well, that and it was cursed."

"Wonderful," Aidan groaned. "What was the curse?"

It was Slaíne's turn to show dismay. "That's where we're headed, innit?" When he did not respond, she swore, jumped to her feet, and took to pacing. "Ludland comes from a northern tongue and it means 'movin' fire'. Some myths say the place moves every morning at sunrise, so no poor fool stumbles on it by accident." She stomped her foot. "That's why we ain't been traveling the same direction e'ry day, innit?" She groaned.

"In the Beyond," Aidan began carefully, "Treevain said that I should follow the Pull of magical blood, that it will lead me to the Ludland. If I am following the correct Pull, it must be moving. I'd thought I was imagining it."

Slaíne scoffed but stopped pacing and threw herself back down onto her makeshift bed. "Treevain again. An' we trust her now all o' a sudden?" She spat onto the ground. "Brilliant."

In the dark of the night, Aidan could only just make out the narrow slits that were her eyes. He shuddered. "I don't care for it any more than you do, but the truth is that I had need of outside counsel."

"Coulda asked me," she said.

Aidan raised his hands in truce. "What has passed has passed. Let's dwell instead on what is to be. Are we still seeking the Questing Goblet?"

"'Course."

It was difficult to tell if she was speaking her mind on the matter or not, so he prodded. "The last time I spoke of it, you seemed uncertain if we should seek it or not." He was prepared to wait for her to mull the issue over, but the girl answered at once:

"If it's what takes down Meraude, I'm all for it. 'Sides, I reckon we don't want her findin' it first."

With that settled, Aidan lay back down, turning as well to face her. Still sensing the creature out there, he Summoned the silver sword and laid it between them. "I think one of us should keep watch." Why the creature would choose the night to strike above any other time was beyond Aidan, but he trusted Slaíne – as much as he dared to – with the weapon. He had seen her with the sword, and it was obvious that it was no stranger to her.

"You want me ter take first watch?" Slaíne laughed. "What sort of gentleman do that make ya?"

"I never said I was a gentleman."

Her laughter stopped. For a moment she was still, but then her Pull moved nearer. In one swift movement, she possessed the sword, and Aidan mused that he was not afraid, not as she swung it at him, bringing the blade half an inch from his face in one long slashing movement. She swore in surprise. "You trust me, then?"

Aidan swatted the blunt edge of the blade away with his hand as if he were ridding himself of a yellow fly or some similar nuisance. "If you don't want first watch, then say so. No need to launch one of your attacks on me."

"If I'd been attacking ya, sir, you would now be dead." She lowered the blade and walked away. "What time should I wake ya?"

"I don't much care." He shrugged. "Whenever you're too tired to carry on." It was perhaps a dangerous move, trusting her so. But he needed to trust someone, and this was as good a test as any. Slaíne had never made a move against him at either of the inns, or when they'd slept tangled in each other's arms to keep warm in the wild. The sword added a new element, however, an unknown.

For someone who had been sleeping just ten minutes prior, Slaíne seemed to have a lot of energy. She paced to and fro, swinging the sword, the wind cracking around it every time she pulled off a quick-enough swing. "You rest, sir. No harm'll come ter us."

He fought off a grin and then a grimace, before turning his back to her and allowing himself to sleep. "Good night, Slaíne."

* * *

In the hours following, Aidan slept lightly. Every little sound in the wilderness roused him, and made him wonder if they were under attack. The night grew dark as the moon disappeared behind clouds, and he could scarce make out his hand in front of his face, but he sensed Slaíne's Pull nearby every time he woke, and that gave him some measure of comfort. At last, when several hours had passed and it was fast approaching sunrise, Aidan fell into a deep sleep. He dreamt of cackling elves, of hags and wizards, and creatures with strange Pulls moving about in the dark.

Aidan was torn out of a particularly upsetting dream about a sentient wreath of fire when Slaíne cried out. He sat upright, and was alarmed to find that the creature that had been following them had returned, and its Pull was accompanied by another.

Metal clashed on metal, and Aidan rolled out of the way as the silver sword went sliding toward him. Not waiting to see what had transpired, Aidan snatched the sword from where it had landed and scrambled to his feet. He spun around and saw the creature, whose shape he could make out in the dimness of the early morning. Slaíne had soared out of its reach.

The man or creature was standing below Slaíne. In his hand was a bronze blade, which he swung out in a great arc, taking part of the hem of her dress. Aidan charged at him, hoping the soft metal of his own blade could take on the force of something so sturdy. The man turned and extended his blade, effectively stopping Aidan's long sword with his own broad one, forcing Aidan to retreat. If he hadn't possessed the power of Summoning and Calling, the blade might have dropped.

The man came at Aidan again, slashing.

Aidan blocked the blow and tried to remember his training from when he was nine. That had been twenty-some years ago, and he knew he was too out of practice to fight this brute off. He would have to use his gifts. Aidan retreated well away from his assailant's reach, Dismissed the silver sword, and Summoned it, hoping to bring it back from Nothingness and into the man's chest.

The other seemed to know what Aidan was doing, for he stepped out of the way at just the right moment, and the silver sword clanged harmlessly onto the ground. The assailant went to retrieve it, but Aidan Called it to himself before the other could even touch the grip.

Slaíne chose that moment to drop from the heavens and wrap her arms around the man's neck, squeezing. It was now the dawning, and as the light hit their faces, Aidan blinked and was startled to find himself looking into his own eyes.

It took him a moment to recover, and in that time, his look-alike managed to throw Slaíne off from around his neck. She sailed backward into a tree, and Aidan thought he heard bones cracking.

But the man wasn't coming for Slaíne. Again he raised his blade and again he charged at Aidan.

Aidan became aware of the second Pull he had sensed moments before. It was making a straight line for them. "Wonderful," he gritted out, blade locked with the other's. If he could hold the shape-shifter off long enough, maybe he could Summon one of his daggers into the fellow's belly. But the look-alike was strong, and it took all of his concentration not to be run through. Aidan was forced back. There was no movement from Slaíne.

"Nelead cunwiladaff," the man growled.

It was strange hearing such ugly, rough words come out of seemingly his own mouth. "What do you want?" Aidan Summoned his dagger, but it fell short of where he had intended it to land.

"Leave the witch," his rival snarled. He pushed his blade nearer to Aidan.

The second Pull had arrived in the clearing, and though Aidan could not see the woman, he knew who it was. "You picked an interesting time to reappear," said he.

"Oi, brute. I don't think this was what your master intended," said Larkin the seer.

Something hard thudded against the shifter's back, and the creature turned, giving Aidan the perfect opportunity to Summon his dagger, which he did, and drove it through the other's throat.

Sputtering blood, the creature collapsed upon Aidan and vanished, leaving behind the bronze sword. All was still for a moment.

Aidan drew in large gulps of air as he pushed away the sword and staggered to his feet. "Is she all right?" he asked Larkin, who was bent over Slaíne.

The seer muttered something and then straightened. "She's all right. Might've broken the tree and perhaps some of her pride, but...."

"Broken the tree?" What the devil? He looked beyond where Slaíne lay unconscious, and sure enough, there was a great crack running down the middle of the trunk where she had hit it. If she had hit it that hard, surely she was dead and the seer was mistaken. Aidan hurried to her, dropping the silver sword.

"She's fine, milord, just had the wind knocked out of her." Her eyes would not quite meet his for a moment, and Aidan wondered if the seer was hiding something. But then the moment passed, and she approached him. "Strange times have come upon you, methinks."

Aidan laughed without humor. "You might say that." He knelt next to Slaíne. The warmth of her breath tickled his hand, so he knew she was alive, as the seer had said. "Are you all right?"

In response, Slaíne let out a tiny groan. "Give me a moment."

"The lass is made of sterner stuff than you think," said Larkin. "Come, tell me all that has transpired since you left me stranded in Abbington." There was a coolness in her words, and Aidan knew he was not forgiven for leaving with Slaíne in the dead of the night some weeks ago.

He grimaced, but rose and faced the woman. "I did not trust you, and I was wrong. I'm sorry."

The seer smirked and folded her hands in front of her. "Well?"

"I did not realize the town would turn against our kind. Rather, I was certain you would betray us to Dewhurst or someone in authority if we did not set off on our own. I realize now I was wrong, and I ask for your forgiveness."

Larkin nodded. "That's fair enough. Tell me what has transpired since then."

Aidan drew a deep breath then launched into an explanation of what had happened between that night and now. He told her of the town turning on them for using magic to protect themselves, of trying to take Dewhurst by surprise and being captured. Aidan left out the bits about his communicating with the magical dead in the Beyond, though he guessed she suspected something. He also made no mention of the man, Salem, taking over his body from time to time. Since his last visit to the Beyond where he talked alone with Treevain, Aidan had not been aware of any strange presence in the back of his mind. Perhaps that was gone for good.

When he got to the part about finding his parents' corpses in Dewhurst's stables, the seer became visibly upset, but he pressed on, and recounted his journey up until before he had woken to find his camp under attack.

The seer was silent for a moment, perhaps sorting through all that she had been told. When she spoke again, the woman merely said, "I need to sit down." And with that, she lowered herself to the ground and shook her head.

"What happened after we left you that night?" Aidan asked.

She looked up at him, and her face and person, he noted, seemed to have aged since they had last crossed paths. "Oh, I left that night too." Larkin tapped her right temple, as if to remind him of her gift of Foresight. "Luck was surely with me that night, for you are a slippery fellow, Lord Ingledark, and you surely churned the waters in that backward town." Her eyes narrowed. "As thou knowest, there is a price for being a Blest, and I have paid that price time and time again these past several weeks."

Aidan simply nodded.

The seer continued. "Seeing has taking its toll on this old woman." She patted her hip. "Fits and seizures are my nightly companions. That is what I get for using a gift I never asked for."

Slaíne began to stir. "Where is the body?" she said, her voice as rough as a cat's tongue.

"All magic folk go to the Beyond when they die, dear," said Larkin.

Aidan shuddered. He hoped he would never come across the shape-shifter if his soul ever visited that place again. It had been disorienting to fight himself...to say the least. Aloud he said, "What are you going to do, now that you've found us?" It might be useful having a seer on their side if they were to find the Questing Goblet and emerge from the cursed place unharmed.

Larkin was shaking her head. "It's the strangest thing, but every time I try to look too far into any future with you, everything goes dark. I am not accustomed to this strange occurrence, and I fear its meaning. Surely there have never been holes in the veil, not in my lifetime."

"Holes? What could it mean?" Slaíne asked. "What 'bout my future?"

"Oh, Slaíne, surely you see how closely both of your fates entwine?" She gestured between her and Aidan, rocking slightly. "Yours, I fear, goes dark as well at some point."

Aidan was not going to give up so easily. "What happens before our futures disappear? Maybe if you told us, we could avoid what is to come, whatever that might be."

The seer turned her piercing gaze on Aidan and, sliding the water bladder's strap over her head, she offered him a drink. When he refused, she took a long pull from it and came up panting for air.

"There are many paths, milord, that lead to where you'll eventually and hopefully end up. But if I tip you in one direction, all of those paths could so easily diverge into different ones." She wiped her mouth clean with the hem of her cloak sleeve. "The future is far from set, and I do not want to upset things any more than they have been, apparently." She turned the bladder upside down over her mouth, and only three tiny droplets fell onto her waiting tongue.

"I'll fill that for you," Aidan offered.

She held the vessel out to him. "That would be very kind of you. I fear I've traveled lightly since my narrow escape. Fortunate am I for some clear streams running through the land."

After refilling both of the woman's water bladders and purifying them, Aidan returned to the camp to the two women talking, their voices low and tense. He hesitated before reentering the clearing when he heard his name, followed by:

"Be careful not to kill him."

"I don't want to kill nobody, 'specially not him."

Larkin laughed darkly. "Be careful all the same. Many things can go wrong in the heat of the moment...especially when you're not quite yourself."

What the devil were they talking about? *Should I be worried?* He waited in silence to see if his question would be answered. But he shifted his weight to his left foot, and a twig snapped beneath his boot.

"Ah, he's back," said the seer.

Aidan adjusted the expression he knew he must be wearing and returned the bladders to Larkin, who took another swig. "Is there nothing you can tell us?" Perhaps if he kept her talking, she would give away what they had been speaking of before.

"Let me look." She held up her hand for him to be quiet and closed her eyes. Her body shook a little at first, her eyes visibly moving beneath her eyelids. Whatever she saw, it made her frown, but whether it was out of concern or confusion, Aidan could not tell. After some time, Larkin opened her eyes again, her face set in a grim expression. "It's going darker even sooner."

"And you nay know what that means, yes? When does it happen?" Slaíne asked.

Larkin hushed her. "You've already asked me that. I cannot say, for fear of unraveling the future." She shuddered and turned to Aidan. "There is someone out there looking for you."

That was alarming news, to be certain. "Meraude?" Hot dread dropped to his stomach like lead, and he chastened himself for it. Did he not wish to find the mage and finish her? She had, after all, been responsible in some way for his parents' deaths. He was no coward. Where was this fear coming from?

But Larkin shook her head. "No, I don't think so. Meraude believes you will come to her, that you are working under her orders. Nothing has led her to believe otherwise. It is a woman who seeks you, but her path is hard to see and has many holes in it as well. It's almost as if someone is interfering with my Sight. But how could that be possible?"

"Does she work with or for our shape-shifting friend?" Aidan nodded toward the bronze sword, which still lay on the ground nearby.

"Neither, milord. I believe she is working with another man, and from the bits and pieces I have seen, I assume he is a guard of some sort. They seem harmless, but that means nothing in this world. Most flowers are as lethal as they are beautiful."

Aidan could only too readily nod his agreement. "And what of Cedric's tomb? Do we find it?"

Again the seer made a hushing sound. "Do not ask me, milord. You do not want to know."

He did, in fact, want to know, and he said so. "What is it with you women and your mysteries?"

"A 'flattering' tongue like that leaves me in little wonder of why you are still a bachelor." But she smirked as she said it. "I will tell you this, though, for I think this will have the best impact at the vital time: in the heat of the moment, when all seems lost, two minds and hearts joined together are better than two torn apart when you need to make a sudden departure." She looked at him meaningfully, but the riddle's answer escaped Aidan.

He stared at her in baffled silence. No words would form on his lips that could express how very much he wished to strangle the woman right now. After small talk, riddles were his least favorite form of communication.

Slaíne broke the silence with a string of colorful words. "What the devil is that? Some useful seer you are." She swore some more.

Larkin was unmoved, but sat there and looked on as if she were watching two children throwing a tantrum. When Slaíne stopped swearing, the seer got to her feet. "Well, now that that's out of the way, I'd best move on." She stretched her legs and put a hand to her lower back.

"What? I thought you might come with us," said Slaíne, her face falling.

Admittedly, Aidan had thought the same thing, but he hid his surprise and made no protest. "How are your provisions?"

The seer pulled her pack from her back and showed Aidan the contents. "Plenty to last me 'til I reach the next town." Her eyes crinkled around the corners and she turned to Slaíne. "Our paths will cross again…if we don't all die first." Perhaps it had been meant as a joke, but Aidan was unsure. She laughed, and Slaíne joined in half-heartedly.

"Where are you bound?" he asked, hoping for no more riddles.

"I think I'll head north for now." Larkin adjusted the strap of

her pack. "I have some unfinished business that needs tending to."
A shadow passed over her features and did not leave, though she
smiled. When she spoke again, her voice was strained. "I suppose
it would not be breaking any rules to follow you a little ways. That
Pull, where is it leading you today?"

Aidan was not fooled by her cheerful demeanor, but he did
not press her, though Slaíne seemed barely able to contain her
questions and concern. "The Pull," he said, "is leading me north
and a little ways west today. It feels like we're getting closer...but
I cannot be certain."

Of course the woman's face betrayed nothing, curse it all. "Very
well. Let us travel north and a little ways west. Once you've broken
your fast in due course, that is. Eat slowly, though. Fighting assassins
first thing in the morning can be trying on the stomach."

"I'd imagine so."

"Not fer me," said Slaíne, rising as if she had not just put a crack
in a solid oak with her body. "I'm half-starved."

On that announcement, Aidan Summoned some of the foodstuffs
he had stolen from the Spinning Cup Inn: half of a ham and some
more brown bread. He had been clumsy with his aim, and the meat
landed not on a stone as he had intended, but in the dirt. No one
seemed to mind, though. As Slaíne hacked into the meat with a knife
from the seer, they broke the bread and ate of it, talking merrily and
catching slabs of the sweet and salty meat that Slaíne would toss
them from time to time. Before long, more than a quarter of the
ham was gone, and he Dismissed the leftovers as they downed the
last of the somewhat stale bread. Aidan passed around a bladder
twice, and then Dismissed the rest of their camp.

"You should take it," Larkin said, nodding at the bronze sword.

"You foresaw something?" Aidan asked half-jokingly, his lips
twisting up in a sarcastic smile.

The seer said nothing, but winked and began to walk the exact
path he had intended to take. Slaíne stood there, watching as Aidan
bent over and retrieved the shape-shifter's blade.

"This reminds me of your sword," he said, testing the balance of it. "Different metal, different Pull, but...."

Slaíne stepped forward. "Lemme see."

He made to hand her the blade, but she shied away from it. "What's wrong? You're paling."

She shook herself and pulled away. "I dunno. It just don't feel like it wants me to touch it. Better not. It did, after all, try ter kill me."

Aidan shook his head and Dismissed the strange blade, along with the silver one. He noted, with bewilderment, that the two would not Dismiss at the same time, Slaíne's disappearing moments later than it should have. He said nothing of it, and followed the seer and Slaíne down the narrow path that was to take him, eventually, to the tomb of Cedric the Elder and the means to his revenge.

CHAPTER THIRTEEN

Aidan

The three travelers walked in near silence for the duration of an hour. Larkin kept stopping mid-step, closing her eyes, and then nodding before moving onward. She did this five times within the first twenty minutes, and Aidan wondered if it had been a mistake allowing her to join their party. The longer she dallied, the farther away the Pull of the magical battlegrounds seemed. It must have indeed been moving.

Aidan said nothing about their pace at first, however, hoping that the seer was merely lost in her thoughts and would soon hasten her steps. The morning was fine, and the air held promise of the hot months to come. There was enough cloud and tree cover to keep the sun off their faces as the way became more uphill. Birds sang overhead. The way was clear, and there seemed to be no immediate problems other than the snail's pace they were keeping. Then why was Aidan feeling so anxious? Gritting his teeth as one hour melted into the next, he set his eyes on Slaíne, whom he had been avoiding since they had left the encampment. It was no better with her. Something strange was afoot, and Aidan could neither discern what was happening nor what might yet happen.

At last, when the third hour of their journey approached, Larkin stopped and sat down at the base of a tree and motioned for Aidan and Slaíne to do the same. "This is where I leave you, I'm afraid. My own curse will allow me to go no farther this way."

Aidan frowned.

"What do you mean by your own curse?" Slaíne demanded.

The seer rolled her eyes and leaned back against the trunk of the tree. "Just what I said. Never you mind the rest." Her expression softened. "I know you're angry with me for keeping such a slow pace, but I can say everything has a purpose in the end. Why don't you rest for a while, the both of you?"

It did not sound like half a bad idea. Aidan rubbed his shoulder, which had begun to prickle, indicating that he was about to be dragged into the Beyond. Still he hesitated. "I don't know." He gave Slaíne an uneasy look, but she seemed to be avoiding him as well. "There's still a lot of daylight left, and I would very much like to make it at least another ten miles before nightfall." In truth he felt ready to fall over and knew that traveling ten miles uphill before night was out of the question.

Slaíne decided for him. "I ain't movin' another step until I've et and slept." With that said, she sat next to the seer and at last looked in Aidan's general direction with expectation.

"Seems as though we're not going anywhere for a while," said Larkin, grinning. "Summon a feast, milord, for I feel we'll need all the strength we can get for the hours ahead."

What was meant by that? Aidan wondered.... Still, he did not argue or voice any of the many questions pressing on him. Instead Aidan Summoned the remainder of the ham, some cheeses, fruits, and bread, plus one of the waterskins. Two had been drained in their hike that day. He would need to find another stream soon and replenish their supply.

"Are you sure you shouldn't sit down, milord?" asked Larkin as Slaíne tore into the meat.

Though he fought the pull of the Beyond, Aidan was reluctant to give in to it. The thought of his soul leaving his body still frightened him somewhat and was a disorienting sensation. But it would seem that he was being left little choice.

Oh, quit being so dramatic, said the voice of Salem in the back of his mind. He gave Aidan another tug, and Aidan almost blacked out right then and there.

"All right," Aidan said after a moment, moving to a tree to the left of Larkin and Sláine. He knew it was no use fighting the supernatural in this instance. No sooner had he sat down than the world around him went black and he faded into the Beyond.

He stood in the middle of the orchard back on his childhood estate, and, as expected, Salem was waiting for him. The two men regarded each other in silence for a moment, before Aidan swore at him. "What the devil did you mean by hitting me in the head with a shovel?"

The young man's face went red and he shook his head. "I'm sorry about that, Aidan. There would be consequences if you stayed here too long, for you and for the Beyond. Can you forgive me?"

Aidan waved away the other's words. "What consequences?"

Salem drew in a deep breath and began. "Well, to begin with, you'll be unable to leave if you stay too long."

"Oh, brilliant."

The young man's expression darkened further. "Oh, that isn't the half of it." He ducked his head, as if reluctant to confide. "No one but Treevain and I really want you visiting here. Nare've was particularly upset to find out that I've been bringing you here." He must have read the confusion on Aidan's face, for he said, "The Nymph Queen. She's power-mad, Aidan. And you're a threat."

"But she was the one who stabbed me with her ice blade in the first place," Aidan said, spluttering slightly as he spoke. *He recalled trying to escape the murderous nymphs, how Sláine had realized the connection between light and the creatures' life-force. He'd Dismissed the wood powering their fires, causing the beings to die and vanish in moments. Before the nymph queen's time was up, she had hastily stabbed Aidan in the shoulder with her blade. At the time, Aidan had assumed it was out of revenge. It had caused him to have many strange visions, and that is when his conversations with Salem in the Beyond had begun. "Why the devil would she make the connection between the Beyond and me possible if she didn't want me visiting?"*

"I don't know, Aidan." Salem motioned for Aidan to follow him into a cluster of trees, and lowered his voice. "Some strange things are going on here, things no one is talking to me about. Armies are on the move."

That startled Aidan. "There are armies in the land of the dead? For what purpose?"

"I told you I don't know," said Salem, and Aidan knew him to be truly upset and afraid. "As I said, no one is talking to me." The man took to pacing, his hands balled into fists as he made trails in the tall grass. "The elves are shunning some of us. The nymphs are training in camps, though I know I was not supposed to see them."

"What are their numbers?"

Salem threw his hands up in the air. "I don't know. I can only hear them from the valleys when I can sneak close enough. Their numbers are great." He turned to Aidan and stopped his frantic back-and-forth walking. "But that is not anything for you to worry about. You are alive." His tone was bitter, and Aidan could not think of what to say in response. Like a dog Salem shook himself, his composure returning. "How is your progress with the—" He looked around them first. "Is anyone nearby?"

Aidan shook his head; he felt no Pulls. "Continue."

"Have you found…it?" He hesitated. "When you find it, Aidan, Treevain says to use it at once. She seems to think something bad is about to happen, and she wants you to have all the luck you can get on your side."

Aidan grimaced. "We were attacked this morning."

"By who? Did Tristram follow you?" The name was like sulfur coming from his mouth, full of bitter heat and ash. He motioned for Aidan to sit, throwing himself to the ground.

Aidan watched as the man tore at long blades of grass, stopping when he found the size he wanted, apparently, and began knotting it.

"A shape-shifter has been following us. It killed a man back in a town we were staying in, and it caught up to us, taking my form and…. Are you all right?" Aidan was driven to distraction, watching Salem tearing and knotting grass with such vigor and hatred, as one quite distracted and disturbed.

The man gave him an abrupt nod. "What happened with the shape-shifter? Where is he now?" Salem did not look up from his hands' task.

"Dead. He attacked me, I stabbed him in the throat, and he vanished."

Salem's hands stopped working on the knot, and he looked at Aidan, eyes wide. "What? That's impossible."

It was Aidan's turn to be distraught. "What do you mean by impossible? Don't all magic folk disappear from my realm and come here when they die?"

The man's face had paled considerably, and there was a wobble in his voice when he spoke. "They do, Aidan. But the last arrival into the Beyond was a week ago. We have had no shape-shifters join our numbers for years."

The two men looked at each other, eyes wide. "Are you sure—"

"I'm certain. Everyone knows when new kin take up residence here. You're different, since you're not actually here, per se." Salem jumped to his feet. "Your shape-shifter assassin is still out there, Aidan." He began to chew on his lower lip, and then swore. "Blimey, I shouldn't have brought you here. I had no idea. Your – your mind has been harder to latch on to lately. It's almost as if someone or something powerful is getting in the way."

Aidan tried to hide his shudder, and clasped his clammy hands behind his back. "Slaíne's Pull is very powerful. Perhaps that is interfering." He had enough to worry about. There was no need to add to the drama surrounding his current quest.

Shaking his head, Salem took to pacing again. "No, Pulls are all on you. They're how you perceive things. It must be the shape-shifter interfering with our connection."

The thought was unsettling, but it was the best explanation, as reluctant as Aidan was to accept it. "The...the land where the Goblet lies feels close. We should be there within—"

"Do not speak so freely, Aidan. Keep information from everyone, even your lady friend. Information is power." Without warning, Salem leapt to his feet. "I am sorry about hitting you with the shovel. But I might have been cast out, had I been found with you."

That made Aidan start. "You can leave the Beyond?"

Salem pulled a face. "I-I don't think it's quite like that. More like forced to cease existing in any capacity." He shuddered. "In case I don't see you again...."

"I'm sure our paths will cross again. You always seem to show up at the strangest of times...wanted or not." Aidan had meant the words in jest, but Salem's scowl deepened.

"Fine, then. Just go." Salem turned his back and started to walk away.

"It was a joke, Salem. That's all."

Salem turned around and smiled sadly. *"That's not my name, Aidan. Farewell."*

Aidan awoke to a darkened sky and hunger pangs wringing his stomach. Droplets of water prickled his skin as he sat up and tried to reorient himself with his surroundings. He was alone, but for Slaíne's Pull in the near distance. Larkin was nowhere to be seen or sensed. "Hello?" Aidan called out, his throat dry and hoarse. No one responded. "Is anyone near?"

The only human Pulls within ten miles were his and Slaíne's. *How long have I been in the Beyond?* he wondered. It had only seemed like half an hour, if that. Here, things seemed to have changed drastically, as if hours had passed him by.

"You're awake," Slaíne said, emerging from the wood, whence Aidan heard water flowing. "Praise be. I thought you were going to die for certain." Her face was pale and her eyes were red, as if she had been crying or deprived of sleep. As she swayed on the spot, Aidan assumed it might be the latter. "It's been half a week, Mr. Aidan, since you was awake. Larkin's gone. Drinking water's gone. No – no food in days."

Taking in what she was saying, Aidan wasted no time in Summoning two water bladders, one of which he handed to Slaíne, who drank greedily. "I am so sorry, Slaíne."

The girl came up for air, gasping and sputtering water. "Not your fault. Can nay control it, can ya?" She went back to drinking, and Aidan joined her.

Next he Summoned food: bread, berries, and a roasted game hen. They drank and ate in silence. When the two bladders had been drained, Aidan Summoned another. He would replenish what they had used up before they moved on, which goodness alone knew when that would be. Having eaten until his stomach felt ready to burst, Aidan tried standing, but his limbs were stiff from having lain in the same position for as long as he had. He looked at Slaíne more carefully. "You haven't slept all this time, have you?"

The girl muttered something, but she scarce seemed able to push out any words. Her eyes blinked furiously against the failing light and the droplets of water falling from the sky.

Aidan Summoned two of the animal skins. One he laid across her lap and, after lowering her from her sitting position into a lying one, he folded the other skin and propped it under her head for a pillow. It wasn't long before Slaíne's breathing grew deep and slow. Her eyes fluttered closed, and her form relaxed.

Lightning crackled in great forks across the slate-gray sky, and thunder rumbled its reply. But the storm seemed to be passing; he would not need to make a shelter or move Slaíne out from the open. Though certain there were no human or large animal Pulls within the near distance, Aidan Summoned the silver sword and laid it next to Slaíne, in case he was lost to the Beyond again. He also Summoned the remaining water bladder and enough food to last her for a few days. Then, confident she would be provided for, Aidan stretched his limbs and prepared to stand guard for the night.

★   ★   ★

Night crept by, as did the storm. Winds blew, lightning flashed, but the rain mostly missed them, just as Aidan had hoped it would. Ashamed for being useless to Slaíne during the days previous, he managed to get to his feet and scouted around the area. There was not much to be seen in the darkness, but he used his abilities to feel out their surroundings. The Pull from the magical battlegrounds pulsed in the distance, a startlingly close distance. While he had slept, the Ludland must have moved closer. Aidan's stomach knotted.

At the dawning, no birdsong filled the air, and the sun itself seemed reluctant to make its appearance. Over all there hung a silent dread, as if all somehow knew the cursed land had drawn nearer.

Aidan shook the night's moisture from his hair and took the empty water bladders to the stream, where he refilled and purified them. He did not wake Slaíne upon his returning, but Dismissed what he wished not to carry and Summoned some food with which to break his fast.

When the sun did rise in earnest, Aidan thought the girl might wake. She did not, but slept on, and he let her.

As his traveling companion continued to sleep, Aidan Summoned the remaining food from Nothingness and sorted through it. There was enough to last them another week. It would seem that most of what Aidan had Dismissed from the inn's kitchen were inedible objects, such as plates and spoons and the like. Of what was edible that remained had yet to be cooked properly. Could they risk a fire with the shape-shifter out there? He knew they would have to, if they wanted to eat again any time soon. Now was as good a time as any.

After taking stock of the Pulls surrounding them, Aidan went about building a fire. He gathered what dry wood he could find along with tinder, and he soon had a modest blaze sputtering sparks and smoke. Blinking his watering eyes, Aidan built the fire up a bit more, and then let it cool down a little so he could roast a chicken and some potatoes. As he manually plucked the feathers from the carcass, Aidan tried, unsuccessfully, not to think about the shape-shifter.

None of it made any sense. Why had the being chosen that moment to attack, when it had been following them for a few days? If the creature was still alive, he must be too wounded to return, so that's why he hadn't attacked further.

Tired of plucking, Aidan Dismissed the remainder of the feathers from the chicken, Summoned a knife, and went about butchering it. By now the sun was high in the sky; he would have to wake the girl soon so they could eat and move on.

It was when Aidan thought about moving on that something tugged in his gut. Startled, he leapt to his feet and turned to face this new Pull. No one was there, though it felt as though someone were standing right next to him. Aidan shuddered. "Slaíne," he said softly at first.

The girl stirred slightly but made no other sign of rising or waking.

Veins pulsing, Aidan Dismissed the chicken and the potatoes and the knife. He kicked ashes over the fire, successfully putting it out and Dismissed the wood. "Slaíne," he repeated, this time more loudly.

"I heard you the first time," she muttered. "Give me another hour, yes?"

He growled at her, and Dismissed the skins and the remainder of their camp. "There is no time to be wasted."

"Hey!" she said as he made to pull her to her feet.

Aidan ignored her as she took a swing at him. "Get up. You have three minutes, and then we move out." He checked to make certain the Pull had not moved, and was relieved that it remained. "Hurry."

She hissed at him like an angry cat, but stumbled to her feet. "What's all this about?" Slaíne took a step back and stared at him. "Your face looks funny." She made a face of her own. "What's wrong?"

"We've found it, Slaíne. Or rather, *it* found *us*." This was the moment he had been waiting for, so he tried to ignore the knots his stomach had tied itself into.

"What's found us?"

Aidan clenched his jaw. "Cedric's burial grounds."

CHAPTER FOURTEEN

Jinn

As they walked, Jinn tried to think of ways her foresight might be failing. And the more she thought and tried to peer ahead, the more certain she became that there was nothing to be done. Not that she was giving up, far from it. It was difficult not to draw Quick's attention to her plight, especially when she stopped him and said she needed to peer ahead again and, waiting until his back had been turned, before drawing out the knife with which she'd slain one hag and wounded another.

Quick caught her in the act of removing the blade, and his brow wrinkled. "Why do you want that?"

"For the starberries," Jinn replied. The lie sounded unconvincing to even her own ears as she continued. "I'm still weak from fighting that merrow. This blade will help me cut the berries from their stems with ease."

Her dear, innocent brother smiled again and pointed her to the path that led to oblivion. "The border is here. We walk in together, yes?" When she did not reply right away, Quick's smile faded. "What?"

"I need one more look ahead."

Quick groaned. "Can't know it all."

That argument might have held weight in the past, but Jinn realized she had been coming at the future all wrong and needed one last look. If she was to die and it was inevitable, was death also inevitable for Quick? He had been the one to say that the 'bad man' was after *her*, after all. What if this mysterious person would leave

Quick alone? If they separated, she might give him enough time to find the Summoner and direct him away from Mother. It was not the original plan, but it might have a better outcome than the one she was currently following. "Give me a minute, Quick. Just one minute."

He did not seem pleased about this suggestion, but made no argument against it, other than to say, "Then Quick eats more fish."

Jinn closed her eyes and looked for Quick's future path. Yes, if she concentrated on them parting ways here, as she had not thought possible nor looked for before, she could see the path. It was a tenuous path, one that she could barely see or define, but it was certainly there. As she watched him leave in her mind's eye, Jinn saw Quick gather starberries...miss her, and then look for her. Blast, but he walked back into darkness. She would have to get him to meet her somewhere. But where? She'd never foreseen this strange land. But Quick had. Jinn would have to get crafty. Without opening her eyes or releasing her sight, Jinn asked Quick, "How far into this place did you go?"

"Quick did not go far," he insisted.

Jinn sighed. "I'm not blaming you for anything, Quick. Just tell me what you saw." He did not respond, so she gave him a nudge. "How about landmarks? See anything interesting?"

Quick's attention at once latched on to that statement. "Big trees. Strange colors. And mountain. Big mountain had lots of berries on it."

"Ah," Jinn muttered, seeing the mountain in her vision. "I see a cave," she lied. "Don't look ahead. I don't want you wasting your energy. We shall need all our strength in order to gather as many berries as we can eat and carry."

His shoulders heaved. "That makes sense. Let's go, then."

A vision of Quick searching among the hills for a cave entered Jinn's mind. It continued, and there was no darkness in the near future for him. That was as much as she could scout, as her end drew nearer. "Show me where the best berries are."

Quick had not been wrong about the strange colors, the tall trees, the out-of-season starberries growing in clusters everywhere. Where had this place come from? It had not been there the day previous. She was certain of that.

Purple leaves the size of her body grew out of trees that could be as tall as the lesser mountains back home. These towered over their path as Quick tramped ahead. This was the difficult moment, the great deceit. Jinn stopped walking and let out a groan.

As foreseen, Quick turned around and started back toward her. "What wrong?"

Jinn clutched her hands to her head and shut her eyes. "Quick."

"Quick here." He came to her side and placed a heavy hand on her shoulder. "What is it? A vision?"

"I'm afraid it is," Jinn said, gasping for air before stumbling to the side.

Quick caught her. "What did you see?"

She hesitated a moment, as if giving herself time to regain composure. When she spoke again, she was ashamed by how convincing her voice sounded. "Quick, you're not going to like this."

"What?" he asked, voice trembling. "Something bad happens?"

Jinn hated herself. "Yes. Something bad will happen to me if we don't separate." She let those words sink in before continuing. "We need to pick berries apart from each other for a while."

Quick just stared at her. "But why? Should Quick look ahead too?"

"No, Quick. I need you with your full strength." She paused. "I saw a cave. If we meet there in two hours' time, everything will be all right." Her voice broke on the last word, but she pulled herself back together and nodded reassuringly at Quick. "All shall be well. Head straight for the mountain and look for the cave."

It was sad, seeing her brother so downcast. He hung his head, tears threatening to spill from his wide eyes as he adjusted his pack. "What will you do?"

If he was going forward without her, he would need both packs with supplies to last him for at least another four days. Jinn closed her eyes and pretended to look ahead. "I need to remain here and use my foresight some more. You'll need to hold on to my pack."

"The knife too?"

Jinn shook her head. She was going to use that knife on whomever or whatever was chasing her. If she was going to die, then they were going to die with her. "No, I need to hold on to this." Had she covered all possibilities? No, not quite. "I didn't foresee you running afoul of anyone, but if you see anything dangerous, you need to run."

Quick threw back his shoulders. "No, Jinn. Not leave you."

"Of course not," she replied. "We'll meet at the cave. All right?"

Her brother gave her a look as if to say that, no, none of this was all right. But he did not argue with her plan. After a moment's hesitation, Quick readjusted both packs and walked away without looking back.

It was difficult, but Jinn swallowed down her panic that she had sent her brother away for the last time. After all, she might not die. Maybe her sight had changed. Maybe she was misinterpreting things and.... "Who am I fooling?" she said to no one. Then she began to count the minutes and seconds. Whoever or whatever was to cause her end was almost there. They would be arriving in five minutes.

Jinn looked around her. There was not a person in sight. She stumbled through the thick clusters of starberries, and looked for the tree she was going to hide behind.

She was down to four minutes, and the nearest tree would force her to cross into the open. Her killer would be able to see her, if they were lying in wait. But she knew she didn't die for the next three and a half minutes, so she walked into the open and followed her fate.

The tree was as thick as seven Quicks. Jinn ran for it, threw herself behind the base, and waited, out of breath. There were two minutes left.

Quick should be well out of the way now. She could no longer see his unmistakable form stalking into the distance. "Good," she told herself, rubbing her hands down her trousers. The last minute had arrived.

Her veins pulsed in triple time. Jinn rolled up her sleeves and readied the dagger. She would throw it as soon as she was within range of this man or beast. Ten seconds remained, and Jinn sensed a change.

The air crackled as if with lightning, causing Jinn's hairs to stand on end. The sky darkened to a red, and the wind picked up to a howl. Her hand on the blade's grip tightened as she prepared to vault herself into the unknown. But as she rounded the tree, dagger poised for throwing, the sky lightened and the wind stilled. Jinn paused. No one was there that she could see, but she did not allow herself to relax, nor did she attempt to use her foresight, which would only leave her vulnerable to attack. Someone was here, she just hadn't found them yet, or they her.

As if in answer to the thought, the unmistakable crunch of vegetation sounded from behind her. Jinn spun around and was prepared to throw the blade, but was hit with a tingling pulse of blue light in her left shoulder, throwing her back a pace. Jinn dodged another ray that had been directed at her, rolling to the right and springing back to her feet. Falling into a fighting stance she had seen Mother's soldiers rely on during practice, Jinn looked into the eyes of her assailant, and tried to hide her surprise. "You?" she said. "I thought I killed you."

The merrow looked surprised for a moment, but then his eyes narrowed in suspicion. He didn't attack again, but stood there, sizing her up. Then he sent out another pulse of blue light, which Jinn just managed to block with the hag's dagger. The magic glanced off it and hit the tall man square in the chest. He did not cringe but absorbed the light, his already-tan skin darkening further still.

This didn't make any sense. Merrows didn't have this sort of magic, according to Jinn's books. They could shape-shift and were incredibly strong, but nowhere had she read anything about them throwing around fistfuls of blue light.

Jinn rolled her shoulder and prepared to take aim. It didn't matter, whatever this creature was. As long as she distracted him long enough, Quick would be able to flee and perhaps find the Summoner.

Of all things, the man threw his head back and laughed, opening himself up for an attack. "We haven't met," he said, white teeth flashing in a grin, "but you seem to know me?" It was said as a question. "That is not possible."

She was about to let go of the dagger, but something told her to wait. If she threw it and missed, she would be defenseless against any magic cast at her. The blade from the hags must have some magic of its own that could repel this man's attacks. It would be prudent to save throwing as a last resort.

The man scratched the base of his neck and frowned, before grinning a wicked grin and hurling a ball of yellow light at Jinn, who only just managed to dodge it. The light bounced off a tree and then rebounded, hitting her in the back and winding her slightly.

"So, you're no wizard," he said. "What are you?"

"Do you always talk during a fight?" said Jinn, wishing she didn't sound so out of breath when she meant to sound fierce. Hand on her lower back, Jinn straightened her posture and watched him, waiting for the next attack.

The man, however, raised his hands as if in truce. "I don't want to fight you. I just want to know who you are and why...."

Jinn let out a stream of expletives that would have made even one of Meraude's soldiers blush. "You've been chasing me. Why?"

He raised a hand. "I can't – I can't *see* you – except through vicarious means – and that's not supposed to happen." He stopped and squinted at her as if that would help him. "Why is that?"

Her blood ran cold. "You're a Sightful."

The man shook his head and his eyes crinkled at the corners ever so slightly, though there was no longer a smile on his lips.

"No, Jinn. I am not. Most of us have foresight, though." He gave her a pointed look.

Jinn swallowed. When she spoke, her voice was hoarse. "How did you know my name?"

He shot another bolt of light at her, now violet, and this time she was ready for it. It bounced off her blade and hit a boulder, and he took a few slow, subtle steps forward. "I know a lot of things, Jinn. I know where you come from, who your mother is."

Her spine stiffened at these words. Meraude was hated by magic-kind. Perhaps he had sought her out as a way of putting a stop to Mother's scheming. If he thought the mage queen would sacrifice anything in exchange for having her daughter back safe and sound, he was sorely mistaken.

"But I only know it because of things I've heard...." He hesitated and gave her a strange look.

"No one is supposed to know I exist," said Jinn, and then grimaced. It had just slipped out. She read his movements correctly, and was able to dodge another band of violet light. Something told her, though, that this man was merely playing with her. Well, whatever would bring Quick time, she would go along with.

The man nodded. "I know." Again he squinted at her, and then shook his head. "I still can't see you properly." He tilted his head to the left. "Have you been having trouble with your foresight?"

Jinn stared him down, refusing to confirm or deny that she possessed any such ability, even though it was clear that he knew. He knew – how? "What are you?" she demanded.

He shook his head, taking another two small steps toward her. "The curse," he said with resignation. "That's why I can't see you, just your brother. My fate and yours are too entangled." He sighed and ran a hand through his long dark hair. "Well, this complicates things."

He knows about Quick. Panic bubbled hot in her stomach. Was he after him too? She needed to lead this man as far away from Quick as possible. While he was standing there seemingly distracted, Jinn took off running to her left, the dagger clutched tightly in her hand. She made it several yards before she ran into an invisible solid wall, which threw her backward onto her bottom. Reeling, she crawled away from the barrier and rolled again, dodging a bolt of orange light.

"I'm sorry," he said, and he sounded it. "I didn't mean to harm you."

Again Jinn was on her feet, ready to lead him away from Quick, but the man threw out a visible wall to her right and to her left, boxing her in. "What do you want?" she screamed. "You killed the hags, y-you put an entire town to sleep."

The man raised a hand, as if trying to calm her down. "The hags were evil, Jinn." His tone was pained. "As for the village, no one was harmed. I don't harm innocents." He took a few slow steps forward.

Jinn began to breathe quickly. She was trapped – trapped like in the caves where she grew up. *Control yourself*, thought Jinn, trying to pull herself together. *You've still got the hag's knife. You're not through yet. Keep him talking.* Aloud she said, "What about the knife? The one that magicked itself into my pack. Was that *your* doing?"

He nodded. "We'll discuss that later. Right now, you need to calm down. Jinn, you're breathing too hard. You're going to faint."

Indeed, even now darkness formed around the edges of her vision. She raised the knife, but before she could throw it, a ray of white light hit her squarely in the chest, and the world began to grow dark, as did the man. A burst of violet hit her, and she knew no more.

CHAPTER FIFTEEN

Aidan

It took Aidan and Slaíne ten minutes to ready themselves and then start moving again. Aidan was prepared to Summon the silver and bronze swords at a moment's notice. With the shape-shifter still out there and the unknown lying ahead in wait for them, he felt better having every trick at their disposal.

The Pull of magical blood was irresistibly strong now. Aidan led the way, skidding every so many steps as he was unable to control its draw. "This is where it begins." He paused and pointed to where the magical battleground joined with the land they had just been traveling.

The change was undeniable. Where they stood was wetland, cool with little sunshine, the middle of spring hanging in the air. Ahead was sunshine and heat, a land in the throes of summer. The sweet scent of ripened fruit perfumed the air. "So those *were* starberries on the map," Aidan mused as he took one step over the line, Slaíne coming up beside him.

"You sure we should be doin' this? We could turn back...."

Aidan shook his head. "We're so close. We can't turn back now." He swallowed and stepped farther into the Ludland.

Overhead, blue tree leaves the size of parasols crackled and swayed in a breeze that Aidan could not feel. The air was charged, dry, full of foreboding. *Turn back. Only sorrow lies this way.*

Aidan turned to Slaíne, who was looking at him with dread. "Did you just say something?" he asked.

"No, sir. I didn't."

The hairs on the back of Aidan's neck rose. He came to a stop. "Stand watch a moment. I think someone else is out here." Aidan did not wait to see if Slaíne was doing as he asked before closing his eyes and reaching out to the Pulls surrounding him. There were too many living Pulls here, too many once-living Pulls as well, for him to discern if any of them were human or magical. A slow scream built up in the back of Aidan's throat as he felt his powers being torn in eighty, ninety, a hundred different directions.

"Sir!" Slaíne shouted. "What are you doing?"

"There are too many of them. Too many strong Pulls." Aidan ground his teeth in agony. If he were stretched any farther, things would start to snap in his body. As it was, his legs began to bow and his muscles cramped. Both arms were pulled out to the sides, and he thought they might be about to be dislocated.

A soft hand rested on his shoulder. "Just focus on my Pull. That's all ye gotta do. Focus on me."

Her touch was reassuring, and it was that that he tried to focus on. Bit by bit, part by part, he drew himself back into himself, centering his own Pull back on Slaíne's. It was no easy task and took his utmost concentration. Maybe she had been right; maybe they should have turned around and gone back. But even now, he felt the land surrounding them, pulling them farther and farther away from where they had made camp.

"Focus," she said.

He groaned, straining himself to the limits of his abilities. Then an idea occurred to him. Wincing, Aidan latched on to Slaíne's Pull and Called her to himself.

Slaíne let out a surprised yelp, but only moved a fraction of an inch. That had been enough, though, to jolt Aidan out of his struggle with the magical Pulls. "Well, you gotta do what works, I s'pose."

Aidan's eyes fluttered open. The Pulls released him, and at last he could breathe easy. "I'm sorry."

"Next time, try to warn me, yes?" She moved ahead, and Aidan followed.

The land had been flat, but now a slow yet steady upward slope began to form. Trees with trunks five times Aidan's and Slaíne's widths combined formed an aisle on either side, as if acting as a reception line. It occurred to him that these things should not exist. Purple fruit the size of Aidan's head hung in clusters from trees shorter than Slaíne and half as wide. He touched one with the tip of his fingernail. Hissing, the fruit shrank and took on the appearance of an apple. "The map directs us to a cave."

Slaíne crept a ways ahead of him, her eyes on the horizon. "There's hills up ahead, yes?" She took a few tentative steps forward and then hesitated. "This don't feel right."

After taking a look to make certain nothing was creeping up behind them, Aidan turned and caught up with her. "I know what you mean."

But she shook her head. "No. I nay think ya do." She held a hand up into the air, and pulled it back, as one burned. Swearing, she stuck her little finger into her mouth. "I can't use my ability here, sir. Can you? I mean, besides Calling me?"

Aidan grimaced. "I can feel everything, but...." There were so many strange and strong Pulls surrounding him, he was uncertain if he would be able to latch on to anything other than Slaíne. Still, he knew he ought to try. He focused on a green rock the size of his fist, tried to explore its Pull, and then attempted to Dismiss it. The rock did not move an inch. He shook his head and stopped striving. "No, I cannot." They looked at each other. He readjusted the sack carrying the Drifting Goblet, which seemed to have doubled in weight within the span of the last ten minutes. Ominous, but nothing he could not manage.

"Are there any people here, sir?"

"I don't know," he replied, a little more harshly than he had intended to. This place was getting to him in the worst of ways. "Everything feels the same, only not."

Slaíne let out a quiet huff. "Well, that don't help us any."

Now was not the time to stir the heat between them, so Aidan turned his attention to walking with care. He had to look to make certain that she was indeed following him, something he had never had to worry about before.

"This cave," said she, her tone measured, "we'll find the Questing Goblet there?"

Aidan pushed through some heavy hanging vines, holding them aside until Slaíne had passed through them as well. "The Goblet should be there, according to the map and Larkin and everyone I've talked to about this." He knew she was getting at something, but he was uncertain as to what.

"And if we find it, we'll be able to take it, just like that?" She snapped her fingers, and the sound echoed in the stillness. "What I'm sayin', sir, is, would a tomb such as this be left unguarded?"

"I don't know, Slaíne," he admitted, half out of breath. "Who would guard it?"

She pursed her lips and said emphatically, "I did not say 'who'."

Cold sweat rolled down the back of Aidan's neck, and he shuddered. "I take your meaning." The hills seemed to be growing farther away rather than closer. After what might have been an hour of walking, they could no longer see them. Panting and sweating, the pair stopped. Aidan attempted to Summon a water bladder, but had no success. It would appear the only thing his magic worked on at the moment was Slaíne and perhaps himself. He shook his head at her, an apology.

Tears might have been forming at the corners of her eyes, as she swiped at them for a moment. "Right," she said, her voice unwavering. "Should we risk cutting a vine and draining it?"

"I think not. There is something malevolent here. Whoever buried Cedric won't have made things easy for us. Come, we've traveled this way before." He pointed to the east, or what he hoped was still the east; the sun had been behind them moments earlier. "The starberries over there seem to be growing thinner

and the grass seems to slope more upward. Let us try that path."
So they did, only to find themselves at a small stream that they
had not seen moments before. The sound of trickling water
ignited Aidan's thirst, but he looked down and saw that the water
was brown. With his abilities arrested, he knew there'd be no
drinking of the water here. He tightened his belt and then led the
way around the stream. Now the ground was sloping downhill.
"I don't understand."

But Slaíne did not seem so discouraged. "We have to try
something else. Walking around like this is gettin' us nowhere
quick." After drawing in a steadying breath, she started walking
backward up the incline.

He could only stare at her for a moment, thinking that perhaps
she had gone mad from thirst. "Slaíne?"

"Just do as I do. There's got to be some magic here that needs
tricking." When he did not follow, she scowled at him. "The
elves did things like this all the time, to break wards and such.
They know more about magic than what's good for a body."

There would be no arguing with that logic, Aidan knew, so he
started backward up the hill as well. It didn't take very long for
him to realize that nothing was happening, except for them falling
over several times. After ten minutes of this fruitless exercise,
Slaíne came to a stop, as did Aidan.

"Still goin' nowhere. Huh." She stood there, feet planted, hands
on her hips, and then began turning in a counterclockwise circle.

Aidan wondered if he ought to do the same, but continued to
stand there, watching. He caught her after a moment before she
could fall over. "Anything?"

She put a finger to her lips, steadied herself, and then started
walking again, forward this time. She stopped sooner this time and
shook her head. "No, that did nothin'. Give me a moment, yes?"
Her face screwed up in concentration as she marched in place.
When that turned out to be useless, she spun in a circle, jumped
up and down, pretended to climb a ladder, and threw herself

into a tumble. Still nothing happened. She walked sideways, and skipped forward, then backward, then threw her hands up in the air and shouted. Aidan decided that last part was out of frustration and not meant to do anything magical. "I dunno, Mr. Aidan. I tried all the usual things. There might be some sort of spell that only a wizard can cast. In that case, we're trapped." Slaíne clenched her fists at her side.

Aidan shook his head. "Perhaps this was a mistake. We should try to find our way out of this place."

Instead of agreeing, Slaíne clapped her hands together. "I don't want to find that stream again," she said, and took off walking.

Frowning, Aidan followed her. "What the devil—"

"Say it too, Mr. Aidan. We don't want to come across that stream again, do we?" She continued to lead the way, and it dawned on Aidan what she might be doing.

"No, we don't want to find that stream again." As soon as he said it, they crested a small hill and found themselves standing at the base of the stream.

Slaíne beamed at him. "It's called contrarian magic. Say the opposite of where you want to go, and you'll wind up where you wish. 'Tis very basic magic for an elf, but it is effective if you don't know what you're lookin' for." She laughed and spun away from the stream. "Right, then. I don't want ter find the tomb of Cedric the Elder."

Aidan repeated what she said, and they took off walking. At first, nothing seemed to happen. They were not walking in circles like they had been before, but the destination did not appear before them.

Several times Slaíne repeated that she did not want to find the tomb of Cedric the Elder, and each time Aidan echoed her.

They were walking downhill now, in the opposite direction of where he'd seen the hills or mountains earlier. That did not seem to discourage Slaíne, though, and her pace quickened.

Finally, out of breath and clutching pangs in their sides, the pair found themselves standing at the opening of a fog-covered valley with a large hill on the other side. "That looks like what's on the map," he said, wishing he could Summon a water bladder. Aidan took a step toward their destination, but Slaíne threw out her arm and stopped him.

"Nay make a move, sir. There might be traps."

Aidan frowned. "How will we know if there are, and what can we do about them?"

That seemed to discourage Slaíne. She stood there, staring into the ether, and then, trembling, took a small rock from the ground and threw it into the fog. Nothing happened. "Right. Grab as many rocks as you can hold, sir. We may 'ave need of them."

So he did as she said. Aidan pulled the Goblet's sack off his back and filled it with stones of all shapes and sizes. By the time he had gathered a sackful, Aidan could scarce carry it.

Seeing his struggle, Slaíne took the other side of the sack, and they carried it awkwardly together into the mists. Again the way sloped upward, and they repeated their false wish about not wanting to find Cedric's tomb. That worked for several paces, or seemed to. That was when the ground quaked.

Aidan felt a strange, powerful Pull and managed to throw Slaíne out of the way and to his left as a giant boulder fell from the sky, landing right where she had been standing. Birds squawked in the near distance, and the mist, which had been disturbed by the boulder, settled back over the land. They looked at each other as the earth began to quake again. "Run!" Aidan shouted, grabbing her hand and the Goblet. Rocks fell out of the sack, and soon the sack itself fell away, leaving the Goblet. The Goblet seemed to have tripled in weight, and another boulder landed in front of them with a deafening crash.

After spitting out a string of swearwords, Slaíne took to singing:

"*Rocks from the sky*
Fall down to the earth
Hey, tiddly-dee-die
Twelve times the size
Of a full man's girth
Hey, tiddly-dee-die
Oh, what a silly wretch
Got in t'way."

Here Slaíne stopped and muttered something under her breath. "Oh, how did the next part go?"

Aidan pulled her around the boulder, as another was headed down to where they were standing. "Is there a way to stop this?"

"I'm trying," she practically wailed. It took her a moment until she picked up the tune again.

"*Oh, what a silly wretch*
Got in t'way
Oh, what a dreadful day
No need to be squashed
The foolish wretch
No need for death
If only he'd remembered
His watch."

It was Aidan's turn to swear, dragging her around another boulder that had fallen several yards in front of them. "What help is a watch going to do us? I haven't got one, and our luck's about to run out."

"No, not *his* watch, *to* watch. I had the words wrong." She pulled Aidan to a standstill and looked up at the sky. "Dontcha take yer eyes off the skies for a moment, sir, and nay do blink. It's the only way ter get out of here alive."

So Aidan cast his gaze to the sky and tried not to blink as they trod across uneven ground, nearly falling more than once. She had not steered him wrong yet with her knowledge of curses, and boulders ceased raining from the heavens, so he tried his best not to blink. His eyes watered and burned, his vision blurring until, inevitably, he blinked. Nothing happened. No boulder fell, the mists had lifted, and the sun was shining.

They stopped walking. The cave was just ten yards ahead, but he now knew better than to blindly tramp ahead.

Again Aidan felt for new Pulls. There were none. "I don't feel anything there. What do you recommend?"

"You nay feel nothin'?"

That was a strange question to ask, yet as he thought on it, Aidan realized that he did not, in fact, feel any Pulls before them. There was Slaíne's Pull next to him, his own Pull, and the Pulls of what he had left behind. Tentatively, he squatted and ran his hand through the air in front of him. "I don't think anything is there." He took one step forward and nearly fell to his death. The illusion of grass and path evaporated, revealing a great gulf between them and the entrance to the cave.

Slaíne managed to grab him, and the Goblet, and they fell onto their bottoms, panting and staring at the chasm before them. After a moment, the illusion of land returned.

"How are we gonna get across?" she asked him, eyes wide. "Ya think we could go 'round it?"

He shook his head. "I doubt that we could. The chasm seems to stretch on far beyond where sight ends."

"But maybe that's an illusion?"

They both knew she was being foolishly optimistic. Aidan shook his head. They had come too far to be defeated by a cliff. He got to his feet and looked about for something with which to build a bridge. It was no use. There were no trees, no vines, and no way that Slaíne could think of to prevent something as unmagical as falling seventy feet to their deaths.

So the pair tried turning back, only to be met by an invisible wall. Irate with himself for bringing them to such a point, Aidan dropped to his knees and clenched his hands into red fists. The grass beneath him responded, and shot up into his hands. Well, his powers had returned. But what good would that do with no bridge-making materials in Nothingness? He was about to Summon everything anyway, just to eliminate the possibility, when an idea occurred to him. "Slaíne, see if you can fly here."

"Huh?"

"Just do it."

She gave him an odd look, but set down her sword, and soon hovered over the ground. "My power's returned."

Aidan Summoned a rope from Nothingness and motioned for her to return back to the ground. "Here, let's see if your powers work over the chasm." So he tied the rope around her waist, making certain the knot was tight, and tied the far end to his wrist. "All right, slowly now, not all at once...."

Slaíne rose upward again and moved a little ways over the chasm. When she didn't fall or sink, he encouraged her to go a ways farther, which she did. The result was the same. "What now?" she asked, coming back to his side and landing. "I can nay well carry ye over. You're too heavy, sir."

He nodded, and then reached for the Drifting Goblet. "You don't need to carry me, though you might need to pull me along a ways." Aidan Summoned a water bladder, and poured some into the heavy Goblet. "Here, drink the rest. We don't know when we'll get a chance again."

The girl did not need telling twice. She drained the bladder as he drained the Goblet.

"All right. We need to move across the gap as quickly as we can manage. I don't want to sweat all of the water out, should the chasm be wider than it appears to be." It could not be his imagination that the Drifting Goblet was gaining weight. It now had become too heavy to carry, and he dropped it, nearly on his foot. When he leapt back, he began to Drift. "Grab the Goblet," he said.

Slaíne came to the vessel and tried to lift it, but it seemed as though she was having the same problem that he had had. "Too heavy."

He thought for a moment. Could they leave the Goblet alone and then return to it? He was unable to Summon or Dismiss any of the Goblets Immortal, due to their magical properties. If they took too long in the cave, surely no one would be able to take it? At least, he thought not. No one would know where to look. It was decided, then. "We'll come back for it, once we have the Questing Goblet."

"Are you mad? We can nay just leave my Goblet there for someone to take."

"And how many people do you think are going to come by here and do that?" When she did not respond but stared at him in grumpy silence, Aidan knew he had won, and gave the rope tethering them together a sharp tug.

She rose and flew off over the chasm, pulling Aidan behind her. It was soon obvious that Slaíne was not used to being slowed down in flight, as she kept turning her head and giving him incredulous looks. "Move faster," she said at one point.

Aidan ground his teeth before responding with, "You know that I can't control it like you can." He felt truly ridiculous and useless, swimming in midair...or, rather, trying to.

Slaíne stopped and, hovering, pulled his rope with all her might. Taken by surprise, he came soaring forward, hitting her square in the chest and knocking the wind out of her, apparently. "Ouch," she said between gasps for air.

This would have made him laugh, had there been anything humorous about the situation. Aidan shook his head. "I am sorry."

"Anythin' you can do on your end?"

Aidan looked beyond Slaíne. They were a mere twenty yards

from solid ground, if that, even. "The more we stand – *hover* here, the more likely it is that we're going to sink. Keep moving."

"Can't," she said. "I'm near out of strength." Despair was evident in her voice, which cracked. She swiped at her eyes once, and then twice. "We can't've come this far for naught." Much to her credit, though, Slaíne turned around and continued to pull him. She made it another two feet, and then was forced to stop and catch her breath.

The sun beat down upon them in merciless rays. Aidan should have drunk more water from the Drifting Goblet. He sank a few inches, as if at the thought.

"No, no, no," Slaíne said, turning and pulling again. "Lot o' good the Summoning Goblet does up here."

"Save your breath," he said, not unkindly. There had to be something he could do. Sweating, he realized he might have to free himself from the rope, so as not to pull her down with him when he plummeted onto the rocks below, for at the rate he was sinking, that surely seemed like a true possibility. "Let me try one more thing before we despair," he said. Closing his eyes, Aidan concentrated. He found Slaíne's Pull over the many strong Pulls ahead, latched on to it, and then sent it hurtling away from himself.

Instead of shooting ahead like a falling star, Slaíne's sluggish pace only increased by a modest amount, but still it was something. It took all of his concentration, but Aidan continued to struggle and Push, and before he knew it, they were both on the other side of the chasm, huffing and puffing and sweating out the rest of the water in their systems. He fell down at the mouth of the cave without ceremony, and then Summoned two water bladders, one for them each.

Neither spoke as they drained the tepid water, but continued to lie there, trying to replenish their strength. Aidan Summoned some food, an apple each, ones that Salem had insisted he Dismiss from the Beyond. Aidan wasn't certain which these ones were, but they looked like regular apples and not of the magical variety, so he thought they would do. They *had* to do, he knew, for they were out of protein, and most every other edible thing that he kept in his cache.

"What do you think we'll find?" Slaíne asked, once they had finished their apples and water. "And how are we to get back across? You haven't got the Goblet over here."

"We'll worry about that once we retrieve the Questing Goblet." Seeing that she was on the verge of panicking, he added, "Besides, the Goblet we seek brings success to whoever drinks of it. It wouldn't be lucky if it left me dead at the bottom of the gully."

Slaíne glowered at him. "Lovely picture you paint, sir." She got to her feet and dusted her hands off on her torn dress.

Aidan rose as well, and they stood there, staring into the dark mouth of the cave. Unwittingly he was reminded of a gaping maw, pointed teeth jutting out to better chew them up and spit them out. "Right. We have our abilities back. If anything goes wrong on the ground, you fly up."

Her expression darkened. "And what about you?"

"I can escape into Nothingness," he said, knowing he would not even consider leaving her to the wrath of her curse. "Is there anything you can think of that the elves taught you about caves?"

She seemed to turn it over in her mind before saying, "Don't get caught in a cave-in."

Aidan looked at her, trying to discern whether she was making a joke or not. The silence became awkward. "Right. Perhaps we should untie this." He held up the rope connecting them.

"Not yet," she said, her voice somber. With that said, they ventured into the mouth of darkness.

No sooner had they stepped inside than the entrance sealed behind them, leaving the way pitch-black. Slaíne cursed.

Aidan thought of Summoning his flint, magnesium, and a knife to start a fire, but thought the better of it. Fate, if there were such a thing, did not seem to be on their side. He might end up cutting off a finger or worse. "I guess we move on blindly." He felt her stiffen by his side. "I'll keep track of the Pulls ahead. We should be fine."

"If you say so, sir." Slaíne did not sound the least bit convinced, but they inched their way forward, waving their arms out in front of them. She hit him twice in the shoulder, and then in the stomach, and three times in the chest.

"Perhaps," he said, disturbing the silence, "we should just rely on my abilities, yes?"

She snorted in derision, but stopped her mad waving. "It stinks."

"I know," he said. The cave was full of the scent of sulfur. The air here was close, wet. Aidan shuddered as gooseflesh formed on his arms and neck.

"What was that?" she asked, treading on his left foot. "Somethin' just scurried up my leg."

Aidan sighed and shook his head. "It was probably a mouse. Its Pull was very insubstantial." Perhaps that had been the wrong thing to say to a woman, but Slaíne expressed no further worry on the matter, and they continued to move inward.

"Eldred," said a voice behind Aidan's back.

He could feel their rank, ancient breath on his neck, but there was no Pull. It was a reflex, but Aidan braced his right fist with his left and thrust his elbow backward. It connected with thin air. "No one's there."

"No one's *here*," the man's voice echoed, this time ahead.

Slaíne stopped walking, and the rope went taut between them. "I nay like this, sir. Somethin' bad's 'bout to happen."

Aidan's terror was strong enough to check his impatience. "We must be getting close. Whatever's guarding this place can't have many more tricks." He knew very well they could.

"Sir, stop a'lying to me. I am no child." The rope slackened, and she caught up with him.

A blue light bobbed ahead in the darkness, only to be at once extinguished. "Melnine," said the voice in a singsong manner. "What brings forth the Daughter of Naught – *naught* – *naught?*" The echo grew louder and louder.

Aidan found himself covering his ears as the sound continued to bounce off walls and boom in his skull. The echoing ceased, only to be replaced by a high-pitched cackle that ended in a wail.

Sláine screamed what sounded like a war cry in response. "Silence, you blight," she said at last, after the apparition repeated her cry back at them.

There was silence, and then the cave lit up as bright as high noon, only to be thrown into an eerie blue light that did not quite penetrate the shadows. Aidan realized at once that the blue was no ordinary flame, in that there was a gust of wind and the fire itself stood still. No shadows danced before or behind them, but he knew they were both ringed in.

"Where is the Goblet, d'you think?" Sláine asked him. "Behind the wall of fire?"

As if in response, the firewall parted, and a shape moved through it, the shape of a man. Aidan squinted, and, thinking a little too slowly, he Summoned the silver sword.

"Won't do you no good against a ghost."

The figure cackled as it drew within ten yards of them and stopped. "Ooh, are we afraid of wee ghosties? No fear, no fear, Melnine. There are no ghosties here."

"Where is the tomb of Cedric the Elder?" Aidan asked, blue light dancing off the silver blade. He studied the figure of the old man.

The man, or ghost, wore dark ragged robes, ones that might have once been a royal red or burgundy. His matted, filthy beard reached the floor, and the toenails of his bare feet were dead-looking and long enough to curl up over the tops of his feet. Aidan gagged, for he could smell the man's long-unwashed flesh from where he stood.

When the stooped figure did not respond, Aidan repeated his question. Again the man laughed, though there was something dark and dangerous in his display of mirth. "No death for Cedric, my dear, slippery fellow." Black eyes glinted in the unnatural firelight, eyes that had seen centuries pass.

"You're Cedric," Slaíne said before Aidan could quite come to that conclusion. She shook violently. "That's nay possible."

"And yet, here I stand. Yes, I stand where you will die, my old foe." He was speaking to Aidan. "Melnine's own might live, should you forfeit your life." The ancient man gestured around vaguely. "I could send her hence without a hair singed upon that fiery head."

"I don't even know you. Why do you wish to kill me?"

Cedric wrung his hands, as if he were imagining wringing Aidan's neck. "Why did you wish to drink of my blood, you lazy, disobliging blight on the face of humanity?" The fire rose with his temper and snaked in closer.

"Kill him, sir," Slaíne said. "Run him through. He's just a powerless old man."

If he had been standing closer to Slaíne, Aidan might have hushed her. "We don't mean that. Please, let us leave here in peace. We truly mean no harm." He gave Slaíne's rope a subtle tug, and they began backing away from the wizard.

"No one leaves Cedric's tomb alive, I fear. Farewell, daughter of Melnine and chosen of Eldred." The man turned, and the flames parted for him as he passed, then closed behind him.

At once the blue flames slithered in toward the travelers. Aidan pulled Slaíne in close, and they stood back to back, as Aidan Summoned all of the bladders from Nothingness and they both covered themselves in water.

"That'll do no good. This's a magical blaze." Her voice was hoarse, and so was Aidan's when he said, "There is no Questing Goblet."

She began to cry. "I'm sorry, sir. I failed." Slaíne turned around to face him. "I'm sorry."

He held her as she sobbed, and the flames drew nearer. There was only one thing left to do, one thing left to try that could be their death or their salvation. "Do you trust me, Slaíne?" he shouted over the roaring blaze. He did not wait for an answer. "Hold on tight to me, and no matter what, don't let go." He grabbed her in his arms, closed his eyes, and as quickly as he could, he Released himself and all of the Pulls surrounding him, all but Slaíne's, whose Pull was his anchor, the strongest thing he had ever felt. And with her pressed against him, Aidan Dismissed them both into Nothingness.

CHAPTER SIXTEEN

Aidan

The strange thing about Nothingness, Aidan had always found, was that you couldn't breathe, see, or feel, and you could hardly move. This place between Existence and the Beyond had only ever been inhabitable by himself, but none of these rules seemed to be true any longer. Something burned so brightly beyond his eyelids, Aidan turned his head away.

Slaíne's grip on him tightened for a moment, before she pushed him away, and he collapsed onto nothing as solid as if it were ground. "Strange," said a voice that was both Slaíne's and not. "What am I?"

Aidan opened his eyes. Where there should have stood a dirty, battered young woman, he beheld a queen, still in rags, still crowned with wild red hair, but somehow changed. "Slaíne?" he asked, pulling himself to his feet as her light dimmed enough for him to get a better look.

Her eyes flashed silver light at the mention of her name, but dimmed again after a moment. "You freed my spirit," she said, amazed, and still not sounding quite the same. "Two souls bound doth unbind. Don't you see, Aidan? The curse is broken." She laughed, and the sound was terrifying.

Every instinct told him to run, to return to Existence and leave her in Nothingness to her own devices. But he couldn't. "Are you all right?"

"Never better."

His soul quaked as she pulled him nearer. Slaíne's sinewy fingers traced halfway down his abs and then back up again, her eyes never leaving his. The light within her flashed brighter still. "It's like seeing you for the first time," she said, her voice devoid of any accent.

Aidan might just say the same of her. *Danger*, he thought again as he allowed her to pull him down lower for a kiss.

"I've always been dangerous, Aidan. That did not stop you from wanting me before." Her lips tasted like honey, something familiar.

He relaxed and kissed her back. But her mouth soon moved to his neck and she firmly bit him, drawing blood. Aidan cried out. "Why—"

She licked away the blood, eliciting a shudder. "Because you are mine, Aidan. Make no mistake on the matter."

Aidan knew he should take umbrage at the thought, but he found himself agreeing.

"Kneel," Sláine commanded.

Aidan knelt.

She grinned a cruel grin. "Give me your blood, your heart, your body." Glowing brighter still, she stood there and waited.

Dread came over Aidan as he realized she meant to consume him. "Sláine...."

"Love?"

He hesitated. "Love? How can you say 'love' when you mean to kill me?"

A flicker of hurt momentarily marred her features. "But I want you." She patted her heart. "In here." Her hands tangled themselves in his hair and gave it a pull. "You have a beautiful heart, Aidan, and I desire it." By his hair she tugged him to his feet. "I'll try not to kill you, since that would make you unhappy." She steadied Aidan without letting go. "Now, will you give yourself, or must I take?" Her left hand smoothed the wrinkles in his brow. "Aidan, I've been waiting over five hundred years for something so exquisite." Apparently she could wait no longer. Her hand glowed blue as she plunged it into his chest, passing through skin without making an opening.

Aidan staggered, but she caught him and drew out a faintly glowing orb the size of her fist. He gasped in shock and reached for it, but his hand passed right through. Bereft, he stood there as she cradled the orb for a moment before slipping it through the skin of her own chest, sighing in obvious bliss. Empty, Aidan shuddered and collapsed.

But Slaíne was not through with him.

She pulled Aidan to his feet and studied him for a moment, concern in her eyes as she said, "Well, this won't do. You're not substantial anymore. I can't have a mate who won't hold his own."

Aidan shuddered as she traced the skin whence she'd drawn his soul. "Empty," he said miserably. "I'm so empty."

"I didn't take it all, Aidan. You'd be dead without a soul." Slaíne's teeth flashed in a mischievous grin. "Kiss me."

What was left of Aidan's own essence roared to life at the command. Weak though he was, Aidan took her into his arms and dipped his head, his lips meeting hers. Slaíne tasted of power, of the sweetest wine and the bitterest herb. Sky and earth were in that kiss. His life thrummed in her breast, and as she slipped her hand through his chest for a second time, Aidan thought she meant to consume him entirely. There was no fear in him, though, only want and need and something he could not name. The kiss faltered as molten iron pooled and settled in his chest. He couldn't breathe or move. Pain he had never known seized Aidan, and he convulsed.

"Shh," Slaíne soothed, sounding more like her usual self as she removed her hand from his chest. "Aidan, focus on my voice." Tenderly, she took his face in her still-glowing hands, though the light had dimmed somewhat. Slaíne held him to her breast as he dropped once again to his knees there in Nothingness. "Listen to my heart. Can you hear it? Try to imagine that heart beating in your own chest. Can you do that for me, my love?"

Eyes screwed tightly shut, Aidan shook his head. He wanted to die. Right there and then, he needed the pain to end. The fire inside his chest would not let him. "Let me die," he said as she continued to hold on to him.

"Aidan, I can't let you die. Here, it should be over in a moment. Just continue to listen to my heart."

He listened, listened as it slowed to a normal beating, with those two separate souls in her breast. Aidan tried to do as she had said, to imagine her heart beating in his own chest, but the pain spiked and his nails drew blood from the palms of his hands.

"Focus," she demanded. There was such pure command in her voice that he could not ignore or deny her.

So Aidan focused as he never had before. Not only did he listen to her heartbeat, he imagined his heart was in her breast and hers was within his, and thought of hot blood pumping through them both, connecting them for the rest of their natural lives and perhaps beyond. The pain stuttered and dulled to something much more manageable. His heart rate slowed.

Slaíne kissed the crown of his head. "It's all right. It's all right. Can you think about Existence again? Bring us outside of the cave, but beyond the chasm. Right where we left the Drifting Goblet. Can you do that, Aidan?"

He did not wish to deny her, but he had never managed it before. "I've only ever managed to reemerge right where I disappeared from."

"You are not what you once were," said she. "You listen to me, Aidan Ingledark. You are no mere Blest anymore. Focus." Slaíne pulled him roughly to his feet and held him close. Though her head came below his chin, she felt much taller and less fragile than she had once seemed.

Aidan held her as well and closed his eyes. The pain was now a dull throb, one he could think around as he attempted to return them to Existence. Normally, he would have to cause emotional and mental friction within himself in order to find his way back to the real world. This time was different. This time he could move and cause friction with his body. He brought his face down to hers, and they kissed as they never had before. Aidan harnessed the power he felt between them and used it to wrench them back to Existence, back to where the Drifting Goblet was waiting for them.

When they landed back beyond the chasm, Aidan caught Slaíne before she could fall over the edge of the cliff. "We did it," he cried, but she was unresponsive. Taking care not to jostle her, Aidan lowered her to the ground and rose, just as he became aware of the Pull of a massive man charging toward them. He had no time to think as he was grabbed around the waist and tossed over the giant's shoulder. "What the devil...?"

"No struggle. Find sister. Where is sister? Said she'd meet Quick here."

Aidan swore. "Who are you? Put me down, you giant. You're going to trample Slaíne."

"Who Slaíne?"

Aidan now became aware that two more Pulls were approaching, along with a strong repulsion. The scolding song of a furious bird filled the air as a tanned man carrying a goldfinch in an iron cage emerged from the mists. With a snap of the newcomer's fingers, the mist evaporated.

The giant dropped Aidan and went for the newcomer, swinging out with his meaty fists, only to be hit with a bolt of violet light, square in the chest. He stumbled for a moment, and with a flash, where there had stood the giant there was now a slight canary. Before it could fly away, the tanned man waved his hand, and an iron cage formed over the creature. It, too, began to tweet angrily.

"I'm sorry," he said to the first bird. "You'll be human again soon, Jinn. I promise." He turned to Aidan, as if asking for commiseration. Instead, he said, "Will you both come with me, or do I need to turn you both into birds?" He held up both cages for Aidan to see, a threat. "I'll send Slaíne ahead, and you can take the Goblet. I'm not toying with that sort of magic."

Before Aidan could think or react, the strange man pointed a finger at Slaíne's sleeping form, and she vanished in a flash of red light. "Slaíne!" Aidan shouted. He turned to look at the wizard. "What did you do to her?"

"I'm Hex," he said in answer. He waved the cages back and forth, and they, like Slaíne, disappeared in a flash of red light. "Your mate is all right, Aidan. She's just resting—"

"What? I know she was just resting until you—"

"—in the east wing."

Confused and unbelieving, Aidan continued to stare at this Hex. "What are you talking about?"

Again, Hex avoided his question. "You and the Goblet are going to have to go the usual way, I'm afraid." He looked around and frowned. "There's just the Drifting Goblet? Where is the Questing Goblet?"

Stupidly, Aidan blurted out, "There is no Questing Goblet, you great idiot." He shook himself. "Bring her back right now."

Hex's expression darkened. "Cedric's still alive?" He ran a hand over his naked jaw, eyes out of focus. "Well, that is a problem. But first, tea, I think." Out of his pocket he pulled a doorknob, which he turned in midair to reveal an empty white hall. Hex motioned to the Goblet. "Fetch that."

Aidan took the Goblet and then, not wanting to lose his one connection to Slaíne, followed the wizard down the long hall. With a great creak, an invisible door shut behind them, and Aidan swallowed his panic.

The way was narrow and bright. More than once, it narrowed farther still, forcing both men to turn and walk sideways.

The wizard named Hex did not speak to Aidan at first. He kept muttering to himself about curses and wizards, and more than once stopped mid-step, causing his guest by force to nearly run into him. After a while, Aidan grew weary of the way and said, "Where are we going, and what have you done with Slaíne?"

"We're almost there," Hex replied. "You can't magic a Goblet Immortal, as you probably well know, Aidan. We have to bring it on foot." Again he stopped, this time putting up a hand for Aidan to do likewise.

"That brings me to another point," Aidan said as the wizard pulled the same doorknob out of nowhere again. "How do you know who I am? Who Sláine is?"

Hex turned and studied Aidan for a moment with frightening intensity. At last he said, "I have known Sláine since she was young – or rather, I *used to* know her." It might have been a trick of the light or Aidan's imagination, but the wizard seemed uneasy about something. "And I know *you* because I've had you followed."

Aidan's fists clenched as things began to fall into place in his mind. "Oh? The shape-shifter was yours?"

The wizard held up a finger. "Save your anger for later, Aidan. I need to focus on what to do now that there is no sixth Goblet, and I can't have someone trying to kill me in my own home. It would be...messy. Can you do that for me? Wait to avenge yourself or whatever it is you are planning to do?" Before Aidan could answer, Hex stopped and turned the doorknob, again in midair. Another invisible door creaked open, and he led Aidan into a foyer the size of Aidan's property back in Breckstone. "This is Vät Vanlud. You are very welcome, sir."

"Where is she?" Aidan again demanded.

Hex sighed, grabbed a torch from a sconce on the wall next to where they had emerged, and led Aidan down a winding corridor with stone floors and colorful tapestries. "You need to be careful. Sláine is not what you think she is." He paused, turned, and looked at Aidan again. "*You*'re not what you think you are." With those ominous words, the wizard turned down another corridor, which dead-ended at an ornate dark wood door. Hex stood back and motioned toward the place. "She should be awake...for now. The change is hard, I'm sure." He handed the torch to Aidan. "A word first. I know you're impatient."

It was an understatement, for certain. Aidan knew himself

to be at the point of performing violence, and on a wizard, nonetheless. "Talk."

"There are five Goblets Immortal. All Blest are products of them." He pointed to the door. "She is not among them."

A tremor ran up Aidan's spine. "I don't know what you mean."

The wizard shook his head. "Her curse is broken, Aidan. Be – be very careful." His shoulders heaved. "There's a reason she had a curse put on her in the first place. It kept things in check, and in balance."

Aidan's eyes narrowed. "And who put the curse on her?"

Hex shook his head. "That is another story for another time. On you get."

Wary but anxious to make certain Slaíne was all right, Aidan unlatched the door and stepped inside. The large room was dim until he entered, the light dancing on the walls as he placed the torch in a sconce next to the doorway. Feeling eyes on the back of his neck, Aidan turned and was startled to find the wizard staring at him.

The wizard nodded, and the door shut behind him and was re-bolted.

Aidan remained standing there, staring at an enormous bed. At first he could not see Slaíne for all the blankets. She lay on the far right side facing a covered window. "Slaíne?" he asked, taking a few tentative steps before stopping.

The drapes flew open, letting in light from a barred window. Slaíne swore, and Aidan knew that she was all right. "Where am I?" she asked, her voice thick and panicked. "How'd I get here?"

"I'm not sure how exactly either of us arrived here," said Aidan, moving toward her. "And I don't know exactly where we are, but I think we're safe…at least, for now."

Slaíne sat up and looked at him, before collapsing back onto the mattress. "So tired."

Aidan knew the feeling. He felt as though he could sleep for a year, and his knees nearly gave way as he closed the gap between them. "Are you all right?" He ran a hand through her hair, and she closed her eyes.

"I think so." She sounded her normal self again, and everything that had happened in Nothingness seemed like a distant dream. The mattress dipped as he sat down next to her. "Where's the Questing Goblet? Did we get it?" Her eyes opened a crack before closing once again. "Blast, but I can scarce stay awake."

Aidan let out a deep breath. "There is no Questing Goblet, remember?" When she made no immediate response, he continued. "Cedric's alive and has been hiding in his own 'tomb' for some time, apparently." The weight of the situation pressed on Aidan. What were they to do next, especially now that they found themselves captives of a wizard? Defeating Meraude felt as far away as if they had just begun their quest, and his parents were nowhere closer to being avenged. Instead of voicing his many concerns, Aidan returned his attention to Slaíne and said, "Let's discuss things later. We'll wait until you've regained your strength before we make our next move."

"Mm," she agreed.

He took her small hand in his and rubbed her palm with his thumb. "What happened in Nothingness? That wasn't real, was it?" Aidan waited, watching her carefully.

Slowly, Slaíne's face took on a glow and she gave his hand a weak squeeze. "I dunno. Feels like it might've been real."

Aidan had been afraid of that. Something deep in his chest thrummed in time to Slaíne's slow breathing, and he wondered if anything would be quite the same again. But when he looked into those gray eyes, which fluttered open for a brief moment, he knew once and for all that he had found what he had lost more than twenty years ago: home.

EPILOGUE

Meraude

Three Goblets sat on a wall: Sight, Enduring, and a regular drinking vessel. Their mistress glared at them. Her anger she reserved for injustice, not dull moments such as the present. No, this was no mere prick of irritation she felt. The mage knew herself well, and knew herself to be restless and impatient. She and her army.

FLAME TREE PRESS
FICTION WITHOUT FRONTIERS
Award-Winning Authors & Original Voices

Flame Tree Press is the trade fiction imprint of Flame Tree Publishing, focusing on excellent writing in horror and the supernatural, crime and mystery, science fiction and fantasy. Our aim is to explore beyond the boundaries of the everyday, with tales from both award-winning authors and original voices.

•

Other titles available by Beth Overmyer:
The Goblets Immortal

You may also enjoy:
The Sentient by Nadia Afifi
American Dreams by Kenneth Bromberg
Second Lives by P.D. Cacek
The City Among the Stars by Francis Carsac
Vulcan's Forge by Robert Mitchell Evans
The Widening Gyre by Michael R. Johnston
The Blood-Dimmed Tide by Michael R. Johnston
The Sky Woman by J.D. Moyer
The Guardian by J.D. Moyer
The Apocalypse Strain by Jason Parent
A Killing Fire by Faye Snowden
The Bad Neighbor by David Tallerman
Ten Thousand Thunders by Brian Trent
Night Shift by Robin Triggs
Human Resources by Robin Triggs
Two Lives: Tales of Life, Love & Crime by A Yi

Horror and suspense titles available include:
Thirteen Days by Sunset Beach by Ramsey Campbell
The Wise Friend by Ramsey Campbell
The Haunting of Henderson Close by Catherine Cavendish
The Garden of Bewitchment by Catherine Cavendish
Black Wings by Megan Hart
Those Who Came Before by J.H. Moncrieff
Stoker's Wilde by Steven Hopstaken & Melissa Prusi
Stoker's Wilde West by Steven Hopstaken & Melissa Prusi
Until Summer Comes Around by Glenn Rolfe

•

Join our mailing list for free short stories, new release details, news about our authors and special promotions:

flametreepress.com